A Light Home

M. Cosmos Newstrom

Cover Painting by Carson Lowmiller

Cover Design by Ryley Wiering

Illustrations by Madison Shorthill

Editing by Copper Coin Editing

Proofing by Dustin Meriwether

1st edition 2026

Paperback ISBN: 979-8-9941602-0-6

eBook ISBN: 979-8-9941602-1-3

CONTENTS

To Grace.
My Light,
My Heart,
My Home,
Forever.

CHAPTER 1

Owyn struggled to push the small rowboat out from the dock. The oars didn't seem to work, and he kept spinning. The dockmaster above him smiled, though he didn't say a word. Owyn avoided his eyes. He focused on the two oars. He took a breath, letting the small vessel spin about itself.

He hadn't stolen it. That would have been so easy. Owyn had thought of half a dozen ways to steal it on his walk to the docks. He didn't act on them, though, and that was what mattered. He had bought and paid for the boat, and if he could do that the correct way, he could propel the awkward thing the correct way. Owyn looked up at the dockmaster still standing on the great stone platform along the shore. Owyn nodded, matching the silence of the man, and then put hands to the oars and rowed. The small boat still tilted to Owyn's right, rocking and propelling itself at a slight angle, but it had moved. He hadn't balanced it, but it had moved. Owyn rowed again, tilting the vessel at the same angle again. There was a change in the dockmaster's smile. There was an almost parental joy along with the laughter it hid now. Owyn smiled, too, and rowed the oars again.

He pushed out a little further this time, and the rowboat stayed straighter. The dockmaster waved a hand before turning away and heading back to shore. Owyn took a breath. It was glorious and sweet. The slight breeze carried a salty taste to it; the cool air felt crisp in his lungs. His smile grew as he rowed. A feeling swelled in his chest he hadn't felt in a long time. He was free. This boat was his, justly and legally. He'd all but forced the dockmaster to write him a copy of the receipt of the sale, which sat now in the breast pocket of his loose shirt.

When he had left the immediate shores of Kudra, Owyn stopped rowing and let the boat drift for a moment. The city of Kudra was marvelous and shone in front of him. At the confluence of the Annwyn River delta washing out into Turtle Bay on its west, with the Shrinking Desert halting its expanse to the north, and with imperial farms and the great Kudran woodfarm spread out in every direction they could, the city rose and gleamed as if a keystone, holding the many landforms together. In the center of the city stood the God's Tower. Looking up in the clear blue sky, Owyn could almost imagine he saw the top of the Tower. Men had not built the Tower, at least not according to the histories that Owyn had heard in taverns and tales. The structure pulled attention onto it, drawing the eye with force. One could either look at the city below, willfully ignoring the structure, or allow their gaze upward, seeing only the Tower. There were cracks in the Tower, gashes that split the stonework vertically. Visible even from this distance, they were wider than many men across. Timber beams held together some of these scars. No one knew how they had happened as the cracks had been there before the city had grown. The expensive wooden fix had happened after. Owyn briefly thought of the cost of the repair, and the cost of his own wooden boat. He pushed money from his mind, and the image he wanted to see returned. The image Owyn held in his head wasn't the God's Tower, but rather something of his own design. His wouldn't fail. It couldn't.

He turned away from the city behind him to look ahead. There was nothing for Owyn in the past, nothing behind him worth seeing. So he turned forward, straining his back, spinning to look ahead, and stopping to turn his body back towards the city with a wince at the needle of pain by his spine. Triph had always told him to stretch before doing anything, even eating or getting a drink at the pub.

Cocky bastard, mused Owyn silently as he thought of the man. He shook his head, stretching his back in an arch before using one oar to turn the boat around, letting him look forward, away from the city. He rolled up the sleeves of his faded green shirt, the creases in the cloth holding the memory of how he had done it a thousand times before. Careful not to tip his new boat, he leaned over and cupped seawater in his weathered hands before wetting his dark, curly hair. The thin, new stubble on his face caught slightly against his hands. They had been roughed up against the stone oars as he had worked today, but they didn't need to be smooth anymore. His hands would never sneak into pockets and purses again.

The ocean opened out in front of him as the rowboat spun on the water. The land trailed on the horizon, sinking further away towards the far edge of Turtle Bay. Then it was gone. The horizon was blue, and it was endless. Small waves rocked the little boat; he rose and fell with them, bobbing as they dictated. What a difference it was, looking out at the sea from land compared to now. He hadn't owned the dock; he hadn't owned the land or the city; he had never felt a part of the city, or any city or town or village he had visited. Owyn owned his boat now. Where he sat was his. He touched the wooden boat. He'd never touched so much timber in a single space, and now he owned it. He looked out at the freedom of the ocean, the entire expanse of the world open to him. It was bigger—so much bigger—than the God's Tower behind him.

He was free.

Carefully setting the oars to rest, he triple-checked that they would not fall off of their mounts before pulling a sheet of vellum from the small satchel at his feet. Owyn unfolded a map of the bay. It was a rough drawing, with ink atop ink marking and remarking the shoreline. It showed the coast of Kudra and Turtle Bay, ending with the coastline going to the north off the page. The map was dotted with little cross marks, some with notes or names, most with nothing next to them. They were shipwrecks, warnings of where other vessels had met with disaster and fallen beneath the depths. By following the marks, Owyn roughly knew where the sea floor rose and where it was safe. He hadn't paid for this map. He hadn't known it was even a thing one could steal until he and Triph had already stolen it. Triph thought nothing of the markings on the vellum, but they'd given Owyn an idea. Something he'd carried for years. These little markings on a map gave him the biggest idea of his life. Another sheet sat beneath the map. One far more important to Owyn.

Turtle Bay was not a safe place to sail, but there was little option for the city. The profits of shipping by the coastal sea rather than by land were immense. Owyn and Triph had always thought becoming a sailing thief would have been where the real money was, but neither man had taken the time to learn the knowledge for seafaring.

They couldn't have started that endeavor on their own and so stuck to the terrestrial variety.

Owyn looked at the circle he had made on the map in vivid, green ink. The circle surrounded the densest area of crosses, a small peninsula of rocks that extended south from the edge of the bay. It was a turning point for the coastal ships that ran north and south along the edge of the continent: take the turn too close to shore and any chance of profit sank to the rocky sea floor. That was his destination. The most dangerous place for a ship. The best place for his dream.

The map showed the edge of Kudra, and Owyn looked from the city to the vellum again and again, trying to orientate himself in the empty space off the coast that marked the open bay, trying to find his circled spot in the vast, open world. How did sailors do this? Finally, swearing under his breath, he put the vellum back into the satchel, turned his boat, and rowed once more. He didn't know if the direction was right, but sitting still would get him nowhere.

Owyn kept on rowing, staring at Kudra as it shrunk slowly into the horizon. The act of rowing was growing on him. A part of Owyn would always hate facing backwards, but it was nice seeing where he was leaving, a place that was smaller than the vast openness the boat was headed towards. An hour went by without thought, then another. When his arms tired and his back started to seize, Owyn stopped, turned the boat with an oar, and marveled at the world around him. How could he not smile? He was still only in the bay, yet there was so much nothingness around him. The water splashed against the wooden rowboat and its stone oars and the breeze swept across his face, cooling the sweat that had built up on his brow. The sun beat down on him, yet it lit the blue skies that were visible no matter where he looked. How can nowhere contain so much? He looked again at the map. There was still land in the distance, and the city and its Tower were visible, but deciding where in the small space on the map his little dot of a ship was located seemed impossible. He put it away again and continued on in his initial direction.

It was in the third hour that a grin cast itself on Owyn's face once more. He turned and looked around as he let the muscles in his arms relax. As the boat spun, an impossible sight greeted him. In the distance, beyond the endless blue of the water, where it met the sky in a seam that adjoined the disparate domains, Owyn saw a ship rising out of nothing. First, the mast appeared, just a dot without purpose. Something new on the horizon. Then it stood taller. A sail appeared, then another smaller sail grew in front of the first, until finally the whole vessel was in sight. It seemed to fly across the water, white foam breaking as the bow cut through the sea. Owyn didn't need the map anymore. That was southwest, where ships rounded the coast into the bay. That was where he needed to go. Checking over his shoulder, he turned his own vessel to face the approaching ship and he rowed once more.

It felt good. It was work with a purpose. Owyn rowed now with renewed vigor. The smile on his face may have faded with the strain of the work, but he still beamed within. It would work. This would work. He'd build something for himself.

"Ho!" screamed a voice behind him. Owyn jumped and turned to see the ship was much closer now.

"Ho!" screamed the voice again. It was definitely coming from the ship, though Owyn wondered how anyone's voice could travel so far. The ship was massive, its white sails gleamed in the sunlight, and the bow was painted and ostentatious. Bright colors reflected in the surrounding water, reds and oranges and yellows. Were he closer, the reflections paired with the paint itself would assault Owyn's eyes. It seemed both haphazard and intentional. There was so much wood used in the making of ships, they cost more than multiple farming estates combined. Who would cover the most precious resource in the world with paint so gaudy?

The ship was coming towards him quickly, yet as Owyn turned his boat to get out of its way, he saw the sails were being furled. Men atop the masts were lifting and folding the cloth sails, affixing them to the wooden towers that held them aloft. The ship was slowing as it approached.

"Ho!" screamed the voice again. "Flag for help if ye need it!" Owyn saw now that it was a man on the frontmost point of the ship, holding something cone-shaped. He must have shouted through it.

Owyn didn't need help, but he didn't know how to flag for that. In truth, he wouldn't know how to flag for help either if he had needed it.

"Raise oars if ye do not need aid!" shouted the man on the ship. *He knows I'm crazy*, thought Owyn. *He knows I don't know what I'm doing out here*. Owyn raised his oars anyway. The stiff leather paddles affixed at the ends of the stone rods dripped and glistened in the sunlight. The man put down the cone he held and spoke to someone behind him. Owyn could not see who, but he saw the men atop the masts, holding the furled sails up. They were watching him. How odd he must look, alone out here. He still held the oars high.

"Gods' speed to you then! *The Small Journey* wishes ye well!" shouted the man on the ship, once again putting the cone to his mouth. At his call, the men atop the masts let the sails drop. It was amazing how quickly they caught the light breeze and were full of wind once more. The ship almost seemed to jump as the breeze propelled it forward. Owyn thought about sitting and watching it pass, but that seemed juvenile. He refused to look that far outside his element. Instead, he dropped his oars once again into the blue beneath him, turned his vessel, and rowed. It was only moments later that the ship passed him by. He looked at the brightly painted vessel and saw dozens of men standing at the edge of the deck. They were all waving at him. Owyn smiled, matching the expression of the men. How could he not? He raised his oars out of the water and held them in a wave of his own. He saw one man aboard the ship who was not waving, but his smile was as bright as the sun as he held his hat in his hand. The man wore a regal green jacket as garish as the paint on the ship, and the only one of its kind that Owyn had ever seen. He didn't match any of the other men on the ship in appearance or manner, nodding as the ship passed by before returning his hat to his head. Owyn figured he must be the captain; he looked as if he had stepped straight out of a pub tale with all the exaggeration that the storyteller could give. The ship moved by in seconds. Owyn put his oars to the ocean again and the men on the deck resumed their work. Only the Captain still looked out at the strange man in a small boat rowing his way into the great beyond.

"I need a name for you," said Owyn to the boat beneath his feet. "*The Small Journey*—that's a good name for a ship. What to name a boat, though?"

He thought over a few names to pass the hours as he rowed and rowed towards the horizon where the colorful ship had risen from but nothing stood out to him. Looking again from horizon to map and back again, Owyn finally saw his green circle's place in the world: in front of the rowboat, still a ways in the distance, was a peninsula of hard black rock that stood resolute as waves crashed against it. As he looked from the land to the north, down along the coast, to the gap of ocean before the rocks he had circled, Owyn could imagine the devastation caused by the shallow waters and hard rocks hidden just beneath the surface that led to the point he now saw. This was it. This was the tail of land at the western edge of Turtle Bay. The hidden hook that had caught so many merchant vessels and sent them to their graves. This was where he was going.

Despite the being in sight of his destination, Owyn still had more rowing in front of him than he had thought. He felt every time he craned his neck to see behind him that the land would be only two strokes away. Yet while the horn of the bay grew every time he looked, it remained ever distant. Another hour passed before Owyn felt the sea floor scrape against the centerline of his boat. He wanted to smile and jump for joy, but a part of him pushed against happiness. Owyn didn't want to be let down. Not again. He kept his face blank as he turned to see that he had, in fact, arrived at the rock he had circled on the vellum map—or close enough to leave his thoughts behind. Emotion won out at last. His hands had never shaken like this before. Always steady in his old life, they were excited now. He was excited. Owyn leapt out of the boat.

His arms cried as he pulled his boat ashore, but Owyn bore through it, noticing to the cry and doing his best to work anyway. He didn't want the pain to matter to him. He wanted more important things to make the decision. He got the boat high on the rocky shore and left it to survey the land. The ground felt odd beneath his feet after the day on the water. His legs wobbled and did not want to obey him, yet he made them. He hobbled in a weak walk along the entire length of the small rock island south of the peninsula. It was larger than it had looked from the water. It was perfect.

Returning to the shore, Owyn removed his bag from the boat and carried it up to a flat spot uphill, away from the water. He set down his bag and looked out at the surrounding land.

This will be a corner, he thought, smile showing again. The sun was still high in the sky, though it had begun its journey towards the horizon. Owyn began emptying his bag. First came food—flour for bannock, sausages, some roots, just enough for a few meals, tucked in a small satchel with an oilstove—then came a tent. Before removing anything else, Owyn set up the tent. He used stones from the island to weigh down the lines for the canvas tent since the ground was far too hard for the stakes he had brought.

Shelter built, Owyn emptied the rest of his bag into his new home. He kicked off his thin leather shoes and felt the cool of the rock beneath his feet. He had never been a man for boots. Too heavy, too loud. Owyn rolled up the cuffs of his pants and felt the sun hit his calves. It already felt so good on his shoulders. He had taken his shirt off as he had built the tent. The worn green cloth sat next to the bag he'd used to carry everything he now owned. He wondered what he looked like now. Not quite a sailor, but not quite the man of his old life either. That was good enough. He looked back at the tent. Owyn didn't have much—necessities, mostly. The last item he removed was a small bundle wrapped in an oilskin cloth. Sitting on the ground of his island, looking out at the water and the blue sky, Owyn opened the final bundle. Inside were vellum sheets. Unlike the map, he had drawn these himself. They were his plans. They were his new purpose.

Owyn marveled at the work on the sheets as the sun slowly fell. This was good. This felt good. As the sun approached the horizon and the sky glowed, he put away the sacred papers. There would be hard work tomorrow. He cooked a modest meal and ate, watching the sun set over the sea. Owyn slept well that night on his new island home.

CHAPTER 2

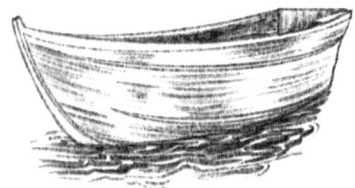

B efore he had even opened his eyes, Owyn noticed that his back hurt from the thin bedroll set atop the rock and that he was freezing, even under the woolen blankets he had brought. But still, he woke up happy.

The thin beginnings of sunlight crept under the unsealed bottom of the canvas tent and he had woken in an instant. Owyn's body hurt as he stood. Not only his back from the uncomfortable sleep, but his arms screamed in pain as he pushed off the ground. Everything was sore. Even his legs were sore, despite the fact that he hadn't walked more than an hour total the whole day yesterday. But the pain wouldn't stop him. He shook his head and limped outside, feeling each step.

Owyn was a man of the mornings. His eyes were bright as he looked out at the bay. His face, while not young, did not show much of the wear of his life before. Age had just begun to crease his skin and pull his tight curly hair further away from his brow. He felt so much older than he looked. Thin without being wiry. Short without being diminutive. His lightly tanned skin may not blend in with the peoples of every town, but his face was an unassuming one. A forgettable one. Not ugly, but not beautiful. Perfect for his old vocation.

Now, the world was beautiful. There was the littlest slice of the sun peeking out from above the horizon and the sky was a golden yellow. The ocean was alight with the sunrise, its water still, reflecting the sky like a mirror, while adding something, too. The sunrise was more than the sum of its parts here. It was quiet on the island. It was perfect. Turning back towards the tent, Owyn saw that the sky opposite the sun was just as beautiful—no, more beautiful than the sunrise. The violet and red colors of the sky danced atop the deeper blue that would show its face during the day. Owyn watched the colors change with awe.

"This is it," he said. He never talked to himself. It almost felt wrong breaking the silence of the morning, but it would have felt worse not saying what he felt. "Thank you," he said. "Thank you."

He cooked a quick porridge and a hot drink for breakfast before packing the oilskin satchel and heading towards the rowboat sitting high on shore below.

"*Morning Sunshine,*" he said. "That's your name." He said as he sat in the water beside the boat. The cold felt so good on his groaning muscles. He'd wanted to leave earlier, but some things took time.

Triph would have recommended more stretching before Owyn finally stood and pushed out the boat, his muscles still aching, but the pain was lessened after the rest; besides, Owyn knew he would not be able to sit still any longer while his dream was so close to within reach. He rested his hand on the *Morning Sunshine* as the boat glided and left the rocks to float on the water. Oars sitting high, it looked like a painting as it sat alone on the smooth sea with the sun rising behind it. Owyn hadn't seen many paintings. He'd once had thoughts of filling a home with them. But he'd never had a home. There had never been a chance. Never the time or the money. He looked back towards his canvas tent now, flapping gently in the breeze. He could have a home here. Maybe. Owyn pushed down the hope, swallowing the emotions that came with it. There was work to do first.

Owyn had a million loose plans in his head. Hope and drive had gotten him to this island; now he needed to act on his plans. His eyes ran across the vacant island. It was a hill of stone, jutting out of the water. The sea lapped at its edges as the breeze began to pick up, but the base of the island was dry. He'd found one corner for his dream, set his tent up on it. Now he could survey the rest. He could stop. He could plan. He was tired of planning.

Owyn's smile faded as he stretched. His body would not be pleased, and was not pleased as he stretched now, but it didn't know what was coming next. Plans were fine, but what was the point of merely planning corners of the building when he could get the material to start building it? A sore body wasn't a dead one. Owyn set the satchel in the boat and hopped in.

The smooth water felt unreal beneath him. His hands found the oars as if they had never let go, and he spun the rowboat towards his destination: East-Noreast. That's how the sailors would say it on *The Small Journey*.

"*Morn'*, are you ready?" he said to the wooden boat beneath him. He sat still, as if waiting for a response. A cool breeze began on the other side of the bay and pushed across the water, rippling the perfect surface before reaching the back of Owyn's neck. He hadn't known what he was waiting for, but this was it. With a breath, he paddled towards Kudra.

Time didn't seem to pass as Owyn rowed across the opening to Turtle Bay. The sun rose behind him and his neck grew warm. The wind continued to push gently against him, yet the water remained relatively still. He watched his island disappear into the horizon, sinking into the sea. He smiled. To travel so fast with so little effort, no wonder all the prominent merchants of the world traveled the rivers or the coasts. Hours had passed, and he had felt nothing but the soothing of the pain in his arms. The warmth of the sun cooled slightly, and Owyn turned to see that he had almost reached the city. He'd rowed straight into the shadow of the God's Tower; it blocked the sun. The immense Tower seemed to pierce the sky. Owyn was unable to see the top. He wondered if anyone ever had.

Owyn had reached the docks of Kudra once more. He felt something as he hit the edge of the stone docks and knew he'd crossed the bay. Joy? Owyn's heart didn't quite know what it was processing as the smile lit his face.

"Two coppers for the mooring," said a voice behind him.

"What—" began Owyn, looking to see who spoke.

"Two coppers, sir, for the day."

Owyn turned to see a boy. "The dockmaster made no mention of this when he sold me the boat yesterday."

"Well, that was yesterday. He may not have expected you back. Two coppers, no matter what he thought. For the day."

"You'll moor it yourself for the two bits?"

"That's extra—three in all—if you want me to do any labor myself." The boy grinned a wide, gap-filled grin.

Owyn shook his head as he reached into the satchel, grabbing three coins from an inside pocket. He tossed them to the boy, one at a time.

"I appreciate your help," he said. The boy caught the coins and, without hesitation, tossed a rope to Owyn and had the boat to the edge of the dock, where, in seconds, a ladder appeared. Owyn climbed out, satchel over his shoulder, and the boy clambered in.

"Thank you, sir," said the child as he hopped down into the boat. He watched the child row his boat inward along the pier for a few seconds before turning towards the bustling docks. Owyn walked towards the city above, slowly at first, then briskly, as he had to avoid people at work on the docks. The world around him had grown busy in an instant. There were so many people, moving and shouting. The noise was deafening.

Owyn made his body smaller. His shoulders hunched forward, his arms held close to his side. His pace quickened. He was used to this. Hiding had been his life. Cities brought out all the old feelings and habits that Owyn wished to leave behind. Still, he made himself small. Unseen.

The markets at the edge of the docks were some of the best in all of Kudra. Owyn and Triph had always investigated the markets at the edge of cities first but rarely made them a target for their work. They were the first to get fresh goods—well, the freshest goods not specifically meant for the mayor, the governor, or, in this case, the King.

The King.

Owyn wove through a throng of people, under and past them, as he thought of the monarch. The King who sat in Kudra was not only the leader of the city, but of the entire empire of Breiar. Owyn had never learned where the name of the land had come from, but he knew where the law came from. The palace at the seat of the God's

Tower was both divine and secular, and that was the source of the King's right to lead.

Owyn ached. Habit made his body small, but he had not stretched nearly enough to be the kind of limber necessary for his old trade. But he wasn't here for his old trade. Owyn tried to stand straight. His back and shoulders yelled within as they were stretched out once more. He stood tall. Tall and uncomfortable. People moved about, sound and bodies all too close. No one had bumped him yet, but people were close. The city didn't stop moving on his account. Being in the city was beginning to sour his mood. Too much of his past was here. He thought of the last city he'd worked in. It was the people and the buildings and the noise. It was all of it. All the things that could be stolen and all the saps who held onto things without thought. There was so much more to the world than things. He shook his head, but no thoughts cleared. He hated feeling this way. The noise in his head dwarfed that of the city. He thought of going back to his island, but that would be a retreat. That would be hiding. He stood up straighter, despite muscles in his back and core manipulating him into a sore hunch. Owyn was done hiding.

He felt the slightest of tugs at his satchel and, before he knew what he had done, Owyn had grabbed the pickpocket's arm. The boy, no more than ten, looked up at him, fear and shock in his eyes. Owyn shook his head and glared at the child before letting go of his arm. The would-be thief ran, disappearing into the crowd. Cities. He patted the shoulder strap of the oilskin satchel he carried and walked forward. That was why he couldn't smile, not here. He could not get away from his old self. The city wasn't for him; his old life wasn't for him. He had plans and he would see them through. He'd get away from here soon.

First, he had to visit the King.

***

The line began outside the palace, off the main street, winding out through an alley and back to main, then down another alley. It promised several hours of standing and waiting, but Owyn found the end and positioned himself there.

It wasn't long before a body took a place behind him, and a person behind that, and another, and so on, until Owyn was nowhere near the back of the line. As the line continued to build, he lost track of people behind him. They didn't matter. No, he didn't want to think that way. The number didn't matter. The wait didn't matter. He patted the satchel again. The plans mattered. His plans mattered.

"How long will you try today, Elvah?" said a voice beside Owyn, outside of the line.

"Today?" cackled a response. "I brought food and water. I won't end my wait today."

"Good for you, Elvah. You may yet grace the King with your pleasant demeanor," said a third voice.

"Don't you crack wise with me, Willem!" snapped Elvah.

A group outside of the line laughed. They were merchants, dressed richly, in a poor sort of way, walking past the line. The rich cloth covering them had faded, and the plated metal buttons were chipped. Owyn didn't need to pick their pockets to know they carried their wealth in ego more than in coin. Elvah turned away from them, her scowl making Owyn regret that he had even looked. He turned ahead, avoiding the eyes of the angry woman and the laughs of the bullies. His eyes fell on the line. There were so many people here. Did that woman say she brought food and water?

Suddenly, Owyn's satchel, filled with plans and papers and dreams, felt very light for the line that loomed in front of him.

Hours passed.

The sun that had been behind Owyn when he had entered the line now fell in front of him. It wearied his eyes, but he always looked forward. His lips were dry, and he hadn't heard so many noises from his stomach since he'd been a boy. He could not look away from what lay ahead of him, though. The palace was so close, there was just a crowd between him and it. Just people between him and his dream. Same as it always had been. That would end soon. His stomach growled once more, rumbling his ribs and almost covering up the murmur traveling down the line of people. Before he heard what was being said as it passed down from person to person, he heard another sound. Hooves clopped against the stone road. Riders from the palace were going down the line. The first time they shouted, Owyn heard only sounds. When they repeated what they had said, they were much closer.

"The Court of His Majesty, Rigney the Second, King of Kudra, Emperor of Breiar, has closed to the requests of the public. Be merry and know your King carries your voice in his heart." They rode for three paces of their steeds before repeating their message: "The Court of..." Owyn stopped listening. Closed. The Palace was closed, and he was barely two blocks closer to being heard by the King.

People started to disperse from the line. More behind him than in front.

"Be gone, you lazy wretches!" shouted the woman behind him. Elvah. Her voice cackled now as it had in the morning. "Give up now. Give us a chance to speak for once."

Owyn had almost given up upon hearing the criers. But not everyone was leaving the line in front of him. Many remained, moving forward as those who had given up and left the line disappeared down alleys off the main street. The sound of so many feet moving and leaving felt as though a load was lifted off of Owyn's tired shoulders. He had almost left with the first wave. He was so hungry.

So thirsty. Yet now he was moving forward faster than he had during the day.

Elvah was now behind him in line. "When does the King begin his reception tomorrow?" he asked, turning to see her as they walked. His voice was hoarse and didn't want to work. He almost stopped to apologize for how he sounded. He wasn't himself. But the glare she shot him stopped him from the apology. It wasn't the answer he wanted, but it was familiar enough. Owyn turned and followed the line of moving people until it stopped. There were still so many between him and the palace, and they were prepared. Owyn's stomach yelled out once more. Its cries distracted from his sore body. At least he hadn't paddled the rowboat with his gut.

The sun dipped further on its journey towards the horizon. It would be behind the buildings of the city soon. Their shadows were already growing long. Owyn absentmindedly touched his satchel again and again. It was always there, but that didn't stop him from always being worried. It didn't carry food, but it carried something more important. His stomach would survive the lapse in food, but he wasn't sure that he could survive without his dream. So Owyn waited, even though the sun did not. Soon it was nighttime. There was a chill in the air that he had not expected from the summer day.

Minutes turned into hours. The line moved, but it was erratic. Only when someone left did anyone get a chance to step forward. The movement was immediate, though. No soul wanted to lose their place this far into the wait. It was past midnight that the line moved again with some regularity. Owyn's head had nodded once or twice as he stood still with eyelids heavy. He shook away tiredness when he realized why the line was moving. As those whose heads nodded more than once dipped into accidental sleep, they were quietly removed from the line. Sometimes it seemed to the side of the road, but Owyn stepped over more than one person dozing on the cobbled street. He forced himself to keep his eyes open, to stop his head from nodding. He stretched upward, moving his whole body, feeling the tendons in his hands move and his calves tighten. Hunger had distracted from his sore body, but it didn't cure a thing. He would sleep so well when this had passed. But when would it pass? He patted the satchel once more, reminding himself of his dream. He didn't need sleep. He didn't need food. Owyn had something better.

No one spoke. The sounds of the surrounding city slowed but did not stop. There was only silence from the line.

Night passed slowly as Owyn waited. More fell asleep. Any who remained awake stayed in line. He almost didn't believe his eyes when a pink and orange glow tinted the sky. The sun was rising. Dawn had come.

He patted his satchel and listened to his stomach groan with want before he looked around. The world was the same, but he was closer, closer to the King, closer to his goal. He smiled a tired smile. Owyn was closer to happiness.

***

It was an hour past sunrise before a rider came from the palace. He shouted and called, announcing that the King would listen to his subjects this day and telling them to form a line and wait their turns. The line remained. Owyn didn't turn to see how much it had grown behind him. He only looked forward, his smile barely touching his tired eyes as he finally set foot on the palace steps. The palace had been built on a small hill. They always were, thought Owyn. The seat of power in a town or village was always above the rest of the town. Why not for a kingdom, too? Within the city and the sight of the God's Tower, the Palace did not look quite so high and mighty.

The Tower loomed above everything. *Loomed*. That was the biggest word that came to Owyn's mind, and still it wasn't big enough. The structure disappeared into the sky. There was no top to it. He knew he'd been told stories of the God's Tower as a child, back when those around him thought religion would help a young boy grow up. While he grew up just fine without the stories setting in, he felt the stories now. So close to the Tower, nothing made by men seemed to matter anymore. *Well, nothing made* yet *by a man*, Owyn thought to himself. The stones stacked by the gods would have a partner soon enough on his island.

Owyn's head nodded. His eyes felt like they'd been stabbed with how much they wanted to close. His stomach ached and his muscles screamed. But his feet still carried him forward with slow steps as the line moved. Tired and hungry, he hardly believed it when he crossed the final threshold and stood before the King.

Chapter 3

"I like your proposal," said His Majesty Rigney the Second, King of Kudra, Emperor of Breiar. His voice was soft, not without feeling, but quietly spoken, as if on the edge of a whisper. It was the room, crimson and gold, massive and domed, closed around the King and open around the court where Owyn now stood. The room carried the voice of the King. He was not sitting on the dark red throne, but stood in front of his seat as he spoke. Owyn tried to listen. His head nodded as the King orated, but his body couldn't keep up. This moment was so important. The King liked his proposal! But the man sure became poetic as he spoke, and Owyn had never had an ear for poetry. The King's voice paused and Owyn realized that he hadn't heard a word that he had been saying. He wanted to slap himself awake, but that wouldn't fit with the poetic scene. He blinked hard and tried to focus on the King's words. Still, his mind wandered further.

The King was young—younger than Owyn had expected— only in his mid-thirties. And while his hair may have been thinning unseen under his crown, there was no grey in his beard. What he lacked in the appearance of wisdom, though, he made up for in demeanor. He spoke with a soft, controlled voice. His ministers and advisors stood around, listening now. They'd whispered their thoughts before the King had started this speech. Gods, he was still speaking! Owyn's tired eyes wandered on their own about the throne room until he noticed a young girl, as inattentive as him, on a chair behind the standing King. She wore a crown and livery but looked as though she wished to be covered in blankets and sleeping rather than beside the King. Her head lolled as she stared out at nothing. Owyn was jealous. Though the advisors had whispered, the King was not quiet now. His next statement was loud despite the King's soft voice.

"However, the Crown must decline this request."

Owyn sunk where he stood. It was as if the words had placed a weight on him. His shoulders sank and his head drooped. The weight of the last two days wasn't held up by anything now. The hope was gone, and Owyn almost fell where he stood. He had not noticed how tall he had been carrying himself lately. That was no more.

"This dream may be worth something. To you it may be worth a lot, but to my council and my judgement, it is simply not worth the cost. Materials, labor, time. We simply cannot allocate what would be necessary for such a project with limited civic value. I thank you for your time."

With that, the King sat. A man of the guards approached Owyn, but he ignored the hint. His tired mind did not have the strength to stop his mouth speaking.

"Daughtn has its lights on the hill. Telnir, its flags and lamps, and Hof, the reflection of the ice on the Frozen Plateau. I need of no labor. I can do this myself."

The King looked surprised at the outburst. The girl behind him looked up, finally intrigued enough to pay attention. The King did not stand as he spoke next: "The crown will not spare the expense to one man and I cannot spare expense to builders. These other harbors may be safer for their ships, but merchants of Kudra are of stronger stuff."

"Sir?" said a small man at the door to Owyn. He wore the same attire as the advisors standing next to the King. Now the King looked annoyed. The girl beside him grinned, but the King saw only his advisor speaking to Owyn and settled in his chair to await the next citizen. He said something to the girl, but all Owyn overheard was a name: Agatha.

"Sir, if you please," said the advisor, quieter now. The man was stately and clean, with a regal air to him, though he seemed timid as Owyn turned towards him. "If I may, can you leave a copy of your plans with me? I'd like to review the figures and hold onto the idea." Owyn lit up as he removed sheets of vellum from his satchel.

"Thank you!" he said. "Thank you!"

"It never hurts the kingdom to hold on to an idea," said the small advisor. "Who knows if this king or the next may wish to act upon it." With that, the guard at the door placed a hand on Owyn's shoulder, and he turned and left the palace.

This king or the next. Owyn sulked through the busy streets of Kudra. It was loud, so very loud, as the cacophony of sounds from people and animals bounced off the stone buildings and echoed around the city. His body wanted to fall over. His feet were so tired, and he was going nowhere, so why bother walking? He stopped and was pushed forward by a man hustling behind him. An expletive was shouted at Owyn but all he could do was stare at the ground. His feet would not move. Another shove from behind as those walking the road could not deal with their impasse. Owyn didn't look up. He looked at his hands.

This king or the next. These hands were cracked and held scars; they had lived many lives. His deft fingers felt like they were slower than before. Maybe that was age, maybe that was his desire. He had left his old life and had no need for quick fingers. Now Owyn wanted strength in his hands—strength like his heart, like his dream.

This king or the next. His hands were not yet old, but they could not wait for the next monarch. They could not wait another day. *He* could not wait another day. Owyn let his hands fall to his side and looked up at the surrounding signs beyond the palace stairs. Taverns and inns lined the streets. Many people walked about him and the line that led towards the King, but a group of young men sat at a table on the edge of the street, eating strips of thin bread, steaming and dipped in a dark sauce, pungent with the smell of fermentation and fish. Opening his satchel, he felt the bag of coins it carried. It was for his project. It felt wrong to spend any of his savings on his stomach.

Owyn wanted to stop. Cease everything. He wanted to lie down on the stone. A breeze cut through the buildings. Coming off the sea and winding through the city, it blew against Owyn's back. His weak body took a step forward to brace against the gentle air. Was that enough? He took another step forward, eyes still on the ground, watching his feet start to move without his mind.

"I need to sleep," he said, his hoarse voice talking to no one. With effort, he lifted his head. The city moved without him, shouts and calls and conversations above footfalls and the noises of movement. It was all too loud. Owyn shrunk, shoulders moving forward, arms tucking in. He was becoming himself again. His old self. He'd been tired before, so he knew what to do now. He made himself think of his tiredness instead of the words of the King. Tired was now, and those words had passed. So, he walked.

The city of Kudra was ancient. Kingdoms had come and gone through it, and it was built as though each generation had hated the plans of the last. But it was still a city, and Owyn had learned cities. What was a thief without direction? He felt history fighting itself as he wove his way through the expansive city. He'd been on his feet for longer than a day and they were aching. At least his stomach had stopped growling. That pain had moved up to his head.

Shouts carried from apartment to apartment above the street as Owyn walked. People were angry. And loud. He was close. Every town he'd ever been to was the same. Why should Kudra be any different? He'd walked minutes away from the palace, crossed a few streets as the markets thinned and the voices of the city grew quieter, until they grew louder again, but different this time. He'd found his old life. Owyn had walked into the slums. He was too tired to know whether to thank his old life or be angry with it.

He walked until he heard the jeers of women from a building. These slums did not know him, but he knew them. There were certainly pickpockets and beggars at the edges of the alleys, but they did not target him, the small, tired thief. The calls came louder and Owyn walked into the brothel.

"A bed, please. No girl. Just for the day," he said to the woman sitting at the open door to the building.

"Gotta kick you out by nightfall," she said.

"You can wake me before then," Owyn said, pulling a coin out of his shirt pocket, not the satchel. There weren't coins in there now. If he didn't think of them, then they would not be. Not in the slums. "If you have food, I'd take everything you've got." He tossed her the coin.

"Room at the end of the hall upstairs. Left side. No girl?"

"No girl."

Owyn forced himself up the stairs and to his room. He fell on the bed and was asleep before his body hit the lumpy mattress. His mind was too weary to provide him with anything but oblivion as he sank deep into darkness.

He woke to a shove and a call. Owyn woke quickly, ready to run before stopping himself and realizing where he was. The girl who'd shouted at him was different from the one in the entry earlier. She watched him. No time to dally, it seemed. It was an hour till sundown and he'd have to clear the bed for work. Owyn stood and tapped his shirt where a few coins were stored. Still there. He picked up his satchel and heard the quiet jingle of the coins stored underneath his plans. It was an honest brothel.

"Food?" he asked. His mind was already on the plans in his satchel.

This king or the next.

He didn't hear the words the woman said, but the gesture looked positive, so he followed her down the stairs to the ground floor.

He smelled the food before he saw it, and he was not sure if his face wanted to smile or grimace. The smell was all too familiar. Owyn had lived in slums his whole life. This was practically an old home.

The gruel he had tasted before. The warm watery bowl of yellow and white nothing was as awful and as marvelous as any he'd ever had before. It smelled only of warmth and removed any memory of taste from his mouth.

The King's words rang out in his mind again, but it wasn't the denial that hurt. "This king or the next," said the advisor. They didn't care. They didn't have the time for him right now and so they'd make Owyn wait until they did. Maybe wait until he died.

But his dream wouldn't die.

Owyn felt the satchel at his feet. The money within took years to earn. Years of hiding profits from Triph. Years of building up an idea into a dream, then refining it to a goal.

Damn the King. Damn the advisor. Damn the—

Owyn stopped. He wanted to damn the right way of doing things. He thought of his little boat, *Morning Sunshine*. His escape from an old life into a better one. He'd always planned to work alone. He'd needed the King's blessing because it was the right way to do things. Well, he didn't have to do everything the right way. Now his work would just take more of his coin. Owyn looked up from his gruel and saw some men coming in with the evening. They spoke to the girls, each going upstairs with his pick. None of the men were rich. This wasn't a place for wealth. Never would be. Owyn felt his satchel. He didn't care for wealth. He'd never been a thief for the money, anyway.

The King seemed to have thought that without his help, Owyn would abandon his dream. If Owyn could do that, what made him different from the men walking in here? What made him different from the women? Men paying to feel something, women taking payment to survive. He wanted more than survival. He needed more than money. He had a chance to feel something real. He had felt something real on that island.

Damn the King.

Owyn wanted his help to do things the proper way. The right way. At least he wouldn't do them the wrong way. He would not return to his old life. But there was more than one right way. There was his way. And his way was alone.

Gruel eaten, Owyn stood. He walked to the door and saw the woman who had let him in.

"Any stone quarries in town?" he asked.

***

The walk to the quarry took until the sun started setting. The woman's directions were good. Not many stoneworkers frequented that particular slum—Owyn walked through others as he had traveled—but the women knew of a few clients. His feet were still sore, and his bones and muscles hurt so much they didn't feel his own. But he was full, and he had slept. Damn the King. Owyn wouldn't stop at the word of a king.

He would have to travel through the city later that night on his way to the dock holding *Morning Sunshine*, then the long row home to his island. Could he do that in the dark? That didn't matter. The darkness and the words of kings were two things on a new list of things that wouldn't stop Owyn. There was work to be done here first, and he pushed the list from his mind.

Owyn stood at the edge of a great opening in the ground, one of Kudra's stone quarries laid out in front of him. Men worked it now with no sign of slowing, though the sun was about to set. There was a small set of buildings at the top of the mine that Owyn approached. Some men stood around outside talking amongst themselves as workers moved about them, approaching or leaving the pit in the ground.

Owyn cleared his throat. He had meant to ensure he could speak after a day with many miles underfoot, but the men before him stopped their conversation and looked at him. Their silence cut into him. How was the quiet more deafening than all the cries of the city behind him?

"I'd like to speak to the foreman, please," Owyn said. Though he had cleared his windpipe, his voice still came out quiet and cracked.

"Aye, that'd be me," said a tall, broad man in the center of the group. The man looked like he was cut from the stone he worked. His clothes were finer than those of the others in the group. They were cheap to be sure—cloth instead of leather—but they were not worn through as if he worked in them. His boots reflected the sunset in the distance. "You come for an occupation?"

"I, uh, come with a proposition," said Owyn. Why were words coming with such difficulty now? He jerked as he removed some sheets from his satchel. "There is waste stone in your quarry, correct?" he said while fumbling with one of the sheets in the bag. Two unwanted sheets were coming with it, and he tried to push them back into the satchel while disturbing nothing else. Dammit, what were these nerves?

"That's true, son," said the foreman. The surrounding men did not move. They stood and watched Owyn. "The crown's marked the waste to be milled into road cobble."

Owyn stopped fumbling with the sheets halfway out of his satchel. *Damn the crown.* "But it's only chosen for such purpose, correct? Not painted?" He thought he caught the hint of a smile at the corner of the foreman's mouth.

"Aye, there isn't a physical mark."

"And you certainly have not measured it in any amount yet, if it's only just chosen for road cobble?"

"You question if we do our job?"

"I assume that isn't a part of your job."

The foreman thought a moment before relenting. "That's true."

"Well then, I don't see an impasse here."

"An impasse to what?"

Owyn pushed the sheets of figures back into his satchel. "An impasse to our deal." Owyn shifted his weight, throwing it in a known way. The coins in his satchel danced as he wanted them to, clinking against one another in the song that every man liked. The foreman stifled a grin.

"Would you like a drink, son?" he said, gesturing towards the building behind him and his men.

Owyn had not been great with numbers growing up. Words had come even harder. Speaking, convincing, storytelling—those had never come naturally to him, so he'd left the talking to Triph. Triph hated numbers, leaving that to Owyn who taught himself on the job. It'd been a fair trade. Well, fair until Owyn had started saving money on the side for himself.

"I can pay you a copper and a half per load," said Owyn, running the expenses through his head. The foreman merely held a full cup towards him with his hand and shook his head. Owyn took the drink, and the foreman sat. They were on two chairs outside the building facing the quarry. It was as if they were both alone and in the thick of the workspace at the same moment. The foreman took a pull from his drink and Owyn followed suit. He held in the immediate urge to spit the liquid back up.

"I knew you weren't a working man," said the foreman as he kept himself from laughing.

Owyn gulped down the foul liquid. "It was never the path in front of me. I choose to do some work now, though."

"And what work are you planning with the leftover stone?"

"A lighthouse," said Owyn. It felt good to say.

"A what?"

"A tower of sorts, off of the coast. I've got the island to build it. I've got the will to build it. I look now for the stone to build it."

"You are asking for stone that is suited for no tower."

"Then you've no reason to worry. The King can't ask about stone for his road if my tower never gets built."

The foreman nodded at that. "Folks in this city don't much care for towers," he said under his breath, before taking another sip of his drink. Owyn refrained from joining in the drink this time. "So we have a deal then? Three coppers per load of leftover stone?"

"I won't—" Owyn stopped himself from saying what he wanted to, pivoting the sentence. "I won't be able to disagree with two." Those figures still worked out.

The foreman eyed him slowly. Owyn nearly spoke again as the seconds ticked by before the other man held out his cup. "Cheers to a deal!"

Owyn clinked cups with the man. "Cheers," he said before forcing some of the fiery drink down again.

"Now, how do you intend to transport these loads?"

The foreman spoke with a smile and took another drink. They'd toasted to the deal. It was done. Now another needed to be made. Owyn had been had. He shook his head and took a drink from the cup without a grimace. "I'll rent a cart," he said after his drink. "If you have one."

"That we do, but how do I know you'll bring it back? You've no credit with me."

"I'm buying the stone."

"Correct, bought and paid for." The foreman held out his hand. Owyn looked at it as the seconds dripped by before removing three coppers from his satchel pocket and placing them in the man's hand. "But the cart is a rental, and I don't know if you'll ever return with it."

"Can I buy it?"

The foreman did not turn towards Owyn. Even so, he saw the man's eyes widen with greed before closing again to the negotiation at hand. "It isn't for sale, so I guess there's nothing to be done for you."

"Everything is for sale."

"Not the cart."

"A man, then. What if you sent a man with me to ensure my credit, and that your cart returned to you safely?"

"Waste a whole man for this? That I cannot afford, and I do not think you wish to, either."

"I'll watch the cart," said a booming, low voice behind the foreman. An enormous figure had emerged from the building that Owyn and the foreman sat in front of. Owyn had heard the door but thought nothing of it.

"I won't pay you for it, Tulbër," said the foreman.

"My work here was done in a week anyway," said the figure, his deep voice sent vibrations through Owyn's ribcage. As he walked around the corner and stood in front of the seated men, Owyn realized that the figure speaking, Tulbër, was not a man. He was a giant. Owyn wanted to speak but couldn't say a thing as the conversation unfolded in front of him.

"You'd leave early?" said the foreman.

"Will you pay me?" Tulbër turned, eyes locking with Owyn's.

Owyn's mind raced with thoughts, but he distilled it to one. "Will you help carry the cart?"

Tulbër smiled. It was a brilliant grin, as large as Owyn's entire face. "I'll watch the cart."

It was done, and Owyn didn't know how it had happened. Before he and the giant continued their discussion of wages and the giant's last week, the foreman shouted down orders; a cart of waste stone was pushed out of the quarry. They mentioned a return in the rainy season, but Owyn only watched the work as the cart full of stone came up out of the hole in the ground. It was massive, nearly as tall as Owyn atop its stone wheels, and was piled high with the heap of stone he purchased. It was wide enough to take up half an alley within the city, and was twice as long. It was a lot of stone. More than Owyn had imagined when he'd ordered "a load." He should have specified that before the purchase, but luck had saved him. Words were not his strength. The men who pushed the cart looked at him and then the foreman who nodded before walking away. Alone with the cart full of his stone, Owyn kept calm. Excitement brewed within and he wanted to race to his stone—worn body be damned—but he walked to the cart instead and started to push it.

The thing wouldn't budge.

It was so heavy the stone wheels sat frozen still. Owyn turned and saw the Tulbër and the man still talking. He planted his feet, put a shoulder to the cart and heaved. It felt like nothing was happening, then, just at the moment Owyn saw the bead of sweat at the edge of his nose fall towards the ground, a catch; the wheels freed themselves and the cart began to move. Owyn wanted to cheer, he turned to look at the pair, but before he could, the cart had started to roll away. Once it started, it didn't seem to want to stop. Stone wheels, free as ever, played with that freedom. The cart was rolling away from him and Owyn started after it.

"I'll just get a head start!" he shouted as the cart barreled out in front of him, his hand barely holding onto the back wall of it. The thing was on a slope. It wouldn't stop now. Owyn's fingers strained just to hold on as he raced behind the thing.

He saw where the slope was headed.

The quarry pit.

Owyn pulled again, getting a second hand on the cart and heaving with all his strength. Planted feet slid forward and fingers hurt. The cart wouldn't stop. What was he doing?

"Give me this, little one," said a booming voice as a stone-gray hand, larger than Owyn's head, landed beside his at the edge of the cart. The thing stopped moving and Owyn crashed into the back of it. He turned to see Tulbër smiling down it at him.

"You'll watch it, eh?" said Owyn. The giant gently brushed his hands away from the cart and pushed it, turning it away from the quarry pit and towards the city. The carved-stone wheels of the cart groaned as they rolled under the weight of a full load of rock.

"It was sad watching you struggle, so I changed my mind. You may watch me for a while." said the giant. Owyn held in a sigh and wiped the sweat from his brow. How had he thought he could do this himself? He shook his head and followed the giant pushing his cart of stone. They had already rounded the road entering the quarry. Tulbër moved quickly, and yet had total control of the cart. Owyn had seen a few giants in his life, but never one so close. He was almost double the size of Owyn, and his reach could more than cover the width of the cart.

"Why are you helping me?" asked Owyn.

"I just said, your struggling was making me sad."

"No, back at the quarry. Why'd you choose to help me?"

"I'm tired of the quarry, and I like giving chances."

Owyn didn't know what to say at that. He wasn't used to help. Not here. Not ever.

Tulbër continued, "Your negotiation with the foreman made me want to as well. Three coppers for a load of this stone is far too much. I want to see what other mistakes you make."

Owyn had never thought to hear a giant laugh. It shook the walls of the buildings at the edge of the street, which is nothing to say what it felt like in Owyn's ribcage. It didn't hurt, but to feel laughter... it was too much for Owyn.

"How did you hear my negotiation?"

Tulbër stifled his laugh enough to speak. "I've got big ears, little one."

Although Owyn had never met a giant until now, Owyn had seen them. Many people feared the giants. With dark hair and gray-colored skin, their features were larger and harsher than those of humans, though their faces were not mean (unless that particular giant wanted to be mean). But what usually scared humans about the giants was their size. Tulbër seemed to match the descriptions Owyn had heard, but he was so much more than that. His light gray skin looked like rock tanned by the sun. His hair wasn't dark, but sand-colored, and lay in a beautiful mess atop his head, somehow wild and controlled at the same moment. What struck Owyn was the bright lavender eyes that looked forward as the giant carried the cart—so bright they seemed lit from within. Tulbër had a big smile, to be sure, but he didn't need it; his eyes smiled for him.

"What brought you to Kudra?" said Owyn, breaking the silence that had formed as they walked.

"I pilgrimage," said Tulbër. Even as they walked, his voice shook in Owyn's chest. It almost sounded musical, as if the giant was refraining from singing as he spoke. "What is a lighthouse?"

Owyn missed a step, stopping, but Tulbër continued moving the cart. "Did you hear that from inside the building?" he said as he caught back up.

"Big ears," said Tulbër.

Owyn smiled. "It's for ships," he said.

"How can a tower be for ships?"

"The tower is just to raise up a flame, something lit atop the tower. It's for ships arriving at night, to avoid the rocks."

"Hmm," said Tulbër. The reverberations seemed to shake the stone in the road under their feet. "This is a good thing."

Owyn looked up at the giant.

"I am glad to help you with this. No. I'm glad to watch."

Not having words to respond, Owyn simply smiled at the joke. He'd done that a lot recently, but he was still surprised. People hadn't made him smile in a long time.

"What tales of this lighthouse can you tell me?"

"It's a story from an old life." Owyn looked about the city. The streets were quiet, but talk of the past still felt too loud.

Tulbër looked down at him, purple eyes bright in the evening. "If you do not wish to share your tale, would you like to hear of my travels?"

"I feel you're going to tell me about them anyway."

Tulbër laughed. "Yes. And with my voice, you have to listen."

Man and giant both smiled as they walked through the city at night.

CHAPTER 4

"Copper or coin for a blessing of Irnam?" said an accented voice.

Owyn's eyes blinked open to see a short, wiry man standing on the docks at his feet. The man repeated the question as he saw Owyn wake.

"No," said Owyn. His voice still half asleep. "No. No, thank you." He didn't mean to wave the beggar away with such disdain, but he had just woken up. The man's face soured, and he shook his head before turning away and heading back up the docks toward the city.

Owyn's joints creaked as he stood up from the hard surface of the dock. Water gently splashed against the shore while boats and ships creaked as they gently bobbed up and down on the morning waves. Tulbër was still asleep, lying atop the pile of stone within the cart.

Owyn and Tulbër had to sleep at the docks. They'd arrived past the point of anyone being there except the personal guards for the merchant ships.

"Tulbër," he said, pushing the giant's shoulder. The giant's body felt like it was made of stone, his gray skin adding to the feeling. He didn't move. "Tulbër, it's daylight." Owyn resorted to a punch instead.

"Huh?" groaned Tulbër. Owyn decided that his voice definitely sounded like a song. Like something he hadn't heard before, but that felt somehow familiar. Like a memory unlived. The giant rolled over and opened his eyes to see Owyn standing by the cart. He went to sit up, and Owyn stopped in awe. Again, the giant's lavender eyes took him by surprise. They looked like pale amethysts set perfectly in stone.

"You make for pleasant conversation, little one," said Tulbër. "I slept wonderfully last night."

"You slept on stone."

"And good stone at that. Your lighthouse will be strong once built."

"It's good?" said Owyn. He would work with what he could get, but the foreman's mistake surprised him.

"It's stone. The shape is wrong, but the material is good. The foreman was not wrong in the work you take on, except to dismiss stone so quickly due to the shape. Do you not know how you are building?"

Owyn thought to lie with bravado, but all that came out was a shrug.

The giant laughed as he hopped off the cart and landed on the dock with a thud that shook the entire platform. "You're a funny man, little one. I want to see this lighthouse built by inexperience."

Owyn wanted to feel bad but something about the giant's mirth kept any dark feelings at bay.

"Have you found a dockmaster yet?" said Tulbër.

"I only just woke."

"Well then, I shall guard the cart while you look for one."

"Aren't you missing work at the quarry?"

"I miss it not, but I am missing payment, tell me tales and I may count them as payment for the work I miss."

"You want stories?"

"Of course. But you seem like a poor storyteller."

"I haven't told you any stories," said Owyn, confused.

"Precisely," laughed Tulbër. The laugh felt good as it boomed through the air and the dock and Owyn. "I want to hear more of this builder who hasn't built. Now, go quickly little one, find a dockmaster. I cannot wait forever," said the giant with a smile. As Owyn turned and walked towards shore, Tulbër turned to watch the sea.

Finding the dockmaster was easier than Owyn had expected. The man was the same from his first visit, when he had purchased the *Morning Sunshine*. He brought him back to Tulbër and the cart.

"I need to rent something that can carry that."

"I hope it's helping you row," said the dockmaster with uncertainty, glancing at Tulbër. There was a weight to the word *it* that Owyn caught, like the man hoped for agreement, but without saying so.

"No, *he* won't be joining me," Owyn responded in kind. "Tulbër is just guarding the cart. I need something for the stone."

"I'm glad you see me as more other than an 'it', little one," said Tulbër. He was still a fair way down the platform, but his voice carried to Owyn and the dockmaster as if he stood next to them.

"I apologize, sir." The dockmaster said towards Tulbër as he bowed slightly. "I only try to match the tone of my customer."

Owyn cut in, seeing a chance before Tulbër could respond. "And now that you've upset me and my partner, what consolations may this salesman give us in our rental?"

The dockmaster frowned. He hadn't meant to talk so much.

In the end, the rental was cheap, but Owyn still felt the weight disappear from his coin purse. He had never planned to make money on this endeavor, but he had hoped his savings would not disappear quite so quickly. Doing things himself cost more than he wanted, but he hadn't gone to the King for money. This way was still right. Tulbër had stayed to help haul the stone into the loadboat Owyn had rented from the dockmaster. It was a large, flat platform of lumber with walls designed for loading ships with cargo. That lumber would have cost more than Owyn could afford. A second wooden boat. The wealth in wood was more than gold or jewels, even here, in a city with a woodfarm nearby.

With the boat loaded up, Owyn watched Tulbër take the cart back up the dock and into the city. He saw the dockmaster watching him, however. The loadboat was not meant to be pulled by a crew of one. Owyn had secured it to the *Morning Sunshine* by two thick ropes on each corner. He looked back at the full boat behind him and he rowed.

The first few strokes were easy. He was only pulling out the rope. Then the rope grew taut. The resistance of the loadboat made things exceedingly harder, yet it did move. Once again, Owyn saw the dockmaster smile as he gained distance away from the shore and towards the sea.

He was already more comfortable in his little vessel. Rowing without turning about to see where he went, Owyn watched the ships at the port as he and his first load of stone crossed Turtle Bay together. He let out a whoop of joy and heard his voice echo across the water. There was no way of hiding his emotion. He reveled in it, the joy. He'd have never done such a thing in his old life, but he was beyond that. Owyn was on his way to building his lighthouse, King and Kudra be damned. His dream had to come true. He would not pause. He would work. Owyn would make it come true.

As he looked back across the bay, one ship in the row anchored a short way from the port stood out. Its bright colors called and assaulted the eye as the morning sun reflected off the garish paint covering the ship from the sea line to the top of the mainsail. *The Small Journey* was there.

The wind picked up now. The day was yet to become hot as the sun rose up on its own journey, but the light breeze felt good against Owyn's face.

Water in the bay rocked the boat gently, pushing it up and seeming to pull it back down. The little ripples of the seawater could never be considered waves, but the wind was against Owyn and the loadboat refused to move. His arms, still tired from two days ago, screamed at Owyn to pause, to stop—just a little rest would feel so good—but he couldn't. If he stopped, the wind would push his boats back towards the Kudran Port. Back towards where he came from. The wind was taking him from his goal and he didn't know what to do.

Fear spiked along the back of Owyn's neck. He was alone, out in the center of the Turtle Bay, with a rowboat and a loadboat full of stone. He could not stop rowing for fear of returning to the city, but he knew his arms would give out eventually. They had to. He was nowhere near land, and further yet from the land he wanted to reach. And Owyn did not know how to swim.

Owyn inhaled. Taking a deep breath into his lungs through his nose, feeling his chest rise, his ribs push outward, and his shoulder—still rowing—shift and pop. He closed his eyes and listened to the laps of the oars hitting the waves and the wind passing his ears. He could still hear the city he wanted to leave behind, but he tried not to let it worry him further. He focused on the sounds of the water. It would be ok. He would be ok.

Owyn let out the air in his lungs, opened his eyes, and continued to row.

The day passed as he rowed the *Morning Sunshine* ever, albeit almost imperceptibly, closer to his island. The design of the boat annoyed Owyn. Who thought to make a boat where you cannot see the direction you are rowing? Efficiency be damned. His arms were tired and he wanted to see where he was headed. Instead, he looked at the sun, setting behind Kudra. The God's Tower set an infinite shadow across the bay and the world. A line of darkness from the ground to the edge of the horizon touched the base of the Tower that rose endlessly into the sky. It was a marvelous sight, and one that Owyn had never imagined seeing. He hated it now. He hated everything now. His arms were tired.

The wind had pressed throughout the day, waxing and waning, but never ceasing. Damn the wind. Damn the Tower. Damn Owyn's weak arms. He did not want to turn and see his lack of progress towards his island. The motion hurt his back and stopped him from rowing efficiently, but he wanted to turn so badly. He needed to see how far he had yet to go. Night was coming quickly.

The *Morning Sunshine* groaned as it scraped against the shore.

Owyn almost didn't stop rowing. His mind couldn't register the sound. He couldn't feel joy, he could only pause and feel that the boat was not moving backwards. He smiled. It wasn't moving at all.

He'd made it to the other side of the bay.

He had not made it to his island though.

Owyn looked about. He was on the other side of the bay, Kudra a misshapen darkness in the silhouette of the sunset, save for the Tower looming as it always would. But Owyn was not on the correct part of the other side. The shoreline stretched much too far up and down the bay. He was still on the rocky peninsula that formed the horn of the bay. He sighed. His arms felt like weights pulling on his shoulders. They were limp and hard to move. Owyn's stomach must be too tired to growl, for the pangs of hunger hurt more than his arms. There was nothing left to eat in his pack. He had only meant to visit the city for a day, and he'd now be gone for a third night. No part of him wanted to imagine what would waste away first. And it was no more pleasant to think of the food back on the island. He sat on a dry stone on shore, tired and dejected. The sunset was fading, the colors in the sky dancing their final beautiful dance before darkness approached from behind. There were no clouds in the sky. It would chill, but it wouldn't freeze.

Another sigh, another exhale and Owyn's eyes left the sky and looked out at the pair of boats. The *Morning Sunshine*, moored on the stone of the peninsula, and the loadboat, full of stone—full of *his* stone—bouncing on gentle waves behind it.

Why do this thing if not for the work of it?

He stood, legs wobbly; but, unlike his arms, they listened, obeying the command to walk over to the boats. He led the rope tying them together around a few rocks. Owyn did not know any sailing knots but hoped what he had tied would hold. Then he adjusted his satchel on what looked like the softest of the dry rocks on

shore—where was Tulbër for this?—and laid his head down. The
night swiftly followed the sunset and Owyn slept.

***

It took him till midday to find his island the next day. The boats had
remained in their place into the morning, but paddling in a way to
skirt the shoreline rather than approaching from the bay was not
as easy as Owyn thought it would be. Rocks jutted out and little
bays and dead ends in the peninsula seemed to never cease. His arms
were dead and the noises his stomach made sounded like those of a
monster in a story, but at least he had stayed out of the wind.

He shouted with joy when he saw his canvas tent flapping gently
in the wind.

All in all, Owyn had been able to singlehandedly bring the first
load of stone to his island. He smiled as he thought about telling
Tulbër the story sometime, now that he finally had a story for the
giant that he'd want to share. There were so many that he wouldn't.

Owyn lingered on that thought, mind flashing through moments
of pain and memory. His old life. Old life. Another sigh let out,
letting none of the memory go, but forcing the body into thinking
so. He pulled the *Morning Sunshine* up onto the shore of his rocky
island but could not get the loadboat to move even an inch up the
rocky surface. He worried the bottom would break if he forced the
fully loaded boat up on the shore. He left it there for now and found
his tent, still standing where he had left it. He went in and slept. The
bedroll was bliss after two nights on the ground.

When he woke, his body felt no better. Soreness and aches and
hunger were all he knew. He had lost count of the days, and were the
sun not above, in open sky, he would not have been able to tell the
time. The pain, the discombobulations; they were a reprieve from

the memories. He mixed cold water and oats to satiate the hunger, then it was time to get his feet wet.

Owyn walked out into the sea to the loadboat, still tied to the *Morning Sunshine* and still far too heavy to drag ashore. But stone could be carried. So he walked into the sea to remove a stone and bring it up onto the island.

Then he did it again. And then again. One at a time.

It took three days to unload the entirety of the stone, the piles growing half-sorted as Owyn carried handfuls of rock up out of the water to the flatter parts of the island. Yet the monotony of the work did not sway his morale even once. This was work. This was good. Each load he walked into the cool water of the bay, feeling the sunlight reflect up off the water onto his skin. Sweat worked to make the stone slippery in his hand, but he only lost a few pieces to the drink. Most were easily gathered back up from the rocky ground beneath the surface. The piles grew without his notice. Each load's focus was the work, not the steps, not the discomfort. The water felt good and the sun felt good. The stone felt good in his arms. Work felt good in his heart. Owyn had to stop partway through the second day to relocate some of the stone he'd already brought up. The stockpile had rolled onto one of the foundation corners he had mentally marked. It was less comfortable carrying the stone on land without the sea to cool his feet, but he did not mind.

Owyn had intended to rest on the fourth day. His body was tired, torn, but not broken. He needed more sleep, but when he awoke to the sun shining through the walls of his tent on the fourth day, he couldn't help himself.

Owyn rowed the *Morning Sunshine* and the loadboat back across Turtle Bay before most of the city had finished their morning meals. Leaving coin with the dockmaster, who this morning was a man

Owyn had not met yet, Owyn left the two boats to start the long walk through Kudra towards the quarry.

"Copper or coin for a blessing of Irnam?" said a voice, interrupting his walk. It was the beggar from days ago. Owyn frowned as he dismissed the man. The man returned the frown with a scowl, muttering something as he walked away. Owyn tried to shake off the experience as he left the docks and walked through the great city. He'd forgotten about it halfway through his journey.

"Back already?" said the foreman. He sat atop the quarry enjoying a drink of fruit juice. He hadn't offered Owyn one.

"I'm ready for another cartload," said Owyn.

"Same rate as before?"

Owyn nodded, and the foreman stood and shouted down into the quarry. A brief wait revealed Tulbër, climbing out of the work area.

"Back so soon?" he said, his voice singing through the stone that surrounded them.

"Load up a cart for the man," said the foreman. "If you still volunteer, you can watch the cart when he takes it tonight."

"I'll go with him now," said Tulbër.

"I'll dock your day's pay."

"I can go with him now."

The foreman looked surprised, but he said nothing as Tulbër loaded up the cart.

"One more thing," said Owyn before the foreman could walk away. "Can I buy a pick?"

The foreman shrugged and sold Owyn the tool at far too high of a price. Owyn placed it atop the cartload of stone, and he and Tulbër began their walk through the city.

They talked, and Tulbër told more stories. He had traveled all over Breiar on his pilgrimage, and Owyn learned that many young giants do the same. "Though most return home quicker than I," said the giant. They drew some looks from citizens of Kudra as they walked, but most men and women simply avoided the pair and the cart, opting to leave the street and take another. Owyn frowned, but Tulbër seemed to take no notice.

"You work quickly for such a little one," said Tulbër as he looked at the empty loadboat upon reaching the city docks.

"I—" began Owyn, but he stopped. He couldn't think of anything to say.

"I like this," said Tulbër. "You're doing good. It is not for yourself, but the work will bring you along, too."

They finished loading the boat, and Tulbër watched as Owyn rowed again, back across Turtle Bay.

Rowing had gotten easier. Unloading the boat had not. Owyn worked for another three days, building his stockpile on the island and lightening the weight of the loadboat. On the fourth day, Owyn looked out at the sunrise as he ate his small breakfast. The sea was calm and wonderful as it reflected the colors of the morning. It was as if the entire world glowed. Owyn thought about getting another load, but the morning on his island seemed so perfect. He looked to the stockpile of stone he had and to the area he'd marked in his mind. Owyn could see the lighthouse it would become. He could almost feel the joy of the completed work. His body ached as he thought of the work yet ahead of him.

Leaving the boats moored on the shore, Owyn instead grabbed the pick he had purchased and began the proper work.

Seeing the first corner, the one he had spotted upon his first arrival on the island, he swung the pick down and chipped away. He had begun construction.

The work felt good. Owyn had been at it all day, stopping only for food at midday and again when the sun had begun its journey into evening. He'd seen two ships that day. One left Kudra and one had arrived. Both rounded the horn of rocks at the edge of Turtle Bay, where Owyn was building, both effortlessly flying on the water. It was a smooth day, and the wooden structures seemed to slice the ocean as if they were a knife scoring the surface of bread dough. He loved watching them, yet worried. They were so close to the rocks of the horn as they turned to head north up the coast. Rougher seas could very well have taken either ship too close to the edge and cut their hulls far worse than they cut the water.

This made him work harder. The work felt good, but his body felt ragged as he watched the sun fall below the horizon. Owyn always woke with a sore body, but he never stirred through the night until the sun rose each morning.

On the third day of cutting the foundation, Owyn heard a call. He left the pick on the ground and walked to see a dinghy approaching his island.

"Permission to come ashore?" shouted a man standing on the boat. Two men sat rowing. Owyn looked beyond the dinghy to see a ship, stopped off the edge of the horn of the bay. He would never forget the garish colors of that ship. It was *The Small Journey*. He looked back down at the approaching boat and realized he hadn't said a word.

"Come ashore!" he shouted back to them.

The wait for the boat to reach shore felt horrible. Owyn didn't know whether to stand and watch or return to work and wait. He opted to stand in his awkwardness as the boat slowly approached. The man standing aboard didn't break his gaze as he looked at Owyn. He was tall, wearing a bright green coat that was long and had tails. The cornered hat he wore made the man look taller. The whole look was capped with a red feather that must have been as long as Owyn's forearm. The man could only belong to that ship. Owyn couldn't imagine anyone else dressing like that.

The boat slid up the shore with momentum from the rowers, and the man in the hat stepped off without so much as a stumble. "My name is Captain Doman Sutherland," he said as he walked towards Owyn, removing his hat. "And my hat is off to you, good sir."

Owyn felt the strangest urge to bow. He stopped that feeling and held out his hand instead. "Owyn's my name." Doman took his hand with a firm shake and put his hat back on.

"So this is where the tower to light the night will go?" he said, looking out at the area Owyn had been cutting.

"A lighthouse," said Owyn. "How do you know what I'm building?"

"Word travels quickly through the city if the topic is interesting enough."

"So you stopped to see if the rumors were true?"

"No, my good man, I knew they were true," Doman turned and looked at Owyn. "I came to give you this." He held out an envelope with a red wax seal.

"What's this?" said Owyn, taking the envelope. The seal looked like a simplified version of the King's Palace standing small and centered in front of The God's Tower.

"A letter from old Rigney." Owyn looked up to see Doman smiling widely as he spoke. "The good King will allow you to live and work on this island."

"He'll help?"

The Captain laughed. There was no malice in the laugh though, simply genuine mirth. "Certainly not. He simply allows you on the crown's land here. You were poaching land before." The Captain's smile could have cut cloth in the wind it was so sharp.

"I was?"

"You cannot simply squat on land in Kudra. I believe old Rigney would like that to be a fact for the rest of his empire. No, you will find no help from the King. His mind is occupied elsewhere for the time being." Doman trailed off slightly at the end, but Owyn didn't hear it. His eyes were fixed on the ship in the distance.

"A man just jumped from your ship!" he cried.

Doman barely turned. "That would be young Husted. He always finds the most creative ways to avoid his problems."

"Is he swimming towards us?"

"That appears to be his plan."

"All that way!"

Owyn kept his eyes on the man, swimming in the distance. The smallest point disappearing and reappearing as waves between the island and the ship rose and fell. How hard it would it be to find a man swimming if there were more wind!

"You may not get help from the King..." started Doman, with a smile in his voice that even Owyn noticed, despite his distraction. The Captain pointed to the swimmer. "...but may *he* help you?"

CHAPTER 5

Aerdethin was a budding city that did not quite know how large it was yet. It was on the cusp of truly overwhelming the simple farmers of the Crescent Fields who had lived there for generations. The only paved road out of town led to Kudra, so far away, yet the street name survived—Kudra Way—a vestige of an older time in travel. A time Aerdethin was leaving. Loose rock buildings, held in metal frames and thatched in grasses from the fields sat awkwardly next to newer, grander buildings, made with mortared brick and tan stone from the quarries to the south. The world of the north, the ranchers and the ice farmers and the poor mixed with those of the south, the seat of government. The confluence of trade and the world. An Empire, they called it. One land with people from everywhere, forced under a single crown, yet trading their individual goods as if they were still from different worlds.

Triph sat atop a pub watching the crossroads of commerce happening below. A budding city never noticed newcomers. Triph saw all the things that made him smile.

Then he remembered why he was here.

He cared little about the business of moving goods—well, until he got to moving the goods how he wanted to, but that was not happening now. Triph had more pressing things occupying his mind. He thought about the situation he was in and the people he worked for. And he thought of the danger he had become to those he called friends.

Breathing in the city air, the smell of movement filled his lungs. Fishermen and river workers, merchants and servants who led beasts of burden—simply the stink of those who had traveled and had not yet had the chance to bathe. Each had its own note, its own emotion. Triph inhaled them all. He was a man of people. As he looked around the crossroads of Aerdethin, he did not see the city that had sprung up only decades ago from a small trade town. He saw the people. He saw the people and the wealth they each carried.

Walking silently, Triph crossed the roof of the pub away from the main street it faced. He stopped in the center of the flat stone roof—a new pub, richer that way—and paused. He arched his back, tensing in muscles and feeling the blood flow before completing the opposite stretch, down towards his toes. He hopped twice on the balls of his feet and grinned. His body still felt good. Owyn had been wrong; they weren't so old yet. He walked to the edge of the roof over to the side alley behind the pub and dropped off of the roof with a grace befitting his slight frame. There was a thud when he landed. Others may have heard it, but he didn't. He thought in silence. He lived in silence. Of course, that was when he chose to.

Brushing off the dust from scaling the rooftops, Triph rounded the alley corners to the entrance of the pub. It was called The Right of Way, the name on the banner above the door spelled out in three languages. He walked in. He had little right of way in his life anymore. He made the choice to walk in there, though, and that mattered to him.

"Istar wine," he bellowed as he walked towards the bar. Expensive and foreign, it would turn heads. He'd make enemies and have attention on him, two things Triph hated, but he'd have the bartender's ear the entire night.

"No tabs," said the bartender. He grabbed an unopen bottle from the top shelf behind the bar and set it down next to an empty glass. He didn't open it.

"No tabs, I understand," said Triph, sitting down in front of the man. "But you ask me to pay up front?"

The bartender nodded. Triph counted the seconds in his head. He knew what he had ordered. He'd known the process. He waited now to only add to the performance.

"If I must," he said, removing more coin than the drink would require from the purse hanging on his belt. He set it on the bar top and watched the bartender stare for a moment before remembering his job.

The man swiped the coin and removed the metal covering on the bottle before pouring a glass. "Change?" he asked.

"Keep it for the next glass," said Triph. Parting with that much money hurt him. He felt it in his chest, a lump that even the exorbitant wine couldn't push down. *It'll be worth it*, he thought. *It would be worth it in the end.*

He downed the wine quickly—well, as quickly as he could. Istar wine came straight from the mines in the Weeping Mountains. Those men worked hard and drank even harder. Triph had even met some of them. He flagged down the bartender with a raised finger outstretched from the hand holding the empty glass.

"Not enough change for a refill," said the bartender, walking closer. He no longer spoke loud enough for the bar to hear.

"What?" Triph slipped. He hadn't wanted to let anything out, but the price shocked him.

The bartender told him the cost of the wine and it took all of Triph's self-control to keep his head from shaking. The prices had been steadily rising as he moved south. Closer to people, further from the places where things were made. He set down the coin requested with some money to spare.

"The tip is for a question," he said.

"Yea?" said the bartender as he picked up the coins and began pouring another drink into Triph's glass.

"I'm looking for a man who'd have traveled this road. Not as a tourist or a merchant, but on a mission."

"Lots of men travel the crossroads."

"He'd have been short and quiet. Carried a satchel close to his heart, as if all the wealth in the world lived within the bag."

"Maybe," said the bartender, pouring himself a shot of the Istar wine. "Lots of men with bags come through the crossroads."

"You have two options. You either entirely missed the man, or you noticed him. He'd give nothing in between."

The bartender tapped the bottle. "Another drink?"

Triph knew the game. It was fine. He'd end up ahead in the end; he always did. With a nod, Triph set out the coin for the drink—and more.

"He went south," said the bartender, having another shot of the wine. "Was quiet, and cheap, but if any man had something in his heart it was this one. Had plans for the coast he was trying to keep to himself. Important plans, the way he was acting after he'd had a few drinks."

That was Triph's man. He nodded, but lolled his head as he did, before swallowing the glass of wine in front of him. That'd be enough to convince anyone. He said nothing, but mouthed the word "thanks" and nodded again. The bartender looked him up and down before capping the bottle of wine and placing it back on the shelf. He shook his head as he walked away, just as Triph furtively grabbed the forgotten coin purse, safely stored in a carved notch in the stone bar top. One of the places impossible for a common thief to get at unnoticed. One of Triph's favorites. It may not have been all the money in the place, but it wasn't the barman's anymore. Triph stood, stumbled as he smoothly pocketed his new purse, and left.

Once outside and around the corner, Triph counted the coins held in the small leather pouch he had pulled. It was a tidy profit on the whole endeavor. Plus, now he was almost drunk enough to forget the situation he was in.

South. South meant Kudra. It was the only city on the other side of the Shrinking Desert, and that was the only thing on Kudra Way. He worried about the bartender misspeaking. Southwest could mean Annwyn, or it could mean one of the many farm towns between Aerdethin and Annwyn. It could mean something to the west. The road wrapped north again, forking towards another river town before hitting Daughtn. None of that mattered. Triph flipped one coin from the purse. It rung out in the air, spinning and spinning. Owyn had gone south, and he had dreams for a coast. That meant he'd gone to Kudra.

"Thief!" shouted a voice behind him. Triph caught the coin and turned. He frowned at what he saw: a familiar scowling face, permanent at this point, sitting atop a wire-thin body that the faded leather ranch-hand clothes could not hide. "C'mere, thief!" shouted the man again. Triph rebelled for a moment. His mind, his soul, wanted to run, needed to. He couldn't. If he ran, they'd catch him again. They'd hurt him again.

"How do you do, Wendel?" he said, the sarcasm in his voice laid on thick enough to make one forget the name was real.

"Hmm," said Wendel, disapproving as always. He carried a longknife to his left and a swordbreaker at his right, though, so Triph couldn't ignore the man as much as he wanted to.

"Happy to have caught me again?" Triph held out his hands together, as if asking to be shackled.

"You cannot run off like you did."

"But I've gathered information."

Wendel looked down at Triph with a frown. Truth was, both he and Owyn were short. Maybe that's why they had become thieves. Wendel said nothing as he thought. They had captured Triph for information, Wendel and the posse that hired him. Triph still wasn't entirely certain that helping them would keep him away from the noose, but it was better than doing nothing and still being hanged.

"Where are the rest of them?"

"Gathering information," said Wendel with a sneer. He started walking down the street, headed north. There was an assumption in the air that Triph would follow. He did.

"Well, they're doing worse at it. I know where he went."

Wendel stopped. "If you lie to me, we will end up shackling you, thief."

"If I'm shackled, I'll be far less successful at the job you hired me for."

"We didn't hire you." Wendel was getting angry. He leaned forward, close enough to Triph that they could hear each other whisper.

"Whatever you want to call our arrangement, freedom traded for information sounds like terms of employment to me."

"Where is he going, then?"

"Owyn? I don't know where he's going, but I do know where he went."

Wendel frowned. He still stood too close. The man's breath smelled of stale tea.

"And I will happily share that information with my employer, but that isn't you. We're just coworkers." Triph smiled and slapped Wendel on the shoulder before taking a step back and walking north. "So where is the boss man again?"

It turned out that the boss had been gathering the group himself. The Sheriff. Triph wondered if he had a name. The men called him by his title or simply "boss." He was a large man with broad shoulders and a scowl that had been burned on his face with deep-set wrinkles. Triph wondered if he could even smile after holding that face for so long. His head was starkly bald, yet the man refused to wear a hat, thus reflecting the sunlight about wherever he went. It was the only bright thing about him.

For a moment, Triph wondered how he found time to shave his head on their journey. His own stubble had grown to annoying levels in captivity.

"Where is he headed?" said the imposing man.

"Can't do your own reconnaissance, Sheriff?" said Triph, a cocky grin on his face.

The Sheriff closed his fist and hit Triph in the face. Triph fell to the ground, eyes watering.

"You only live outside the walls of a jail cell because I say so. You'll speak only when I say so." The Sheriff loomed over Triph.

"Kudra," said the thief on the ground.

"Better. Your friend went to Kudra. If we do not find him, then his crimes become yours. As well as their punishment."

CHAPTER 6

"Dinner?" asked Owyn. He spoke loudly despite the quiet of the sea around the island. It had been the second time that he'd said it.

"Aye," said Ost. The young sailor set down the stone he had been carrying and walked to where Owyn had set up the stove. He'd pulled it out of his tent after the second man had started staying on the island.

"Any guesses on tonight's menu?" said Owyn. He'd never been a talkative man, but Ost's quiet throughout much of the day brought out his voice. Ost looked at him without speaking. It was like he waited for an answer even though he could speak one just as simply.

"Bannock and sausage," said Owyn. He'd meant for there to be more humor in the response. It was the same thing they'd eaten the rest of the week. He'd have to row back into the city soon. Looking at the stockpile, they'd need more stone soon, anyway.

All that Husted had told Owyn of his journey thus far was that he had decided it was time for shore leave and that he wanted to be called Ost. The Captain wasn't worried about desertion. Many of his men were on shore leave as *The Small Journey* completed a few days of maneuvers around the bay and surrounding sea. The way he had spoken to Ost almost made it sound like this was normal. The crazed man skipped shore leave to work with Owyn? Owyn had wanted to refuse. This island was his solitude now, but how could he deny a man that solitude if he needed it as well? He must if he skipped time in the city. Owyn hated the city. He understood that much. He lit the flame under the stove and sliced off pieces of the hard sausage as the metal heated in front of him.

Ost looked out at the sea. Even sitting still, he looked as if his body was working. The man never seemed to rest. A question sat at Owyn's tongue. A few, even. But the moment passed and he looked down at the food instead.

The sausage had greased up the metal pan slightly and Owyn tossed in the bannock dough. It fried with a satisfying crackle. Though the food was simple, it smelled wonderful as it mixed with the salt and spray in the air.

The dark stone of the lighthouse looked good as the sun fell. Both men ate in silence as night rose opposite the falling sun. The last golden rays bounced off the base of the little tower, and Owyn couldn't help but look at it. He'd built that. Well, they'd built it. The waste stone did not love to stack—it was irregular, jagged—and they had no mortar. Owyn started the stack within his foundation cuts and Ost sorted. Then the tower began to grow, but slowly as they puzzled out how to stack the irregular stone shapes in a way that didn't fall. Owyn thought Tulbër would laugh; he'd found another man who wasn't a builder to struggle with him.

The tower was growing at least. After four or five collapses, it was nowhere near done, only stacked up to his knees at the highest part, but he had struck the foundation within the island, and they had begun the work on the base. Owyn had started his lighthouse. He'd actually built something.

The sun left the horizon, dipping into the sea to the far west, and Owyn's eyes left the construction project. Before he looked up to see what stars had formed in the sky, he saw Ost putting away the stove. The man was lit by the small burning lump of coal that fueled the flame. Owyn shook his head.

He hadn't built this alone.

It felt important that he not forget that fact.

Ost put away the stove and lay down on the rock, staring upward. The stars started showing their small shining faces. Owyn and Ost stared at them for a while without speaking. Owyn's body was getting the best of him. His eyelids were heavy and the aches had built up against the cold stone. He started to stand when the sailor spoke.

"Why a tower of light?"

Owyn was startled into sitting back down. The other man had not noticed, his gaze remaining on the stars. Though they had worked together for days, his voice was almost unfamiliar.

"To protect the bay and the ships traveling it."

"Like the lights of Daughtn or Hof, I see. Why a tower though?"

Owyn paused. A part of him was sad at having to share the tale. He'd kept it to himself so long. "Have you ever been to a wood-farm?"

Now Ost looked at him, surprise on his young, tanned face. He didn't speak though. Owyn continued.

"Of course not. I'm sorry."

"When did you visit one?"

Owyn thought about his next words. He didn't know Ost beyond the work they'd done, but the man hated the city as much as he did. He'd needed solitude too, whatever the reason. Owyn opened up: "We robbed one," he said with a grin. Ost's look of surprise grew into shock. "The money we got from the job was not worth the danger, but it was something else." Owyn stopped, looking out at the stars. A cool breeze was crossing the bay, chilling both men, but only he shivered.

"Security at a woodfarm keeps a pretty tight ship," Owyn stopped, laughing to himself as he noticed the unintentional pun. "Of course, you know what that's like," he remarked in a vain attempt to make the sailor laugh. "Anyway, the security is good. Though it's not so tight once you get past the perimeter. In the woods and on the manor grounds, you just have to avoid the normal workers and rich folks.

"The perimeter was the most impressive part."

Ost watched Owyn, rapt with attention. The young man no longer looked towards the stars or the sea.

"They have towers for the men to keep watch—for people like me and my partner—but the part that interested me was the towers at night. A guard tower doesn't do much good in the darkness; it merely elevates the blind. But these woodfarmers put fires atop towers. Men stand on platforms kept dark, between those lit and looked around with ease. The edges of the woodfarm were as bright as day in places."

"How did you get in?"

Owyn smiled. "Trade secret. But that is the origin of my idea. I'd heard of shipwrecks in Kudra, and after seeing the lights and flags in Daughtn and Telnir, the idea started to come to me."

"Huh," said Ost. "Alone?" he asked.

Owyn nodded and the man stretched and began to stand when Owyn stopped him: "What of you?"

"What?"

"Sit back down," said Owyn with a smile clear as day on the starry night. He was beginning to understand Tulbër more. "I told you my tale. Tell me why you dove from the ship and joined me."

Ost sat back down, but did not speak. He looked out into the stars and the dimly glowing city beyond the bay.

"Your Captain said you were avoiding shore leave. Seems like the worst way possible to avoid rest is to help move stone."

"Not that," said the sailor. "There was…" He paused; words did not come easy to the man it seemed. "is," he corrected himself, then continued, "…a guest aboard the ship."

Owyn held in a laugh. He saw the young man's face in the starlight and knew that look in a young man's eyes. "What's her name?"

Ost shot him a look of shock mixed with anger. Both emotions faded quickly as he got a hold of his gambling face, but for a moment he would have lost any bet placed. He frowned. "It doesn't matter."

"It may not for me, but for you it does. No sense running away from love. You've got to face something like that head on."

"Yea?"

"Well, that's what I've heard. Triph was the one who caroused. The other sex never held much interest to me. But I've seen many men at a loss for words like you."

"You have?"

"Yes. We robbed them blind."

Both men laughed and talked a bit further into the night. It was good. Owyn felt something talking to the young sailor. It had been so long since he had just spoken with another person without something to gain. He didn't think of the lighthouse or the money or the food. He just lived in the moment. The moment that passed too soon as each man stood before their tired bodies got the best of them and went to the tent to sleep before the day's work ahead of them tomorrow.

The sun rose in the morning as it always had done. Owyn cooked breakfast while Ost began the puzzle of stacking stone. The man would never pause if he could help it. Owyn made him take a break to eat.

"Rain today," Ost said as he swallowed a bite. He was looking up at the sky and Owyn matched his gaze. It was a clear day with a brilliant blue sky.

"How can you tell?"

"Rainy season always comes when the wind turns east." And with that, Ost was done with the conversation. It appeared they were back to their old ways. He set down the small plate and put the knife back into the sheath that sat on his belt, and he went again to the stockpile, to continue the work of the morning.

"I'll visit the city today," said Owyn. Ost looked up from the rock he had been sizing up and nodded. That was all that must need to be said. Owyn shrugged and started for the shore.

"Owyn," said Ost.

Owyn stopped and looked back at the young sailor, arms tight as they held a stone. "Thank you for telling your tale last night."

Owyn smiled and nodded. Ost went back to work as he continued the short walk down to the *Morning Sunshine*, seated on the shore of the island. He saw Ost working on the island as he rowed out into the bay.

Owyn enjoyed being in the *Morning Sunshine*. His muscles still ached, but he found that their protests were weaker and easier to ignore. Owyn watched the birds as he rowed, seeing them glide on the wind, calling to each other and dancing in the sky before diving into the water. He was surprised how quickly he'd made it to the docks of Kudra. The sun had moved a fair amount upward in the blue sky, but not nearly as far as it had on his first attempt.

The dockmaster was slow to react. Owyn didn't even see the man, so he tied up the rowboat and loadboat himself. In the distance, he saw the beggar from before speaking to someone. The men stopped speaking, and the beggar turned to glare across the dock at Owyn. After a moment of eye contact, Owyn walked forward and ignored the man. The beggar returned to his conversation, more emphatically than before. His arms were flying with emotion. Owyn kept to himself as he walked past the two people in their shadowy corner.

The walk to the quarry was becoming old hat to Owyn. He knew the paths, and the alternate routes, depending on what time of day he arrived. Today held a surprise, though. Tulbër was already moving the cart down past the stretch of pubs halfway between the docks and the quarry.

"There's the little one!" sang Tulbër from across the length of three storefronts when he saw Owyn. Dozens of people looked up, but only Owyn looked at the giant with a smile. It was impossible not to smile as he saw the massive body grin as he ran towards him, the cart of stone barreling behind him. "Where have you been, little one?"

"My question first," said Owyn. "What are you doing bringing the stone down now? How'd you know I was coming?"

"I didn't. I bring the stone every day."

"You carry that down every day? I hadn't even paid for it yet and I haven't been to the city in four days!"

"I work the quarry or walk the stone to you. Walking is much less work. I knew you'd pay me back for the load."

"Pay you back?" said Owyn. "Can I pay for the next load too? I don't want your money spent on me." He thought a second. He hadn't meant to take advantage of the giant. Paying him back wasn't enough for what Tulbër was doing. The giant looked down at him with kindness, about to speak, but Owyn interrupted before he could: "Can I buy you lunch?"

***

"You talk so little, little one," said Tulbër as he sat on the stone stool. Owyn hadn't realized that stone could ever groan under the weight of someone. "You tell me nothing of yourself."

Owyn started to speak when the serving woman came to their table, cutting him off.

"Tulbër, with a friend this time!" said the woman.

"Hello, little love!" shouted Tulbër, his voice reverberating through the air in the pub. He flew up with a spryness that Owyn hadn't expected and pulled the woman into a hug. She was taller than Owyn, yet she still looked like a child in Tulbër's arms.

"Don't crush me, now!"

"Never, little love." Tulbër set her down and fell onto his stool with a thud. That could not be good for the stool.

"So who is it you have brought to me?" she said, eyeing Owyn up and down.

"This little one is building a lighthouse."

"A what?"

"A big tall tower that holds lights for ships at night." Tulbër smiled a knowing smile as he spoke. The woman just looked at them both. "I am being rude! Little one, this is Roset, the nicest woman in Kudra. Prettiest, too." The giant's grin was only outmatched by the volume of his voice. The whole pub was a mixture of people blatantly ignoring their table or unashamedly listening in.

"Be quiet, you," said Roset as she punched the giant's shoulder. She turned to Owyn. "I shouldn't be surprised that such a big character comes in a body such as his, but here I am, shocked every time. Now, what can I get for you?"

"I, uh..." started Owyn. Words were a challenge after watching their exchange.

"The wine is freshest, though the ale is excellent. And I wouldn't recommend anything other than the catch of the day."

"Sure."

"Perfect, then I'll get you the wine?"

Owyn nodded.

"Goes better with the fish, anyway. Good choice." She turned to Tulbër. "Don't think you're setting us up." With that, she walked away.

Owyn looked at the giant, dumbfounded.

"The little love is wonderful, is she not?"

"Aren't you going to eat?"

"She knows my order."

"How often do you come here?"

Tulbër pointed up, and Owyn saw the domed ceiling. It was high, reaching up into where a second story would go if the pub were an inn and had rooms. "It's one of the places that fits. Few do."

Owyn looked around. The place was small, despite the rather high ceiling. The other patrons had let their eyes return to their own tables, letting him and Tulbër be for now. Roset returned quickly with three mugs. She set one down in front of Owyn. He quickly noticed how fragrant the fruit smell was that wafted from the wine and set the other two in front of Tulbër. "Enjoy," she said before disappearing again.

Owyn took a sip of his wine. It was crisp with a hint of sweetness. He quickly took another sip. Tulbër pulled a long drink from the first mug.

"The beer here is unmatched. Brewed in back, you know."

"Wine's good, too," said Owyn, taking another small sip before setting the mug back to table.

"Good. Now let it loosen your lips. I've told you many tales, yet you speak nothing."

"You never told me how you found this place."

"It's not a great tale," the giant took a drink. "It could be later, but it is not yet. You must tell me something, little one. Stories make friendships."

Owyn took another drink from the wine. He felt like Ost. "What do you want to know?"

"Whatever it is that you wish to tell." The giant took another drink as well. Owyn thought for a moment. Nothing came to mind, but the wine seemed to come to his lips far too quickly. The mug was half gone already, and they'd only just begun sitting in silence.

"You know where they make great wine?" he said, fishing in his brain for a story, something for the giant. He looked at Tulbër and realized that he didn't want to let the giant down. He'd almost waited too long after his question. Tulbër shifted as if to answer, to break the silence. Owyn didn't let him. He continued: "The Istar Mines."

Owyn let the words sit in the air.

"You've been to the Istar Mines?" shouted the giant. Heads turned again. Owyn saw Roset behind the bar, shaking her head with a grin. "This must be a great tale." Tulbër turned to the bar. "Little love, we will need more wine. For the both of us this time!" Eyes ablaze with interest, he turned back to Owyn.

"It really isn't much of a story," stammered Owyn. He hadn't realized he'd fold under the pressure so quickly.

Roset had reached their table already, setting down two mugs of wine. "Don't worry, he only gets more excitable as he drinks," she said, laughing as she walked away.

Tulbër's eyes never left Owyn.

"We hit it on one of our...travels," he said cautiously. "Well, we didn't hit it, that was the important part. Important to me at least." Owyn saw the interest in the giant's eyes. The hope. The anticipation. He cleared his throat and took another swig of his first mug of wine. It drained the vessel. Standing would feel funny when he'd have to go back to that. He thought of Ost, how the young man's eyes lit up under the starry sky. Did he owe Tulbër the same? Did he owe anything?

"Tulbër... it was glorious. The Mines aren't only mines. They are great and wealthy—sprawling holes filled with jewels and ores. But there is also something more there: a soul. The City of Istar! The Grand Forge!

"I used to travel with a companion. We'd had others with us from time to time, but it was he and I against the world."

"You fought?" said Tulbër before he shook his head, raising a massive hand from the table and waving away his words as if to say, "Don't answer that."

"We fought against our better nature—or at least we used our nature to fight what we thought was worth fighting for. It wasn't worth a damn." Owyn almost caught himself in a thought. He let the story take him back. "What was worth more than the total value of all that it held was the Istar Mines. A forge, hundreds of lengths across. Dozens of furnaces to heat and smelt metals. Hundreds of inspectors, specializing in gems and metallurgy and stonework, each shouting and leading and working towards something great. There are so many parts, Tulbër, and they all move. It should be chaos, but it isn't. They form the whole. The mountains weep—" Owyn stopped as Tulbër raised his cup to that but saying nothing. "But they weep not for lack of majesty within them."

"The mountains weep," said Tulbër, a toast to the air, before he took a drink.

Owyn raised his mug in response. "The mountains weep." He took a drink. Tulbër nodded with a smirk. Owyn had answered the toast incorrectly. "You've never thought to visit the Istar Mines on your pilgrimage?"

"I search for buildings and architecture and materials about the world. I would love to see the mines for what people have constructed there, but a pilgrimage to the Weeping Mountains is something different, something I was not—am not—ready for."

"What makes it different?"

"The father is there." Tulbër looked at Owyn as if he were a child or an idiot. "Donar is the one who weeps."

Owyn just looked at the giant, not wanting to ask another stupid question.

"You don't know your religion very well, do you, little one?"

"It's never served me much."

The giant still smiled, and Owyn was glad. People got so touchy about their gods. He shook his head slightly, dismissing his own thought, and raised his cup. "The mountains weep."

Tulbër raised his wine and touched cups with Owyn. "And so, we live." Both drank.

"Oh good, the first of many toasts I presume," said Roset. They could hear the smile in her voice. "Eat up if you're going to drink that fast." She set down a plate of fish and grains in front of Owyn. It smelled delicious. The light tang of the fish mixing with the nuttiness of the grains smelled full and fresh, like the sea and the sand perfectly balanced in a meal. In front of Tulbër, she set down a massive bowl filled with green leaves, fresh and strange to Owyn, mixed with red and purple and orange vegetables. The colors of the dish were so bright they offset the lack of odor of the salad and made Owyn's mouth still water. "Enjoy, you two."

Owyn and Tulbër did.

***

The man and the giant stumbled out of the pub, a little looser in the legs than they had intended, but much happier in the heart. Tulbër grabbed the cart and began to pull before Owyn could say or do anything. He followed along at the giant's side.

"I'll let the money replace a story this time, little one, but next time you don't get to pay for a meal instead of talking to me."

"I told you a story!"

"One, and barely that. I've told you many as we walked."

"You've got a big mouth, though."

"That aids in volume, but it does not make the storytelling any less wondrous coming from me."

"You've got a big ego, too."

"I'm a giant. It fits."

"You're a good person, Tulbër."

The giant was silent, but Owyn saw a smile still resting on his face.

When the pair reached the docks, they were surprised by a figure seated on the edge of the stone platform looking out at the sunset.

"Ost?" shouted Owyn. The sailor turned to look at him and waved. "What are you doing here?"

"Work was finished, so I figured I'd help with the stone."

"Stone's here," said Tulbër. "Who's this?"

Ost approached and held out a hand to the giant. "Name's Ost." The pair shook hands. "Port is never fun," he said, looking out at nothing before bringing his gaze back to the pair, "but since the stone is here already, let's load it up and get a drink. I know a good pub close by." Ost saw Owyn looking at him. "No advice tonight, just drinks. It looks like I've got some catching up to do."

Tulbër laughed at that. "A perfect suggestion."

CHAPTER 7

The pub quieted as Owyn entered, and only when Ost followed though the threshold did the customers resume living as they had been. And the pub was alive. There had been a murmur when Tulbër entered, ducking sideways through the door that was not designed for his kind. But the patrons kept to themselves after seeing the familiar demeanor, if not face, of Ost. He was a sailor like them. The sailor led them to an open table.

"Beers?" he said. Owyn and Tulbër nodded emphatically, and Ost wove his way through the tables and bodies to the bar.

Owyn took it all in. The lights were dim, but the place was filled with life and shining with colors. None were as bright as Doman's ship, *The Small Journey*, but still the men here wore vibrant colors compared to their fellow Kudran citizens. Then again, he wondered how many of these men actually hailed from Kudra. There was music in the corner. A concertina and flute, Owyn had never heard the combination. And there were games. Men flicked discs across a circular table—the cheering was loudest from those seats—but there was also a table for pocketball, with a line of men waiting to play behind the foursome currently occupying the table. There were cards and dice at each table, even if the men were not playing, and there was even a quiet game of stones being played in the corner. But what caught Owyn's eyes the most was the game of darts against the center of the back wall. His eyes lingered there until he saw Ost out of the corner of his eye with three mugs in hand. He stood to help the man but was quickly waved off. It was only when he had sat again, with beer in hand, that Owyn noticed the sad look on Tulbër's face.

"There must be many stories in this place," he said, loud enough and looking towards the giant.

"Yea," said Tulbër. He raised his mug and touched it to Owyn and Ost's, but there was no joy in the action.

Owyn looked beyond the giant then and saw the table behind him. Three men sat there. Their faces held a mixture of entitlement and anger, and they were laughing. Owyn hadn't heard what they had said, but he knew what that look meant. He took a deep breath and a drink from the mug.

"How did you get to the docks?" asked Tulbër, before Owyn could act on the thoughts in his head.

Ost smiled. "I swam, of course."

"You swam that far?" exclaimed Owyn.

"You've never told me where your island is, little one."

"It's on the other side of Turtle Bay!" said Owyn, still looking at Ost.

Tulbër looked at Ost with a surprised look on his face. "Simply amazing!" he said, his booming voice musical even through the dense sound of the bar. The men at the table behind them whispered something and broke into uproarious laughter once again. Owyn watched Tulbër sink a little further into his seat.

Ost didn't miss a beat, though, and kept speaking. "It really isn't that much of a challenge. Compared to freshwater like the lakes by Gilles where I learned to swim, it's a breeze. The seawater in the bay lifts a ton. Don't you know how much the seawater helps you float?"

The man and the giant stared blankly at the sailor.

"Well, it lifts a lot."

Owyn looked at Tulbër. The giant would not speak, so he continued. "You come from Gilles?" he said.

"You've heard of Gilles?"

Owyn shook his head. "Of course not."

Ost laughed. "No one has."

He stopped. Owyn saw the discomfort. Knew how hard it was to share about one's past. The man was young, but he was still alive. He saw Tulbër, still silent, and knew he'd have to keep the conversation going if they were not to drink in silence. He was fine with silence, but seeing the giant quiet felt wrong.

"Tell me another tale of the woodfarms," said Ost, before Owyn could speak, "and I'll tell of Gilles."

"You've visited woodfarms?" said Tulbër, perking up and taking his eyes off Ost for the first time.

Owyn smiled, "Deal."

Ost let out a small cheer. "I'm from Gilles, born and raised, until I took a riverboat down with a merchant, well, the merchant didn't know I was there, but I was, to Aerdethin. There I hopped on another boat and found my way to the sea."

Owyn glanced at Tulbër. The giant had turned back and was watching Ost speak with such intensity as if willing the story to continue.

"When did you find Doman?"

"A stormy night." The sailor drained his mug of beer and held it aloft for the next few seconds of his story. Man and giant leaned in. "I'd worked the worst sorts of ships, those based in Daughtn—not that all from Daughtn are bad, mind you, but the ones I worked on certainly were." He nodded and set the mug back on the table, having finally gotten the attention of the bartender. "It was during a storm after I'd left Daughtn and had gotten to a small port town called Annmur. The storm didn't start out bad, but it was already bad enough that the ships at sea had all found their ports where they could. I saw this brightly colored monstrosity"—Owyn noticed Tulbër wince at that last word—"sailing out in the distance. It had no thought nor care for the storm and appeared to be making its way to port at Annmur, hell or high water. And there certainly was high water.

"There's a danger in Annmur. Rocks and jagged points jut out of the water just inside the small bay they call port. If you don't know their location, your ship is surely to sink. It's not a good port, and the ship I had just left service of had made use of it a lot. I knew those points. But there was no way that this multi-colored wonder of a ship could. The storm was getting worse as I waited. Watching. Hoping.

"The ship was lost in the waves. And I couldn't let a ship like this crash into land. A ship painted so could not sink against the stone near port. I'd come from such poorly taken care of vessels. I just could not let something that looked so wonderous sail at such risk."

Ost paused. There was a palpable but unspoken "what did you do next?" that hung in the air above the bar table. The small space had not quieted since the story started, but the space around the table was stark and silent. They could have heard a pin drop if it were the distance from the top of a mug to the table. The bartender dropped off three mugs of ale and removed the one empty one, sitting unattended.

"So I swam out to meet them. The lightning struck the sea about the town and the ship, but that did not matter. There was a ship and it needed me. And I was there. I could help. With a rope affixed to the port in case I was lost in the waves, I dove into the tempest.

"I swam harder than I ever had. It took more out of me than any other moment of my life. The waves crashed under me and above me. My lungs filled with water as I struggled for air. It was darkness and darkness alone that kept me company through the storm. Yet at the end of it all, I reached the ship.

"'Man overboard!' I heard the cry. They thought that they had lost one of their own. That was fine. That meant that I'd met my goal, at least the first. 'Man port side!' I heard the call, and I knew my mission was complete. Shortly after the cry, they took me aboard. It was to the credit of this ship's Captain that the men saved me with such efficiency. I later learned that they knew that none had fallen overboard. They saved me at the behest of the Captain and the crew. What men. What men!" With this cry, many of the bar looked at their table for a moment before returning to their own stories.

"I stated my purpose as I got aboard and was brought to the Captain. I aided their navigation and even though the storm fought us, through line and lead, Doman Sutherland, Captain of *The Small Journey*, brought his ship to port. Later I heard it had been the greatest storm to hit Annmur that season.

"It was after a thorough headcount and a few drinks at the local portside pub that I made the acquaintance of the Captain himself and he invited me aboard. And I've stayed aboard ever since."

"Why did you rush into the storm like that?" said Owyn. The words came out without a thought as the question forced itself to be asked.

Ost looked at Owyn, almost confused, like he thought the man would already know. "Because they needed help."

The last of the instinctual words out, Owyn and Tulbër looked at the sailor frozen, mouths agape. Owyn could not guess at Tulbër's thoughts, but he felt a wonder at Ost's tale. He'd heard maybe a dozen words from Ost since the man had appeared on his island, and now he heard this epic tale. He took a drink of his first mug, draining it before grabbing the fresh mug placed by the bartender and taking another sip.

The moment was ruined with laughter.

The men at the table behind them had whispered again, laughing as they stood and worked their way towards the dartboard painted on the far wall of the bar. Owyn hadn't heard most of what they had spoken. He heard two words though: "Monster" and "oaf." The men had been looking towards Tulbër. Owyn stood without thinking.

In an instant, he noticed that two of the three men wore belt wallets, small cloth sacks affixed to their belts. They jingled with a modest amount of coin. Owyn looked at their table. They left nothing behind. The third man hid his money on his person. At a glance, Owyn knew it was near his chest. These men weren't stupid. But they had made a mistake. They had insulted Owyn's friend.

Owyn was already standing. He hadn't thought about what the word meant to him. What Tulbër had come to mean to him. He pushed his stool under the table for the room. "Will you back me up?" he asked Ost. Before he had finished the sentence, the sailor had nodded. Owyn looked at Tulbër and nodded. He didn't think the giant had expected anything, nor had he wanted him a part of the conversation.

He saw the wallet again.

Owyn pushed down the world he had come from and thought instead of the world he had chosen. He would not steal. That was not who he was anymore. He noticed Ost had stood up behind him. He hadn't left the table, though; he knew his role was not intimidation.

"Fancy a game?" bellowed Owyn louder than needed, practically shouting it towards the three men who were currently arranging themselves about the dartboard. The three men looked at him, surprised.

It was the smallest of the three, the man who walked without a belt wallet, who responded: "What's the wager?" He spat the words out. There was an anger there, an anger Owyn would have used in an instant in another life. He could use it now, too.

He pulled out his wallet, a leather pouch held in the satchel at his side. He held it aloft. "My wallet and its contents for those of your three wallets," he said. Owyn noticed that both Tulbër and Ost were standing now. Ost was closer behind him, but he was still not close.

The third man, the small man, had almost spoken. He wanted to speak, but the first man stopped him. "I don't trust you," he said. The words lingered in the air. No one let them fall to either side of honesty.

Owyn did the only thing that he could. He emptied his wallet on the table between them. All of his money fell out and clattered against the stone's surface. It was everything he had. All spread out, it was a wealth beyond that of the men at the table, maybe all of the men in the pub. They weren't carrying everything they owed, only what they would need for the night out. They wouldn't be betting their money for food and stone. They wouldn't be betting their dream.

The noise of the bar quieted. Men all around stared at the coins that now covered a portion of the table. The three men didn't speak.

"There is no fairness in that wager," said Ost. Three pairs of eyes looked at him. Owyn's gaze didn't leave his targets, though. "Kel, what are the rules on wagers?" he said.

The bartender, Kel, leaned closer to the action. "Any gambling here need be fair and sanctioned."

"And would you sanction this wager?"

"Nay."

"I'll request more," said Owyn. The trio's eyes finally returned to him. "You can keep the coins in your wallet. I wager the wealth on the table for an apology. You insulted my friend. If I win, you will apologize to him and never set foot in this establishment again."

Owyn couldn't believe the words from his mouth. Triph would have slapped him. He would never have left the money behind in his old life. Not even for his old partner.

"Put their coin on the table, too," said Kel, "and I'll sanction that."

The three men glared at Owyn. The third man spoke. "What game?" He held out his hands with a smile growing on his face as Owyn feigned thought. The two of his crew handed him their belt wallets, and he removed his own sack of coin from a hidden pocket in his shirt, setting all three on the table next to Owyn's money.

Owyn tried not to stare at the growing pile of coins on the table. It wasn't a lot more, but it was more. He needed it.

"We'll play darts," said Owyn.

The mouths of all three men curled upward into vicious grins. Owyn hid the joy he felt at their confidence.

The first man pulled a set of darts out of another pocket. They shined, even in the dim candlelight of the room. "Arik, hand him yours." The third man, the one who had wanted to speak earlier, grinned a slimy smile. He handed Owyn a set of broken sticks, darts in name only, taken far beyond their reasonable usefulness. Arik would not be competing, it seemed.

"One round?" said Owyn.

"Sure."

"And since you're using your own darts, may I use whatever I like?"

The man looked at the pathetic excuse for darts held in Owyn's hand, realizing that he may not have as easy of a time with it as he had hoped. "Sure," he conceded.

"Perfect." Owyn handed the darts a back to Arik. "Kel, if I may be a bother. May I borrow three knives?"

"Knives?" said Arik.

"You agreed I could use whatever I like," said Owyn. Kel held out three knives taken from behind the bar. Owyn took them and gently hefted them in his hands. The weight was off, but it wasn't so far gone. These would do. "You may choose the line if you'd like."

The man walked across the room, finding the furthest section of space from the target marking the wall. It was still a straight shot, but it was over two tables, which quickly emptied.

"Who begins?" asked Owyn.

"Kel?" said the first man. The bartender flipped a coin.

"You do."

The man smiled. "Ready?" he said. Owyn nodded. The man stood up a little straighter, his back erect and his figure poised. He held his first dart in his right hand. It was an odd method. Owyn wasn't practiced in dart throwing, but he would have never thought to hold it in such a way. It almost looked dainty. With a flick of the wrist, the man's first dart sailed across the length of the bar and stuck into the wall. It was only a dart-length from the bullseye. The bar was silent. Owyn's coins glittered on the stone table to the side of the wall with the target. Tulbër sat where he had been standing moments ago, with Ost at his side, still standing. The men who filled the place watched with palpable anticipation. The second dart almost hit the first, sticking on the side closer to the bullseye. The third hit the outer edge of the bullseye. The man bowed to the crowd. A crook in a bar, playing theatrics.

Owyn flipped a knife in his hand. He'd judged the distance when he'd walked the length from the target to where they stood now. He flipped the knife in his hand again. It had been a while.

It hadn't been too long, though.

His first knife stuck at the edge of the bullseye with a thud that echoed throughout the room. He smiled. Tossing the second knife from his left hand to his right, he gave it a twirl and a flip before sticking it almost centered in the bullseye. No sense in creating more drama. He threw the third knife and watched it spin through the air as it flew true to its mark and clanged against the second blade, hitting the bullseye and sticking right next to its brother.

"Now apologize," said Owyn. His voice held an anger fueled by confidence and a righteous feeling that he wasn't sure he'd felt before.

"Cheater!" shouted Arik. But before anything else happened, much of the bar stood up. The scraping sound of their stools on the floor cut through the heavy silence.

"You three leave. Now," said Kel from the bar.

The first man walked up to the wall and removed his darts before looking at the pile of money and the three wallets sitting on the table. He turned to the giant. "I am sorry for what we said." Then he left, his two cronies following shortly behind.

The men of the bar returned to their seats and drinks. Sound slowly filled the room once more. Tulbër didn't sit back down. He looked at Owyn. His lavender eyes didn't waver as they looked at the man.

"I'm sorry, Tulbër, I—" started Owyn before being cut off with the biggest hug he had ever received. The giant lifted Owyn off, the ground and squeezed him until he thought he may burst before being set back down.

"Thank you," he said. Even whispered, his voice still sang.

Ost set four bags of coin down on their table. "Now that that's over, I say we can afford something fancier than beer. Istar wine, perhaps?" he winked at Tulbër.

"That we can!" said Tulbër, taking some of the coin from one of the newly gained wallets and walking up to Kel.

"You'll have to teach me that," said Ost.

"I'll trade you: teach me to swim and I'll teach you to throw."

"You can't swim?"

Owyn shook his head.

He couldn't tell if Ost was disappointed or was about to burst into laughter. Tulbër returned with a platter in hand: three full mugs and three smaller cups. Ost slapped Owyn on the shoulder. "It's a deal."

"I got us the potent stuff," said the giant. "What deal did I miss?"

"Owyn can't swim."

Tulbër burst into the loudest laughter Owyn had ever heard. "Let's drink to swimming, then," he said, when his laughter finally subsided. He lifted one of the small cups. Owyn and Ost followed suit. It wouldn't be the last one of those this night.

***

The night passed wonderfully, and the trio stumbled out of the bar hours after they had walked in. Reaching the docks, Owyn sobered upon realizing that the *Morning Sunshine* was missing.

CHAPTER 8

Owyn stared at the vacant dock where his boat had been. His boat. The *Morning Sunshine*. It had a name; more importantly, it had a receipt of sale. His boat—not stolen, not "borrowed," not anything other than his. And now it was gone.

He sat down on the stone dock. Hands reaching up for his face when he felt a large hand on his shoulder.

"Do not weep, little one. The world is not ended with the loss of a boat."

Owyn looked up, on the one hand, disgusted at the thought of crying over something so simple. On the other, he felt seen. "It was my boat though."

The giant squeezed his shoulder, the massive hand so much more gentle than it seemed.

"Look at the stars," said Ost. He was pointing out at the night sky. It was a clear night and the stars pierced the darkness as they shined down on the world. Out across the bay, Owyn thought he could almost see the island. His island. He'd be able to see it when a light sat atop it. He wanted to sit with his friend and be distracted, but he couldn't.

The drink still ran though his body and Owyn stumbled as he stood. "We've got to get it back," he said to everyone and no one.

"I can't swim out in the dark," said Ost. "But we can try in the morning."

"You have winnings, little one, they must be enough to replace the boat. Was that boat so special?"

It had been special. It had been his. Bought and paid for, not stolen, not pilfered or borrowed. It had been his, never mind the cost to replace it. "No," he lied. It felt wrong lying to Tulbër. He looked up and saw the giant's lavender eyes, stark against his stone-gray skin in the starlight. "And yes."

"Then we shall sleep before deciding what to do next. I saw you stumble rising there; you humans can't handle your drinks, it seems." His grin lit up the dock. "It is a good night out and the stone is soft."

Owyn was about to protest, but Ost was already down, lying on the dock, shirt tucked under his head as his droopy eyes stared up at the stars. Owyn gave a drunken shrug and lay down next to him. Tulbër shook the stone pier as he fell down and lay near them.

Tulbër snored softly, and Owyn heard Ost's breath subtly change when sleep took hold. He stared up at the stars, unable to sleep, waiting to see the *Morning Sunshine* again. Knowing he ever would

***

Owyn and Tulbër sat on the edge of the dock as the sun was rising. It was coming later and later in the morning now.

"What's winter like this far south?" he asked.

Tulbër waited a second before responding. They were watching Ost, coming back from the edge of the port. He had searched one side and Owyn the other. The *Morning Sunshine* was nowhere. Owyn still hadn't told either of them the name for his boat. It didn't matter now.

"Rainy," said Tulbër. "It gets dreary and cloudy for months and the storms can be nothing, or they can be magnificent."

"No snow or cold, though?"

"It gets cold, but nothing like what is north of the desert."

"Hmm."

Another moment passed as they sat in silence, watching. Owyn's head hurt, throbbing on his top right side for a reason he knew all too well. His throat was parched, and he was tired.

"How much longer before the rainy winter starts?" asked Owyn.

"Still many weeks," said the giant. He sounded slower this morning, too, but Owyn wasn't sure if giants got hungover like humans did. It felt rude to ask.

"How long do you plan to stay in Kudra before your pilgrimage resumes?"

The giant thought on that. "The wise would say the pilgrimage never stopped. Kudra is a part of the journey, as are all others." He looked at Owyn with a grin. "I'm not that wise yet. I stayed in this city for the people."

"Not the money?"

"Money is nice, but I worked the quarry for the stone and the stoneworkers."

"What?"

"This whole city is built of the stone from the edge of a desert. The Gods Tower itself is both different and the same as all of the other buildings."

"You're here for the buildings?"

"That is what I feel right for my pilgrimage, yes. There is life in the stone and grass and wood we all live under. And we all build it so differently. My people always wish to learn more of the world, yet we build so little now in what cities we yet have."

"But you stay for the people?" asked Owyn.

"I did not want to leave on pilgrimage, but I must. The people and friends in the city make it feel closer to home. I hate being alone."

Owyn didn't. All he wanted was to be alone. He could not say that to Tulbër though, especially not now.

"I've never been to any of the giant's cities," he said.

"You must come," said Tulbër. "We have highchairs for our little ones, so you can still eat with me."

Owyn and Tulbër laughed. Quietly, though, because the shaking aggravated his head. The seawater gently lapped against the docks of the port. With the sun rising further, there was a noise behind them of people starting their day. A crew was loading one of the sloops with piles of woven blue cloth, and some men were getting into their own dinghies to bring crates that jingled with brassware to their ships anchored further offshore. The architects of the city had built the whole port on the edge of a massive drop-off into the water, which allowed the ships to get close before they anchored.

"What's your home like?" Owyn asked. The two of them stared out at the water, and at Ost returning. The sailor was deliberate in his gait, taking his time to return to them as he walked.

"It is smaller, and it is poor. We are not far from Novash, but even the seat of the kingdom is not wealthy. Time has challenged my people. Many settle to return home with wealth or money, but to return from a pilgrimage is to bring a better version of oneself. Others become wise, learning knowledge and skills from afar; others, artisans, learning new trades; others, artists. And some never return. I may not be an artisan myself, but I can learn. I can come back with a different sort of wealth. I could help my people build once more."

"Still," said Owyn, hesitant to not insult his friend. "You may take the wallets."

"You won them."

"I won them for you."

"You won them to bring those men down."

"I won them because they insulted you, and you won't get me to believe there is a difference. Take the wallets for your home." Owyn shook his head and stood up, stretching. He took some coins out of his own satchel. "And here," he said, holding out the money. "Payment for your work. I've been cheating you out of money."

"I earned my money from my time at quarry, and you've paid me for the stone. That is enough."

"It's not. Not for all you've helped with."

Tulbër eyed the man. They both knew the *Morning Sunshine* would not be found. That's not how such things worked for Owyn. The giant took the money from his hand after another moment's hesitation.

"You're a funny man, little one."

"You won't bring home anything by helping me out for free." He turned and saw Ost was very close now, within shouting distance. "Now take that cart back to the quarry and do some work today. We've got things handled here."

Tulbër leaned down and gave Owyn a hug. Owyn still felt like a child held in his arms.

"Thank you, Owyn," said the giant. He turned and walked down the dock, taking the empty cart with him back into the city.

Alone on the end of the dock, but not alone, Owyn watched as Ost walked up.

"Anything?" he asked, knowing the reply before he started.

"Nay," said the sailor.

"Could it have sunk?"

"If so, its lost. The bay is deep. Some even say monsters live in it." Ost winked, but the humor didn't stick with Owyn. He thought of the bay and how he had never known how to swim. He took in a breath and pushed the thought from his mind, but found only the *Morning Sunshine* took its place. He would never see that boat again.

The dock where they stood was not alone. There were dozens of stone piers for boats to set off from. The morning work was beginning around Owyn and Ost as sailors and merchants of other vessels moved about, carrying out their work for the day.

Owyn saw the dockmaster walking down the piers and his head dropped. He knew what he had to do, but he did not wish to think it. He wanted to run away. He wanted to shrink to his island, but he could not reach that on just the loadboat.

"Watch the stone, will you?" he said to Ost. The sailor nodded. He also knew what had to happen and watched as Owyn walked down the pier to the dockmaster.

"I see you've yet to drown," said the wiry man. He was only in middle age, but gave the impression of being a much older man. His grin was the grin of a salesman. Owyn knew it too well. It was the same grin as a fence. "How goes the work on your island?"

Owyn was surprised. "Word travels so quickly?"

"Not a lot of strangers claim land out in the bay. Unique stories travel."

Owyn saw the interest on the man's face, but he didn't want to share what he was doing. He hadn't wanted to share it with anyone. "I need another boat," he said. His hand sat against his satchel. It was as if he felt the coins about to disappear.

"Lost yours already?" said the dockmaster with almost a laugh. But when he saw the look of pain on Owyn's face, he paused and his tone shifted. "What happened?"

"It went missing last evening."

"From my docks?"

Owyn nodded and the man took a breath. He seemed to be holding in his anger. He muttered something about a boy before listing the price.

Owyn noted the cost was far less than the *Morning Sunshine*. He looked at the man with not quite thanks, but knowing. The dockmaster did not smile. He did not allude to what he was doing, he simply took the coin from Owyn as he handed over more than his winnings from the night before. His own wallet in the satchel was lighter now. With a shout, the dockmaster called a girl over to help with the new boat. Owyn pointed to Ost and the loadboat and she was off to bring the new boat over.

Owyn walked back towards his stone and saw a man in the distance. The beggar for Irnam from before. The man spat on the stone beneath his feet before shaking his head and speaking to another man seated next to him. The second man glared at Owyn before shouting "Sinner!" and spitting on the ground himself. Owyn caught himself between anger and laughter at the sight of the sitting man spitting between his own legs. Sinner? He shook his head and returned to Ost.

"Tie these together," said Ost to the young dock girl as Owyn approached. She had already gotten the boat over to their dock, near the loadboat, and Ost tossed her the loadboat's ropes to tie to his new boat. "They got the stone, too."

"What?" said Owyn.

"Ship varnish," said the sailor as he gestured to the stone. The pile was covered in an oily, paint-like substance. Owyn held himself steady. His neck was sore from shaking his head, and the hangover from the night before had not yet passed. He would figure out the solution to that problem once he had reached his island.

"All set," said the dock girl as she hopped out of Owyn's new boat. Ost was quick to get in. Something about his comfort on the water, even so simple as being aboard a boat at port, calmed Owyn. The girl held out a hand, and he tossed her a bit coin from his satchel. He was poor. But he was not unkind.

***

"Ready?" he asked Ost.

"Aye." Without asking or waiting, Ost had seated himself in the rowing position. Owyn got in. He hadn't realized how clumsy he was even on his own boat until he had watched Ost get in the small vessel with a grace that he had to admit he envied.

"I can—" started Owyn, but the sailor just shook his head. Owyn sat instead at the rear of the boat and faced the sailor, who immediately began to row.

As they left the dock, there was a splash in the water near the boat. Owyn looked to it, but saw nothing moving in the water. His gaze continued up to the two men from the dock. The beggar had left, but the man who shouted remained. He was standing now, eyes fixed on Owyn and his boat. Owyn knew anger. The man was seething with it. He spat again and walked away, down the dock. Owyn watched him for a while. Both knowing what had happened and refusing to admit it. There'd been a few throwable stones by the man's feet.

He turned to see the bay ahead of them.

With Ost rowing, they were flying across the water despite the slight morning chop. Doman had been standing on a similar boat as his men had rowed him to shore at Owyn's island. The larger dinghy they had used may have sailed smoother, but still, Owyn, feeling the waves more than usual in his present state, marveled at the balance the man must have. He looked back to Ost. The sailor was focused; he looked about. He was watching the sky above them, but his body was taut with effort.

"You're quiet when sober," said Owyn.

"Just hungover."

"You sure didn't seem to be hurting as bad as we were."

"Work helps."

"Hmm."

Row, row, row, they went across the bay.

"You said last night that the men at the pub didn't do this," said Owyn. It was a mixture of question and statement.

"Aye. Sailors wouldn't do this."

"Any idea who would?"

"There were angry folk at port when I came in yesterday. Protestors, maybe."

"Protestors?" Owyn thought of the beggar and the man who shouted.

"You're building a tower."

"And?" said Owyn.

"People get touchy when men try to match gods." Ost gestured to the shadow over the bay cast from the Tower in the city.

That explained little to Owyn. He made a mental note to bring wine to the island the next time he did the out and back trip from

Kudra. He'd need to get the man drunk again to have a full conversation.

"You don't know your religion either, do you?" said Ost.

Owyn looked at him, confusion on his face. "That's the second time I've heard that here."

Ost shook his head. He nodded towards the city behind Owyn. "People are sensitive about religion here. Lots of importance in a tower when you live under *the* Tower."

Owyn turned and looked at the God's Tower looming over the city. "Huh?"

"Ask the giant next time you can."

"You can't tell me more?"

Ost shook his head. "I don't know the specifics. There's a story to the Tower, but I only know people get mad about them here."

"You're not religious?"

"Have to be faithful on a ship."

"So?"

"We're not on a ship." Ost laughed.

Owyn wondered if he'd ever understand the man.

"Whatever god made that Tower isn't who we pray to when storms hit the seas. We'll pray to anyone and everyone. As much as my mom wanted to, I never much listened to the pulpit until I went to sea."

Owyn nodded. Maybe it didn't matter. They made it back to the island faster than he would have on a smooth day without the loadboat in tow. For a few terrified minutes, as the island was in sight but they had not yet reached it, Owyn worried the vandals had reached this place, too. They hadn't, and most of the worry left. A bit would always remain, though.

The two men beached the vessels and began unloading the stone in silence. The varnish had stayed slick on the rocks; they slipped through the men's hands, covering them with grease and slowing their work. They started a separate pile for the tainted stone. Not all was ruined, though. Some of the deeper stones evaded the haphazard toss of the vandals and remained clean. The challenge with these was washing their hands enough to handle them after touching the varnished ones.

"Gods, this stuff gums up in the water," said Owyn.

"Complaining to the gods is sure to please the pious of the city," said Ost.

"Isn't that most of what the pious do?"

The men laughed and worked to clean their hands before returning to the water for another load.

The angry beggar again came to Owyn's mind. He had never paid for a blessing of Irnam from the man and his friend called him a sinner. How much fervor could a beggar have?

"Are you ready?" asked Ost as Owyn put the last stone on the pile.

"Ready?"

"There's no work left today."

The sun was low in the sky, and Owyn didn't want to work on the structure at all today. He was still tired from the morning and the night before. He wasn't following the man, though.

"Well, I'm going to swim. If you want to learn, you can."

Owyn jumped up. "Oh, of course!"

Ost was already walking to shore.

***

"Lay limp."

"What?"

"Lay down in the water and let your body go limp."

Owyn hesitated. He and Ost stood fifteen paces away from the shoreline in the water.

"You're far from the drop off, and I'm here. Lie back."

Owyn awkwardly kneeled down in the water and laid down on his back against the surface of the water. He held his breath and closed his eyes, and nothing happened. He opened his eyes and saw the blue sky above him.

"Huh?"

"Saltwater is easy to float in," said Ost, face replacing the sky as he looking down at Owyn.

"I'm floating?"

The face blocking the sky nodded. "Now you learn to swim."

CHAPTER 9

Weeks passed as Ost and Owyn worked together on the tower. Sometimes one man on the ground below handed stones up to the other on the edge of the tower and sometimes they both worked on the walls. Even though the jagged shapes of the waste stone did not like to be stacked, the structure had only fallen down three times. Each placement was completed carefully, patiently. Owyn admitted to himself that Ost was the more patient of the two of them and so let him take charge of the organization following the second collapse.

Yet the tower still rose.

When he was back on the docks, Owyn could almost see it from across the bay: a little mound of stone, like a tall island on the edge of the world, where things had been flat before. It brought him a smile through the shouts.

"Blasphemer!"

"Heretic!"

"Sinner!"

The beggar had found friends. More than just the first man to shout the word sinner at Owyn. There was a crowd now. Beggars and ragged people, though some dressed cleaner than others. They were not always the same, but more and more shouted towards Owyn as he came to port. Among them he sometimes saw familiar faces shouting; the men from Kel's bar and the game of darts were all to glad to join in too. Their words were different than the religious, but they still felt the same.

Blasphemer, heretic, sinner—the last of the words was the most frequent. And the most painful. It hurt because it was true. Owyn thought of his life, thought of the truth of his sin. It almost pulled him away from the work at hand.

"Little one, are you here?" said Tulbër.

Owyn looked up at the giant. They were loading stone from the cart into the loadboat. This had not been left alone. More than one load had been varnished by the crowd, though they weren't so bold as to throw it on Owyn while Tulbër was here. Yet. Owyn nodded, but Tulbër would not have it. "You cannot let their words get past your ears, little one."

"What if they're right?"

"They speak of gods that they have never met."

"And you've met the gods?"

"No. But we are the children of Donar."

"The gods created men too."

"Not as Donar made us. We are his children."

"I'm going to go talk to them," said Owyn.

"The gods?"

"*Them.*"

"Ah, then I will watch for your safety," said Tulbër with a wink of a lavender eye.

Owyn nodded, and the giant gave a small smile—if any of his smiles could be considered small.

Owyn was not a confrontational man. That had been a major deciding factor in his old life. Why walk towards conflict when you could avoid it and live just as happily? Not now. Now there were those shouting at him and at his friends. Owyn could no longer abide it without a conversation. That's what he told himself as he walked towards the small crowd. This is a conversation, not a confrontation.

The people did not see it as such.

Sneers and jibes flew at him, "sinner" now being far from the worst of them.

"Please," he said, hands held out, placating. "Please, I just want to talk."

A man in the crowd raised his hands high, and the shouts dimmed; they did not stop, but they quieted. The man stepped forward. He was not a beggar, but one of those well-dressed in the group. He was a leader if Owyn had ever seen one.

"What does a sinner have to say?"

"I want to learn about my sins. What I am doing wrong," said Owyn.

"Ignorance shall not save those who disobey the gods!" shouted a person from within the crowd.

The man who had stepped forward turned his head slightly at the call, as if he were about to turn and speak to the crowd, but he stopped and turned back to face Owyn. "She speaks the truth, sinner."

Owyn thought of more than one response, but none would further the conversation without conflict. He pushed down the anger and the frustration he felt. "I wish to know my sins."

The man looked him up and down. He was older. Owyn hadn't seen him before; or if he had, the man had not been distinct enough from the crowd to notice. Were he giving a sermon, Owyn could imagine the congregation behind him refer to the old man as wise. He spat at Owyn's feet.

"You blaspheme. Compete against the gods. Make a secular idol in the image of their lasting creation on Breiar." He spat again. "Ignorance is the least of your sins."

"So, it is the tower on my island?"

"Stop the work on your attempt to be a god or live with your sins. In this life and in the mist."

"I'm not trying to be a god," said Owyn, but the shouts of the mob behind the man grew once more. Owyn turned and left. He tried to keep his composure, but ended up almost fleeing, his pace more than a walk but less than a run. The jeers of the people behind him called him names, commented on the fear he felt. He couldn't talk with their leader. He would not stop his work.

Tulbër stood on the other dock, watching as Owyn came back.

"Are they following?" he said.

"No little one, sit. Sit." Tulbër watched behind Owyn as he sat down on the edge of the dock.

"I just want to be alone," said Owyn. "I came here to leave the ire of people. I came here to be alone. To leave the world and to try doing something good for it. This is what I receive?"

Tulbër turned away from the shouts. He sat down next to Owyn. "You must ignore them, little one. Their attention will pass as time does. You should not put in the energy to match theirs. They are a mob."

"This'll get worse."

Tulbër hummed. "You tried," he said.

Owyn looked at him.

"You tried, and that speaks more than their words. We are all sinners, little one. All kill the gods in little ways as well as big. You tried to speak to your enemy, and they did not return the kindness. This is also a sin."

"So I am right with the gods, if not with men?"

"Are you right with yourself?"

The man and the giant looked at each other. Owyn didn't have a response. He looked back at the bay.

They didn't sit in silence. The water hit the edge of the dock and the loadboat creaked under its weight and the shouts of the mob never ceased. But it was a sort of silence. It all washed over the pair. Tulbër did not speak. He waited. He sat next to his friend.

Owyn slapped the stone dock and stood up. "I should return," he said.

Tulbër stood with him, but did not speak.

"Thank you, Tulbër."

"There will be stone waiting for you as always, when you come back."

Owyn wanted to say more, clarify what he meant, what he had said within the thank you. He thought to speak, to tell the truth, to thank the giant for so much more than the stone. He didn't say a word, and instead took a step towards the giant with arms out and the pair embraced.

"Safe rowing," said Tulbër.

Owyn nodded and began the journey back to his island.

Rowing was good. It was work that left his mind blank. His thoughts could take control, race and shout and fight if he let them, but he didn't want to. Owyn wanted to row, and so that is what his mind felt. It was blank with the moment and the work. He focused on the oars hitting the water.

Halfway across the bay, he turned to see his work, his tower, his sin, his lighthouse. He did not notice his project, though; instead, before it sat *The Small Journey*, anchored a short distance from his island. Owyn's eyes stopped on the vibrant colored ship with confusion. There were two smaller boats leaving the ship and headed towards his island.

Owyn had so many questions, but he turned back to face Kudra and the open water between him and the city. He turned to face the loadboat, filled with stone for his work.

It was not as high in the water as it should have been.

Owyn cocked his head, confused. He'd been staring at the boat for the entire journey, and it'd been a familiar sight over days. He wanted to ask himself what changed, when change happened before his eyes. There was no question.

It had been sinking.

It was sinking faster now.

"No, no, no," said Owyn as he leapt to his feet and went to the back of his boat. The ropes tying the loadboat to his were tightening as the second vessel, full of stone, was falling beneath the surface of the water.

Owyn's mind raced. He didn't know what to do. He couldn't bail water out of another boat, and one full to the brim with rocks at that. He couldn't cut it loose and sacrifice a boat he didn't even own. He wanted to panic.

Owyn did the only thing he knew he could and he rowed. Back in his seat, he forced his arms to work harder than they ever had. He watched the boat sink lower and lower towards the surface of the bay, blue water getting closer to the top of the wooden structure, getting closer to the stone. The weight on the ropes pulled at his boat, each stroke of the oars harder than the last as the loadboat refused to move.

The water reached the stone.

In an instant the loadboat appeared to fall beneath the surface of the bay. The ropes, which had pulled against the cleats on Owyn's boat before, now ripped at them. Wood groaned and Owyn heard a splitting screaming sound that he had never heard before. Timber did not wish to be rent so. He brought in the oars and raced to the other end of his boat. The weight of the sunken loadboat was pulling at the rear, ripping the joints that held his vessel together. His boat would sink too.

Owyn's fingers could not work the knots about the rear of his boat. They were too tight now. He could not untie the rope pulling him downward. His hand reached into an old life but found that the new no longer kept knives where they had always been. The wood beneath him groaned and the water below seemed closer than ever.

He wouldn't be able to save this boat.

Owyn took a deep breath, letting the salt in the air spice his lungs. Fear pressed at his heart, but the air held it at bay. Panic would not take him. It could not.

As his boat joined the loadboat approaching the depths, Owyn pushed out from the capsizing wooden structure and lay on his back.

It felt unnatural, floating as he did. Panic pressed in along with all the doubts he could imagine. He was atop a bay deep enough that ships could sail. Deep enough that ships could sink and keep them beneath the surface. "Some even say monsters live in it."

Owyn took in a breath and felt his body rise atop the water. He let it out slowly and the water rose up about him. In and out. He bobbed and stared at the blue sky above. White clouds meandered on the windless day across the blue above. He worked to not think of what lay below.

The boats lay below.

The loadboat should not have sunk.

Dark thoughts wormed their way past the panic and doubts, unable to be held back. Thoughts of sin and retribution. Thoughts of varnished rocks doing no good.

Consumed in thought, Owyn didn't notice the lapping sound approaching him. His mind turned over ideas as he worked to keep fear away; anger instead crept in. He heard the splash only when it was close enough to feel drops spray on his face. Owyn wanted to jump but feared what it would do to his precarious float atop the bay, so he worked to steady himself.

"Ho, Owyn!" shouted a familiar voice. "Need a hand?"

Owyn didn't want to turn his head. He didn't want to risk anything that would sink him into the water as his boats had.

"I'm going to grab your waist; you put your arm around my shoulder," said Ost, suddenly behind him. "Don't panic, though; I've got you. Don't bring us both down with flailing."

The splash now made sense.

Owyn took a breath and put his arm around the younger man and felt Ost's other arm support him as he lay back beside Owyn and began swimming. "If you can, kicking will help," said Ost. Owyn had no words to reply; he just kicked as they approached the boat behind them.

"This was not the welcome I anticipated," said Captain Doman Sutherland, as he reached out an arm and helped Owyn aboard the boat. Space was tight, between the Captain and another man seated at an oar, but they gave Owyn room to fall into the vessel and a moment to lie at the bottom.

"What are you doing here?" said Owyn. He felt exhausted. His entire body wanted to relax and fall into a sleep. The boat rocked as

Ost hoisted himself up over the side. Water splashed Owyn but he didn't care.

"We heard a man of ours needed help," said Doman with a smile. His voice seemed to sing in a way different from Tulbër's, but with a music of its own. "I did not expect to help him so immediately." The Captain smiled and looked at Ost. The younger man moved to sit beside the second oar, but Doman waved him off and sat there instead. Owyn moved in the back of the boat and faced the Captain and the other sailor rowing as they turned the boat and began towards his island. In that instant, Owyn knew why this man was the captain. There was simply nothing else that Doman could be.

"There was a call from my ship as your vessel began to sink," started the Captain as he rowed. "I had hardly looked in the direction when Husted had commandeered one of *my* boats and a crew of one to leave the island towards you." Owyn saw Ost behind the Captain. The man looked bashful, but his eyes did not leave the Captain as he spoke. "I could not let such a rescue go unsupervised." Doman winked.

Owyn didn't know how to thank the Captain. He didn't know what he'd have done beyond float atop the bay until hunger and exhaustion took him. There were so many thanks he wished to give.

"What sunk the boat?" asked Ost from behind the Captain.

Owyn sat up straighter and looked at the man. "I don't know."

Doman looked at his sailor. "The construction was good," said Ost. "It was not fit for the open sea, but a clear day in the bay..." He trailed off.

"I tried to speak to the zealots," said Owyn. His voice was quiet, hesitant to give voice to the thoughts that had crept in as he had floated.

"Sabotage?" said the Captain, turning back to face Owyn as he rowed.

"It would make sense," said Ost. "A threat to the stone should not have threatened your life."

"At least not in their eyes," said Doman. "There is such resistance in the old cities." The man looked out at the bay behind them. Owyn saw his tower, not much more than a pile of stone, approaching ahead of them. Sailors were leaving their boats, coming from Doman's ship and waiting on the island.

"Why are you here?" asked Owyn.

Doman Sutherland smiled. It was a grin that could make anyone join in. "You've done great work here, Owyn," he said. "Ost spoke highly of you when we landed. It made me smile. I hate deciding something and having to feel like I was wrong after the fact."

"What decision did you make?"

The boat slid against rock beneath them. They had reached the island. Owyn saw that sailors were already at work, not sitting idle as he'd thought. They were moving stone, preparing stockpiles and building scaffolding.

"The decision to help you in your work, of course."

"But why?"

"You are doing something great here, Owyn."

"And the Captain ordered it," said the second sailor at the oars, smiling as he stood and hopped out the boat to push it further ashore.

Ost leapt out of the boat and looked at Owyn for a moment, as if to emphasize he still sat in the boat with the Captain, before heading up the island and shouting towards the men moving stone, directing them.

"There is a...break...in our work for the King," said the Captain. "I don't like idle hands aboard a ship and cannot abide more shore leave for the duration of our wait."

Owyn watched the men as they moved with Ost's calls. They were like a machine as they worked. It was slow at first, but the shouts of Ost grew less instructional and less frequent. The sailors learned quickly and worked well. They moved and lifted and placed stone. It was still only the waste from a quarry, but with care and Ost's instructions, the men got it to stand. Past collapses had taught Ost well. The men grabbed stone and placed it, then did it again and again as Owyn and Doman watched. The efficiency of it staggered Owyn. He would never have been able to work at this rate alone. The sailors sang a song that Owyn had never heard before.

"The murderous horn of Turtle Bay is legendary by those who sail the coast," said Doman. His voice made Owyn nearly jump as it pulled him from his thoughts. "Inexperienced ships can run aground here during the daytime. Even I may miss the rocks of the horn in a storm bad enough. There's something good about a warning. A light to see in the distance. Like the lights and flags along the coast, Kudra should have a light for its own. A sign of home and the danger of arriving there. This structure will save many lives, Owyn." Owyn turned to look at the man. He had put on his hat as he watched. The great feather extending beyond the corners of the hat made him look as tall as a giant.

Owyn wanted to speak, to still ask why. He wanted to dwell on the darkness of losing another boat, and the loadboat as well, but no words came to his mouth.

The Captain patted him on the shoulder as he looked up at the tower, growing slowly towards the sky.

"You are doing something good here."

CHAPTER 10

T riph stumbled through the streets of Kudra. It was a good stumble. He was loose. He was in the right mindset. He was hunting.

The city didn't scare him. It was big, sure, but it was just another congregation of people. Triph was good with people. Well, he was good with them for a time. They always seemed to find some issue with him after a while. Owyn had been the only one not to... well, until he did. Triph wasn't sure what that issue was. Nothing like a friend leaving in the night to bring a smile to your face. He tossed a coin in the air, watching it twirl in the sky for a second before it landed in his palm, forgetting his old friend abandoning him and putting his mind to its task. This city was rich and its people needed to keep a better eye on their purses.

"Alone...alone...where could he be alone?" Triph mumbled. Evening was falling, and the streets were yet moving, but that wouldn't last long. People were finding their homes or their pubs. Triph looked at the buildings. The architecture. He always had an interest in buildings. Particularly, how to best get inside them without using the front door.

Kudra was a big city. It had different kinds of buildings built with different grades of stone. Each area had its own flair, but each was a part of the whole. Tan sandstone walls, large open doorways, wide windows to let in the sea air with thin stone coverings for when they wanted those windows shut in the rain. The roofs in this part of town were poor. This was a cheap part of the city. Small clay tiles covered the roofs, set there loosely in rows without grout, covered with curved tiles to stop water from getting in. They were loud to walk on but easy to break through to get inside. Good things to know.

An angry man was walking in front of Triph and pulled his attention back down to what was in front of him. The man's walk was stiff, but it was fast. Triph knew this man, or rather, he knew enough men like him. Following him was easy. It was like walking in his own footsteps or those of his father. Triph knew that he and the man were walking towards a pub. A quiet pub it'd be. Or perhaps an angry one. Owyn could be at the first, but Triph doubted that he'd be at the second. But he could not doubt enough to ignore the possibility of finding his old friend.

The pub wasn't quiet, nor was it the type of angry that Triph had been expecting. He'd walked in a few minutes after the man and saw him seated at the bar with a beer in his hand. The people by the doorway quieted as Triph walked in and he worried he'd have to buy himself a drink to justify being here now. The pub was busy enough that he could leave without a word, seen yet unnoticed. He scanned the room for Owyn. The man he knew wouldn't be in a pub like this, but you could never be certain after a friend walked out on you like that. A good scan and Triph walked out of the pub. His mind wouldn't leave alone.

Owyn was a bastard. Took half their haul and up and left Triph alone. Alone. Triph never wanted to be alone. Other people always seemed to help him do so, though. *Bastards*, he thought almost aloud. Then that Sheriff found him. Sheriff never would have gotten ahold of Triph if he hadn't been searching for his friend and their goods already. He'd never have found Triph if he hadn't had cause for sulking like he'd been doing.

Well, damn it all, Owyn wanted to be alone and Triph wouldn't let him. Nothing was new, it seemed. Triph never thought about what would happen after they found Owyn. It didn't matter. One step at a time, and make it a limber one at that.

This was good. He wasn't alone if he was working.

He stumbled down the street again. He was getting lower in the city. It physically dropped as he walked forward towards the sea. He could see some of the blue beyond the city wall as he had walked during the daytime, but it was all darkness now.

A light shone outside the next pub in the row and Triph walked in

***

"Stone cuts them, ya see," said the man. The pub was quiet other than him. The sounds of the bartender cleaning mugs seemed to intrude upon the man's words.

"Stone?" asked a man. "Why stone?" It was what Triph had wondered. He took a step closer to the table.

"My faith doesn't speak of it," continued the man. "But the stories do. The folktales spread by giants and those that trade with those kinds. Blades of stone it be—no metal, nor wood, or other work of man. 'A blade of earth,' it must be. It didn't matter to me then. I had no stone blade. Never seen such a thing. I would have had no chance to use it, anyway."

The floor made a terrible groan as the stool in Triph's hands scraped along it. Some looked up at him, irritation in their eyes, but the storyteller didn't stop.

"The woods have a way of entrapping you. It's as if they be a snare, set by something other than man. I didn't want to go in, nay; that would not be my disposition, ye know that. I followed a boy. Stupid village child. He'd heard the stories, he must have, yet he ignored them and went into the woods to have fun, to have a play, as all children do. As all children should do.

"The woods had him without pause or thought. I heard nary a scream nor sound, but I knew there's a dread up there, in the north. The people know pain; they know the weight that death puts on a person. They've lived it. This feeling was worse. The darkness had sucked up the boy between the trees. I was the only man around. There was naught to do but help.

"In the woods, there was no darkness, though. From the outside, as I looked in, there was only the timber and the blackness, the haunting, the death. Inside, it was different. Light shone down from above. Between the branches and the thorns of the trees, there was sunlight, diffused through clouds and a haze that I could see, but not describe to you now. But it was light.

"The light was good. It was the silence that I felt in my soul."

The storyteller stopped for a drink. It was as if the listeners had received an instruction. They all drank. Triph drank too. It felt wrong not to follow the man now. His mug hit the table, and the whole pub leaned in closer to hear.

"There was something about that silence. It pressed in on me. There was a weight to it. I ran."

Every mug was back on its table. The bartender had stopped cleaning.

"I had to save that boy. There was something wrong about this place. A natural forest. There is nothing safe in a natural forest. To survive the impact of humanity? A forest must have something protecting it, something that keeps us at bay. If we cannot take it as a resource, then there must be something keeping us from taking it. That is the way of man. That is the way of those woods."

The man stopped again. The pub drank together.

"The first wisp appeared to me after what felt like an hour. I had not heard the boy. I had no way of knowing where he had gone, what path he had taken. Finding him felt like finding my way out. I thought not of walking backwards, but I did not know which way was forward.

"It looked like an orb, the wisp. It felt good to look at. Floating amongst the trees, I saw it in flashes as I ran forward. It was never in my sight, yet it was always in the periphery. I never looked at it, but I always saw it. It was drawing me towards it. My eyes wanted to look at it. I wanted to stop and see the thing, but I knew that was not the way. I continued forward. Towards the boy, always towards the boy. I had to reach him.

"Another wisp appeared. There was a second light fighting for my attention. The thing of it was, they were not working together. It was as if there was competition for me. There wasn't an agreement. Then, the run forward was easier. The woods thickened, and the wisps were harder to see. They remained behind trees for much of what I ran. I ran and I ran. I ran for the boy. Where had he gone? Stopping felt wrong. It felt like death. I'd be giving up. That wasn't the path for me. Then I saw the third wisp.

"This one was a man among wisps. It did not hesitate, and it did not play coy. The shape appeared in the path I had yet to run. It did not move as I approached.

"I stopped running."

The man paused, though he did not drink. The pub was silent. Not a soul dared move. Triph forgot himself.

"I saw the two wisps from before. They weren't alone now, either. Orbs of light appeared at their sides, though they remained still. It was as if they were watching me."

The man stopped. He looked down at his hands. The eyes of the pub followed his gaze.

"It's as if the veins in my hands aren't mine anymore." This wasn't the story, thought Triph. This was the man. "I see the thin blue lines poke though and I don't know what to do with them. I cannot do anything with them. They're a part of me, a part of my hands, a part of this tale.

"The boy was gone."

The story seemed broken. There was a gasp in the room, barely audible, the sound of the group feeling something. They felt it so strongly that they allowed the feeling to exhale, leaving their bodies.

"What of the wisps?" shouted a voice in the pub. Triph didn't let his gaze leave the storyteller. The crowd ignored the question, and the man spoke once more.

"They followed me till I left the trees," he said. When the sentence ended, it did not lead to another.

Now the pub was silent for a time. Each soul in the place breathed, or drank, or ate what sat on a plate in front of them. It was as if the only functions of the room were those of survival, persistence, life. Then a man ordered a drink. Sound came back, conversations restarted, but life was quiet in the place.

Triph stood up and left the pub.

He no longer stumbled. He'd sobered up some during the story. It had felt wrong to drink much during it, the drinks with the crowd were ritual more than comfort. He walked along the streets, silent. Exhaustion had crept into his body during the story. Triph had been hunting for so long. Searching pub to pub, town to town, all under the Sheriff. He was tired. Before, Triph had been searching, but now it felt wrong to have a purpose. He walked. That was good enough.

His eyes moved under their own command as they followed a giant as it walked from the streets and into a pub. That wasn't normal here. Even in the largest city of the Empire, a giant was worth noting. A man followed the giant into the pub.

No.

Triph felt like he woke up. His stupor left him. He shook his head. He was alive again.

Owyn had followed the giant into the pub.

Triph had found his prize.

He held himself from rushing in after them. He stopped his excitement. His heart was pounding in his chest. Freedom. He'd found his freedom. Voices shouted from down the street, away from the pub. They came from the direction of the docks and the sea. Triph approached the pub he had seen Owyn enter and found a small crowd standing across the street from the entrance. They must have been the ones shouting. They looked angry, and their voices remained loud as they talked amongst themselves.

Triph inhaled as he sized them up, each and every one. That's what he did with people. That's how he was still here, still alive. Size mattered.

"Is there an issue here?" he said, approaching one of those in the group that had been shouting. The leader, he hoped.

"Do you walk in the shadow of the Tower?" asked the man, barely turning to acknowledge Triph. The people around the leader quieted a bit, but the group was too large to all take notice of the disturbance.

Triph didn't know religion well, but he knew the words when he heard them or guess at them, half remembered. Words like that worked to gain the trust of unsuspecting folk too many times. They had power. He was good with words. "The shadow from above blankets me."

The man looked at him now, wariness in his eyes, but with a confidence that only the righteous have. "We protest against a blasphemer and a heathen brother. Will you join us?"

"Pray thee," started Triph, "what has the sinner done?"

"He builds a mockery to the gods. A secular tower as a symbol of his faithlessness. The King dares allow this as well, furthering the corruption of this holy city."

"This sinner, was he the man walking into the pub with the giant?"

"Yes. The Donar-kinder seems to have made a friend of the blasphemer. I thought their kind wiser."

"Why don't you stop them?"

The man glared at Triph. "We cannot commit violence, brother. Not here. Not in this great place." He looked up at the God's Tower, looming above them in the dark sky. "The men of the pub have disallowed us of faith into their establishment."

"They won't know my face. I can enter in your stead."

"What would that gain you?"

"I need to see the sinner for myself. Judge him with mine own eyes."

"Then you will join our cause?"

"Not alone," said Triph. "I've got plenty of help for your cause."

CHAPTER 11

Owyn stood on his island and looked towards the city of Kudra. The God's Tower ascended from the city towards the sky, seeming to cut through it. Owyn wasn't sure where the top ended, if it ever did. This ancient structure was the source of his problems now.

He didn't dislike religion; he'd just never found a need for it, a place for it, in his life. Owyn looked at the Tower and wondered if he was wrong. Should he be more devout? He hardly knew the stories of the gods that he was supposed to believe in. Maybe that was something his parents were meant to have taught him. Or if he had grown up in a steady village, they would have taught him. A village with faith, one with people who cared. He hadn't grown up with either.

Owyn felt a hand on his shoulder.

He looked up and found Ost standing next to him.

"You did not see them in the bay?" he asked the sailor turned foreman.

"No."

Owyn saw the worry still on the younger man's face.

The men who had left the island in the morning to retrieve the next load of stone had not returned.

Ost had told Owyn they could not swim.

If another loadboat had sunk as Owyn's had... if something worse happened in the city...

The Captain had been kind enough to lend use of the boats of *The Small Journey* for a time. Owyn had asked if Doman would miss the men and the boats, but Ost merely laughed and said, "not while he's carousing in the palace." The Captain and the King appeared to be friends beyond a working relationship.

Ost was not laughing now. Neither man was.

An anxiety had come over them on the island after the sinking of the loadboat. The work went well, but every sailor who rowed to the city worried Owyn. Every man *he* sent across the bay sat in his mind until he returned.

Two had not yet returned.

Owyn didn't know what to say. Both men looked at the God's Tower in silence, both men stuck in their thoughts. Things they avoided thinking about bubbled up where the only answer was silence.

"Breakfast would be good," said Ost. "They will return." He gently squeezed Owyn's shoulder before taking his hand back. He turned and walked back towards the construction site and the surrounding tents. Owyn turned back, not towards the tower, but to the sea behind him.

There was so much space.

It took effort to pull the ocean out of sight. Owyn did so and walked towards the construction site. It was truly a tower of its own now. Captain Sutherland's men had done so much work. They were Ost's men on the island. He'd worked here the longest, and though he was only a sailor aboard *The Small Journey*, a seaman of low rank, here he was foreman. The Captain said nothing that put Ost in charge, but the men deferred to his recently gained expertise and Ost led them as a true captain would. It amazed Owyn, their efficiency as they worked. It would have taken Owyn and Ost months to get this far. No longer a minor bump on the horizon, but a legitimate tower atop an island in the bay.

They'd come so far from his drawings on vellum, held safely in his satchel for so long. He'd never known how to build, but sketches of structures on his adventures and questions asked in pubs had gotten him the knowledge to start. Ost and he had learned through crashes of stone falling down, and now they taught the other men to not fail as they had. Owyn let him talk to the men; the sailors he had worked under, he now led.

The trouble was the scaffolding. Owyn couldn't afford timber. Wood was beyond his means to purchase even before the expense of two boats—both now gone—food for weeks, and payment for stone. Wood was an impossibility. Kudra had but one royal wood-farm, and any purchase from there involved directly buying from the crown. Owyn still felt unsettled from visiting the King the first time. He would not visit the viziers in charge of the Empire's timber. He could not afford to, in any case. Instead, the men made do with stone. Tripling the work ahead of them, they built scaffolding of stone, to build the walls of stone. Stairs to build stairs. Without Ost and the sailors, it would have taken Owyn years. He still thought about those years. He had wanted them.

Owyn walked into the tower. The sailors had set up stone scaffolds within the lighthouse now; they were placing interior walls and stairs. Each man he passed would stop what they were doing, for only a second, and put a knuckle to their forehead. People had never saluted Owyn before. They shouldn't now. Not if he couldn't take care of them.

"How goes it?" he asked one man who was leading the others. Owyn could never remember the names of all the jobs aboard Sutherland's ship, but this man was an officer of sorts.

"Well, sir," he said, touching fingers to the brim of his hat. "The oil reservoir is complete, and I've got Pratch and Jack both filling it now. We'll get more towed in on the next city trip, barring any hassle from the locals."

"Good," said Owyn. "Good." The locals. These protestors worried about his nebulous sin, stole his boat, sunk another. What had they done to the two men in the city now?

He walked away, leaving the man to his work.

Stairs wound up the inside of the lighthouse. Without a roof, it was as if Owyn stood inside a spyglass that spiraled and twisted on the inside before allowing sight outwards to the blue sky above.

He nodded to no one before leaving the lighthouse. *His* lighthouse.

Could he say that now? He thought as he walked out on his island. That was a gift, the island, land from the King. But the lighthouse was his to build. And he was not building it.

As he walked towards the Captain's boat beached on shore, Ost stopped him. He was smiling. "Heading ashore?" he asked.

"I can't wait around anymore."

Ost nodded. He felt it too. The men were here because of them. He waved at two men standing near the lighthouse site. He turned back to Owyn. "Check on them at the city. It still may be a good day." He patted Owyn on the back.

Owyn feigned a smile. His mind had already decided, good day or no, he would not simply check on the men in the city. There was more he had to do. Ost and the other two sailors pushed the boat out to sea and the sailors got in. Owyn had been traveling with a few of Sutherland's men each journey as a precaution, since there were so many protestors each time he got to the dock. Now he wondered how safe that actually was. He'd stopped being the man to lead the trips carrying stone to and from sides of the bay. Another thing gone. Another step in his construction, his project, that he no longer did himself, that he deferred to others in his stead. He patted his satchel. He didn't have to paddle. The men took care of that. They took care of everything. Owyn held his breath. Thinking. Grieving. It was his dream, and it was no longer his job. He felt a loss at that, a sadness. Why should he feel this grief? Why shun those who want to help him? The work is being done, but that wasn't what Owyn had wanted. He shook his head.

His thoughts were interrupted as the boat approached the shore. They heard the shouts far out from the pier. There was splashing in the water nearby as rocks flew through the sky. The protesters' accuracy left a lot to be desired, but Owyn still remembered the cuts and bruises some of Doman's men had returned to the island with. They brought back stone, sometimes varnished, but they had always returned.

Stones hit water all around the rowboat, but Owyn ignored them, standing instead to see the docks. His shoulders fell and a smile grew on his face. He saw the men, holding buckets, kneeling on the loadboat they'd taken with them that morning. The sailors were ok. Owyn felt the oppressive weight ease for the first time that day. Owyn noted that the docks they approached were bereft of protestors. Side docks held people shouting obscenities, but not the one for Owyn. Tulbër stood there, smiling with the cart of stone standing beside the two sailors who had left the island early in the morning. The protestors avoided the giant and he ignored them. Were he gone, Owyn wondered what they'd be bold enough to do.

"Ho, Owyn!" sang the giant across the water. "I hoped you would be here today"

The rowers let the boat glide towards the dock with perfect form. Owyn reached out for the dock and was getting out when the giant hoisted the man into his arms.

"Owyn my friend, despite all that happened it is a good day!"

Owyn turned away from his friend and to the pair of sailors on the loadboat. "What happened?" he said, head turning from man to man to giant.

"A leak, sir," said one of the sailors. The other was brushing pitch across the wood. "Like the one that capsized your vessel. Like Ost warned us about."

"Beneath the stone?" said Owyn.

"Aye. Bored holes, small enough that she'll still float unburdened."

"Can either of you swim?"

Both men shook their heads and Owyn seethed. Though he had not mastered Ost's lessons, he could at least float. He could survive the sabotage. These men may not have. This may have been murder.

Owyn turned to Tulbër. "I don't know what could make this a good day."

"Little one," said the giant. His voice came out in a soothing sort of song. There could never be malice in his words. The shouts from the other docks had not ceased. Only Tulbër could speak in his normal voice and still drown out the noise. "All days may be good, despite evils within. Your friends were not injured, nor did they even get wet. And...I bring you a gift!" The giant's smile grew at Owyn's cocked head. "See! Your eyes light up at this. I say you will love it and I say today is yet good."

Owyn's mind left the moment and the gift. "They could have died. They cannot swim," he said. His voice was quiet. Owyn barely heard it himself above the cries from the other dock.

"It'd take more than a few holes in a vessel to sink us," said the sailor.

"See!" laughed Tulbër. "I am not the only one with large ears. Do not forget the work of evil men, little one, but do not also ignore the light in front of you when it arrives. I have a gift, and word of it made you smile, if only for a moment. That is enough to call today a good day."

The man and the giant looked at each other for a moment. "Alright, what brought a smile to your face today?" said Owyn.

Tulbër was already walking towards the cart as he spoke. "I almost asked for help from men at the pub to keep it safe." The giant stopped and winked at Owyn. "But my ears aren't the only big things I have." He flexed his arms. "The fools would do nothing to me."

Owyn could still hear the protestors on the other docks, but he could almost ignore them with Tulbër's enthusiasm distracting him. He could almost forget about the holes in the loadboat. The pair stopped, and Tulbër pointed to a thin sheet of metal atop the cart. It shined brightly, reflecting the day's sun back towards the sky.

"What is it?"

"A mirror, little one!" Tulbër slapped Owyn on the shoulder. "For the light home. It is like a lantern, no?" The giant stopped for a moment to gauge Owyn's reaction. The man felt so much at once, feelings brewing atop one another, bubbling around; the ennui and the anger and the sadness from the work and the shouts and the loss of purpose he felt—they all now contended with something else. "You have seen these lanterns? They point the light in glass cases with a mirror. This one will direct the light from your home," continued the giant. "The flame will be ten times as effective now."

Owyn looked at the giant, his mind and his heart catching up with each other. The confused mass of feelings was not simplifying, but one won above all others despite the battle: "Tulbër, this is amazing!" He leapt up, grabbing the giant with joy, and they hugged once more.

"It is a good day, I told you."

"I hope I can make it so," said Owyn, taking a step back.

"Why hope now? The gift is in hand. Well now, it is soon to be in a boat, soon to be on island." The sailors were testing their repairs, starting to move stone from the cart.

"I've got to wait to see the King."

"What for?"

"This," said Owyn, gesturing out towards the shouting people on the other docks.

Tulbër looked out at the protesting folk. "This is not good," he said.

"It's getting worse. They could have killed those sailors."

"What can the King do?"

"I don't know, but I've got to ask."

"I'll join you."

"No."

"The shouting fools are afraid of me, little one. I will watch you as you go."

"The Cap'n is probably up at the palace," said a sailor as he carried a load to the boats. "He could get you in."

"Ost mentioned that he visited there," said Owyn.

"This Captain is friends with the King?" said Tulbër.

The sailor simply shrugged and continued loading the boat.

"I don't know his story," said Owyn.

"Then we shall go to Captain Doman and the King now to find out?" Tulbër looked at Owyn expectantly.

Owyn knew he would never do this alone now. Tulbër wouldn't let him.

"We'll watch the loading," said the second sailor, returning to the cart for another bundle of goods. They needed many more kinds of supplies than just stone these days.

And so the man and the giant walked through the city of Kudra once more.

It was loud. It was alive. Away from the shouts of the religious zealots, Owyn almost enjoyed the noise. The sound of so many people, so much movement and action, seemed to permeate the air they breathed. The sound tried to seep into Owyn's soul.

They walked the streets, not quite ignored by the people of the city, but not watched by them, either. Owyn and Tulbër were simply two people amidst a crowd of so many already. Two more people among a civilization too big to notice a man and a giant for more than a moment.

That was ok.

It was a quiet walk for the pair. Owyn tried to quell his nerves. He couldn't shake the memory of getting denied by the King at his first request. He tried not to think of going back to the docks and having stones thrown at him or at the men who were choosing to help him. They weren't his men; they were volunteers. These sailors had helped Owyn in his dream and now risked assault or injury for him. He could not abide that. Owyn had to do something.

They reached a corner turn and hit a thoroughfare that cut through the city. Down it, Owyn could see the palace. It sat on its hill, and beyond it, The God's Tower loomed. Before the buildings, though, there was the line. People awaiting their infinitesimal chance at getting their requests granted by the King. Owyn remembered the line. He turned to walk towards the back of the line.

"It is a little palace, but it is built well," said Tulbër.

Owyn said nothing. He only saw the line.

"It is funny, though: even though this was never the land of Donar-kinder, you still build as though for the giants. It is only little to us." Tulbër looked down and saw his friend's gaze. "Little one, if the Captain is already up there, we have an invitation."

"I don't enjoy stealing a chance from all these people, though."

The small group of people in the line nearby watched.

"What about stealing your own chance?" said the giant. They looked at each other, and Owyn nodded. He silently followed Tulbër as they walked past the line.

"You win once and now you skip the line!" shouted a woman who had been standing in the line near them.

"Elvah?" said Owyn as he stopped.

Elvah spat at his feet.

"Little one..."

"Wait a moment," said Owyn to Tulbër before turning again towards the old woman in line. "Why are you back in line? You made it to the King before, too, just after me."

"Don't mean he listened."

"Owyn," said the giant. Owyn held his hand out to Tulbër, saying to wait.

"I know that feeling. What did you ask of him?"

"Food for my girls," the sneer left her face, if only a little, as she spoke.

"Your daughters?"

The sneer returned. "He don't care about our part of the city." Her words grew quiet. Elvah looked away from Owyn and Tulbër, focusing back on the line in front of her. It was then that Owyn knew this woman had no daughters. The girls she took care of were different than that, but Owyn knew that, truly, they weren't any different from daughters at all.

Owyn's hand twitched. He wanted to reach out and touch her, comfort the woman in some way, any way he could. He knew she would not accept it. His hand stayed still. He knew her now. Not all of it. No one could. But he was familiar with her life. He looked up at Elvah. She did not want to see him, did not look at him, but he saw her eyes. There was a longing that became a knot in his chest. He'd lived a similar path, had done more than traveled through the parts of town that she spoke of. He was born there. He remembered Elvah's same story told by his mother. He could see his mother in her eyes. She'd taken care of the girls around them as she'd gotten older, as Owyn had left her on his own, stupid, adventures...

"Owyn?" repeated the giant.

"Come with us."

Elvah looked back at the pair, confused.

"We've got a man up in the palace who may get us to see the King without this line. I want to help you. Come with us to see him."

"Why?"

"Do any of your girls have sons?"

Elvah's sneer faded into understanding as she looked at Owyn. She may not have known his mother, but she knew many boys like him. "If it gets me up there faster to be put down again by his highness, then sure, I'll follow."

"I don't think that will happen today," said Tulbër. His lavender eyes were a comfort as he looked down at the two people standing at the edge of the line. Elvah didn't trust him. Her eyes lacked confidence in his words. There was no lack of self-confidence within their sharp gaze, though.

"Let's go," said Owyn. So the trio did. Owyn couldn't shake his dislike of walking past the people standing still in the line. They had been waiting for so long. But he felt better now with Elvah. There was a fight to be fought and good to be done. That was bigger than his own request. Tulbër may have been right about the day being good.

The guards gave the trio a look as they approached the grand entrance to the palace. They didn't look pleased when their companion returned to the doors and told them that yes, Captain Doman Sutherland was in the palace, and yes, these three were to be allowed entrance at the order of the King. The third guard, the one who had run and relayed the message, was given the task of escorting them to the Captain.

Looking back, Owyn noticed Tulbër didn't have to duck as they entered the palace's foyer. He looked comfortable. Perhaps men did build this place for giants as he said. Elvah still scowled, but there was less anger behind the mask now. Owyn looked ahead again, towards the guard leading them inward. Elvah should speak first. That made sense to him. He took a sharp breath as they continued forward.

The guard didn't take them to the throne room, but cut off to a side before reaching the anteroom and took them down another hallway. This one was thinner—still regal, but less opulent. Through a quick turn and another large doorway, they were standing with Captain Sutherland in what appeared to be a small office room. Even in the rich palace, the man stood out. His green coat had been replaced with an even more garish cloak. Gold trim lined amber cloth that shimmered as the man moved, and the cyan ascot around his neck should have clashed with the colors, but something about the Captain made the contrast and vibrance bearable to witness. The only piece of clothing that remained from before was the hat, tall with the impossibly long feather that made the tall man appear almost as grand in height as Tulbër.

"Welcome to the palace," he said with a flourish. "What brings you here today?"

"Owyn," said Tulbër with a smile.

"I've a request, but first Elvah must see the King."

"What put you on this mission?"

"The King has denied her request."

Sutherland made a face. "The King denies many, I'm sure."

"I'll keep asking until something's done," said the woman.

"And something must be done," said Owyn. Doman looked at him. The Captain was tall, but he didn't give the feeling that he was looking down at anyone. He cocked his eyebrow, but there was no judgment in his eyes.

"Sure," he started, then looked to the guard who had led the trio to the room, "Be a dear and tell Rigney that we must see him."

"Sir?" said the man, but with a look, was on his way out the door and off to see the King.

"Rigney?" said the woman.

"Yes, but don't you go calling him that. We're on a mission for your cause here and you shan't muck it up by stating the King's name in front of him. Drinks, anyone?"

"What's your cause here?" asked Tulbër. Doman smiled at him, that dashing smile that said he knew all the secrets of the world if only he wanted to tell you.

"I'm here at the King's behest, and at another crown's request." He laughed. "And I've been told not to speak of it, so I shall have to silence myself." He turned to Owyn and winked. "Our dear friend

Ost hasn't told you too much of the budding crush aboard my ship, has he?"

Owyn didn't know what to say, but Doman didn't let the moment linger, offering drinks once more. Owyn declined a glass of wine as the Captain poured for the others, but, at another one of Doman's looks, felt obliged to partake. It was a wonderful wine, each sweet, sharp sip beckoning another taste. And so it was good that the guard returned quickly. Owyn left his second glass on the table still mostly full.

With a little more than a glass of courage in him, Owyn once again stood before the King of Breiar.

CHAPTER 12

"You again?" began the King. He spoke from across the room, but his voice was carried by the design of the space. He didn't speak loudly, yet it filled the room. Surprise sat on the King's face, but he wasn't looking at Elvah, Doman, or Tulbër. His eyes sat square on Owyn.

Owyn attempted a bow.

"Sire, I wish to speak with you, but first I come to support a friend." He looked up at the King, then over to Elvah, whose anger had fallen away to a sort of awestruck look on her face. An awe with a bite behind it, but still an awe. Owyn held out a hand, signaling the woman forward.

She stepped towards the King on his throne. Beside him sat a girl in a chair less opulent than his, but which looked more comfortable to sit in for the stretches of time required of royalty. Advisors stood beside the chairs and down a level, on the floor before the King rather than on the dais.

"I've come to you before, sire," she said, bowing slightly. "To ask for food, clothing—basic necessities—for my employees and my neighbors."

The King's eyes shifted from Owyn to Elvah. Owyn saw now how the throne had been built to look down on someone. The King looked down on Elvah with a posture and a face that he had not shown to Owyn.

"You're the whore with the brothel getting robbed." It wasn't a question.

Elvah attempted three responses, each accompanied by a haltingly faint noise from her mouth, before one took and she spoke to the room. "Yes."

"I've given you provisions before, despite my misgivings about your vulgar vocation, yet they are gone now?"

"Yes."

"What good is it then to send more, if they are just to be stolen again? What of the precedent? I frown on prostitution; Breiar frowns on prostitution. My Empire does not condone your work, yet here it happens right under my nose, in my city, and I support it with food and clothing? No. The crown cannot help you."

Owyn had heard that too much. He wanted to leave and shrink away from the palace, as he had once before. Owyn thought of all the times Triph and he ran away from their problems...and how that hadn't changed. Then he looked up and saw his friend. He remembered Tulbër's giant smile after he'd won at darts. He made a friend smile. It had been worth any cost he'd wagered.

"Robbery is a crime," said Owyn. The King looked back at him, face unreadable. Elvah looked at him in shock. "A legitimate crime. Not just a moral judgment, but banned by law. Yet you let it happen under your nose, as you say."

The King just stared at Owyn, as if to say "what is your point?" but Owyn noticed that the girl sitting next to him had perked up. She was paying attention for the first time in the conversation.

"If a thief is murdered, do you let the killer go free in this city?" He let the silence after the sentence ring out. The murmurs of the advisors had stopped. "I refuse to accept rule from those who would not protect the law."

"You refuse my rule?"

"I warn of a precedent, your majesty. Letting criminals run free because they prey on criminals, it is a cycle. Crime begets crime."

"What would you do, were the crown weighing on your head?"

"Guards," said Tulbër. His voice, always musical, truly sang in the throne room. The acoustics built to project the King's voice worked, even for the giant standing on the wrong side of the room.

"Guards?" said the King.

"Yes, not one but maybe a pair or trio. They will go to the rough part of town; the work will be hard there. You should reward them well."

"Now you ask me to pay a segment of my guard more, as well as feed and clothe whores?"

"Father!" said the girl next to him. The room was silent once more, her singular word ringing past everyone. The King looked at his daughter, aghast. His face held a mixture of anger and pride and questioning. It was the face of a father. "Agatha," he said, shaking his head before turning back to Owyn, donning the face of a king once more. The princess looked at him, too.

Elvah spoke first. "I ask for safety, and I ask for dignity, your majesty. With protection, a safe quarter of the city, we can get by without the need to be given goods if what we earn is safe."

She stepped back in line with Owyn, Doman, and Tulbër. Owyn looked at her with a smile. Tulbër watched the King. Doman looked regal and proud. He belonged here, even if he had no stake in the plights he now represented.

An advisor stepped closer to the throne.

"Father," said the princess, and the advisor stopped where he was.

The King looked from his daughter back to the four standing before him. With a twitch of his right hand, the advisor continued forward, stepping up on the dais towards the monarch. The King whispered in the man's ear, which, despite the acoustics of the throne room, Owyn could hear nothing of. The advisor nodded, leaving the room. His footsteps rang out in the room's silence. The King turned back to his subjects. "Guards shall better their patrols of the city. If this is not done, you shall not have to wait in line to see me again. Varsee, the man I spoke to there, will give you a word as you leave. This word will allow you to come to me as you had today. I expect my men to do their duty, but this shall be enforced this with your aid."

Elvah nodded and was about to speak, but the King had not finished.

"Varsee will provide provisions as you leave, and your escort shall assist you in bringing them to your people. These will be the last of the gifts you receive from the King. I only demand one thing."

Elvah looked up at the King. Owyn couldn't see her face, but he could imagine the expression she held perfectly.

"You, and your women, shall not now, nor ever, service an employee of the crown. Guards, advisors, visiting vassals. I will not have it in my kingdom."

Elvah nodded.

"Good." The King made another gesture and one of the guards behind them approached. His eyes told them to come with him. Owyn smiled towards Elvah as she left. She smiled back. It was a strange and wonderful sight.

"So, there's more, is there?" said the King.

"Always, your majesty. There is always more until there isn't, and for a king that day is a bad day indeed," said Doman.

"Captain…"

"It's not for me; I just represent a friend."

The advisors looked appalled. Doman Sutherland had just interrupted the King. The princess was paying attention. King Rigney the Second smiled. The Captain looked towards Owyn.

"Your majesty," began Tulbër, stepping forward before Owyn could. "On behalf of my friend here"—Owyn caught up with the giant and they stood together—"I request the aid of the crown." The last word, *crown*, stayed aloft, filling and bouncing around the room as if a choir had sung it.

"It has been quite some time since a member of the Donar-kinder has entered these halls."

Tulbër bowed. "It is an honor to walk the steps of the palace built by your people to accommodate the work of both our peoples."

The King smiled, then turned to Owyn. "What request do you bring me, Lighthouse Builder?"

"I also come to ask for protection," Owyn started, and the King frowned. "There are protestors, people of religion, who assault myself and those who are helping me. They throw stones and damage my property at the docks. They damage my boats—sabotage in order to sink them. They could have killed someone!" Owyn was panting. His shoulders rose and fell and could not cease moving and he could not catch his breath. He felt so powerless. The emotion had swelled up in him and he needed the King to do something. He needed anything.

"Why do they protest?" he asked.

"They follow a false path," said Tulbër.

"Their religion, your majesty," said Owyn, trying to calm himself.

"Do they not share the faith of the kingdom?"

"I don't know, your majesty."

The King leaned forward. "Do you share the faith of the kingdom?"

"Father, they're assaulting him," said the princess.

"That they may be, but it was not so long ago that Kudra was not the center of an empire, but of a theocracy."

"That was generations ago."

"Yet the faith still survives. It can outlast the monarchy."

"Do you practice the faith of your kingdom, your majesty?" inquired Tulbër.

"The Palace of the King of Breiar and the seat of the Empire are beneath the God's Tower. All who lead must do so under the watch of those above," said the King.

"Then you are astray as well." Tulbër shook his head. He stepped back in line with Doman and Owyn. The advisors, the monarch, and his friends looked at him. His gaze had fallen towards the ground.

"My daughter is right, Lighthouse Builder. We cannot allow the assault of a citizen, let alone one whose work is authorized by the crown. You stretch my guards thin, but they will watch the docks."

"You'll disperse the protestors?"

"I will stop the assaults, but I cannot stop an assembly of free people."

Owyn bowed. "Thank you, your majesty."

"I hope that our next meeting proves to be as interesting as the first."

Doman looked at Owyn and Tulbër, and the man and the giant both bowed before leaving the throne room. The Captain followed them out.

"Well done, lads. You've got the Eagle's own luck catching the King in such a generous mood," said Doman once the trio had returned to the small room beside the antechamber.

"Why does it feel like he dismissed me?" said Owyn.

"Because he did. You were dismissed with success, though, guards in hand." He placed a hand on Owyn's shoulder. "Thank you for wishing to protect my men. I never doubted my judgment of your character, but it is nice to receive confirmation of these things once in a while."

Owyn didn't know what to say. Tulbër had remained silent.

"Well, I believe it is time for you both to leave the palace. Rigney's orders will have been made, and the guards should be ahead of you on the way to the docks. I've got unfinished work here, but I trust my men in your hands, Lighthouse Builder." The man smiled before tilting his head forward, not in salute, but in acknowledgement, and leaving the room.

Owyn and Tulbër left after Doman. They didn't speak as they left the palace in unison. Owyn thought he should feel like he won, but he didn't. Tulbër was silent, and that did nothing to calm the brewing tempest within Owyn. He could not believe that the King had agreed to help put an end to the assault, but the protestors would continue their jeering. He'd won, but he still felt helpless.

Outside it was yet daylight, the sun hanging straight overhead. Noontime. The line of people leading up to the palace had not moved forward. The man and giant walked in silence towards the docks, taking the first turn they could find away from the main road and the line.

"Pub?" said Owyn as they turned down another alley.

"I don't feel like drinking."

"You don't have to drink at the pub."

The giant looked at Owyn. After another two turns down the roads, they entered the first pub they found.

Owyn had yet to stop at this part of the city. It was a mixture of nice and dingy. The stone-cobbled roads were shattered and sharp against his feet. Weeds grew up through the cracks in the road that was only a whisper of paved anymore. The architecture matched that of the palace: opulent, save for the sunbaked paint, faded and peeling. It was close to the palace, so guard patrols walked by with some regularity, but it seemed tucked into an ethnic corner. The people here all had sandy bright hair, tanned skin, and thin eyes. Owyn wouldn't blend in, and Tulbër especially not, but the people did not seem to pay them any mind. Bright red and gold cloth ribbons hung from between the buildings over the walkways covering the faded history.

The smell of the food in the pub hit them first. Piquant spices cut into Owyn's nose. He imagined the tears hitting his eyes if he ate the food, but his stomach protested their weakness.

"Food!" said Tulbër. Owyn saw the same mix of joy and excitement hit the giant's face. Something about food could brighten anyone out of a mood. The more flamboyant the smell, the better, to Owyn at least.

The pub was garnished with a similar flourish of red and gold decorations. As they walked in, the savory and hot smell of the food struck Owyn with full force. He decided then that they must try the food in this place. It seemed so foreign for a part of the city so close to the center, but it smelled good and that was all that mattered. They walked in. The place was empty, save for a few patrons and a sole worker behind the bar, who nodded as Owyn and Tulbër entered. The giant had to bend over to get through the threshold and had to remain slouched inside.

"Grab a seat, I've got us covered," said Owyn. Tulbër found them a table. He looked somehow bigger and more out of place sitting down, but at least he could sit up straight. Owyn went to the bar.

"Do you have tea back there?"

"Tea?" said the man. His accent was not thick, but it added a flavor to his words that Owyn was unaccustomed to.

"What are you drinking back there? I doubt it's the liquor you serve." Owyn pointed to a clay cup sitting behind the bar. It was tucked near the safe box for the place's coin, hidden in plain sight. He tried not to notice.

"That is water," laughed the man. "I have tea, I rarely sell it, though."

"We'll take two. And what is it you are cooking back there?"

"Spiced fish." The bartender was pouring tea into two clay mugs.

"We'll take two of those as well."

The bartender raised an eyebrow at that, but said nothing as he pushed forward the two steaming mugs. Owyn paid and carried them back to the table.

"Good bartenders always have something hot that wakes you up behind the bar. The ones that don't are the places you want to go to when you're poor. Bartenders are usually drunk at those."

Tulbër took the mug.

"Huh," said Owyn. Tulbër looked up at him. "That's not what I was expecting." They both took a sip. Each person smiled. It was an excellent tea. The steam and heat of the drink hit Owyn's nose, smelling earthy, reminding him of the Istar Mines without being so strong as the liquor of that place. "So, what's on your mind?"

"You smile now, but I can feel the worry in your mind, too, little one."

"I wasn't talking about me."

"That doesn't mean the worry isn't there."

"I can still put on a smile."

"I don't like masks."

They both sipped their tea. It wasn't bitter like Owyn was used to. It was smooth and tasted like how flowers smelled.

"A mask of sadness is still a mask."

The giant looked at Owyn from across the table. His lavender eyes could pierce in their depth.

"I talk little of my faith. It is not a faith to the Donar-kinder, but a fact. We are the children of Donar, as you are the children of Osnir. For men to have strayed so far as to forget history, to ascribe it to faith, to forget the purpose of the God's Tower and to call it heresy to mock its image, this saddens me."

"What was the Tower?"

"Even my friend does not know." The giant spoke to no one, gesturing outward in frustration. "The Captain talks of the Eagle as a joke. Men see me in front of them and forget what sin truly is. There are no dragons left, and they worry about honoring the last prison of the true enemy. More than one god lived in that Tower, yes, but the Donar-kinder know not to change how we see a prison because of who built it."

Owyn drank of his tea, he watched his friend talk, then cease, and look down. Tulbër seemed to stare at the table without seeing it, silent. "We're all born without knowledge of history. Your family taught it to you. I had no one to teach me," said Owyn.

"Spiced fish!" shouted the man behind the bar, waving to Owyn and Tulbër.

"I ordered us food," said Owyn as he stood to retrieve the plates. The spices assaulted his nose as he walked back to the table. They were sharp, though pleasantly so.

"I am sorry, friend," said Tulbër. "I judge and become sad. This is not what I wish to do on my journey."

"We all have bad days." Owyn cut into the fish. It was red with spice and laid atop a bed of grain. Hot steam escaped the food as he cut in. The spice hit him again. He remembered how the giant had cheered him up just this morning. "Nothing some tea and a strange dish can't fix."

"Strange dish? You haven't visited the Dragon's Canyon and met the people of the Delta?" Tulbër couldn't hide the surprise on his face. "You were so close when in Istar. This is Delta food, little one, from Rista or Zeltas. Good for the insides." He smiled. "It cleans everything."

CHAPTER 13

"Well done, boy," said the rough voice of the Sheriff.

Triph frowned. He felt he should be happy as he and the posse behind him watched Owyn and the giant walking towards the Kudra docks. Maybe he was happy. He forced a smile. He was alive. He should be happy.

"You said you had a plan," said the Sheriff. He had put his hand around the back of Triph's neck and squeezed. It wasn't a kind gesture.

"Yea, we're meeting at the shadnel near the inn by the docks."

"Good." Another squeeze, this one softer, then the hand left Triph's neck. "Take us there."

Triph wasn't sure he'd ever get used to the Sheriff's voice. It was the sound of gravel churning against itself, or a millstone without grain, yet somehow it made words. The voice terrified him. He heard it sometimes in his dreams. The posse had not allowed him to sleep unbound on their journey to the city. A guard in his tent and rope on his wrists. Not the freedom he had been hoping for, but there was still the horizon. Once this business in town with Owyn was done, he'd be free.

He didn't know what he'd do then. But that didn't matter now.

The sun was below the horizon as they walked towards the shadnel—a small temple, what these southerners called their parishes and churches. Lamps outside the buildings were lit, oil burning with the dim flickering light of lanterns spread far apart. The market near the docks felt good to Triph, a familiar sort of place. It was like a small town on the inside edge of the city, rather than the city itself. It was larger than any town he'd been in, but the darkness helped hide that, too. The market stands were empty, but his mind still raced with the possibilities. So much wealth in one location. He could enjoy this city.

"How much longer?" said the sniveling voice of Wendel. Triph was leading the posse, and the Sheriff walked somewhere in the middle, which gave Wendel the freedom to get entirely too close.

"It's here," said Triph. He didn't want the relief in his voice to show. The Sheriff could think it was weakness. It was annoyance.

"Good job, thief," said the slimy man, touching Triph's shoulder before he walked ahead, leading the way into the shadnel. Triph would have been slower to follow, but the Sheriff stopped, waving the smallest of gestures of his fingertips toward the door. Triph was to go in before the Boss did.

The shadnel wasn't full, but the architecture of the room made the dozen people waiting for the posse feel like an entire congregation. There were stairs to a second floor, but everyone stayed on the first, filling up the simple square space. There were the few familiar faces that Triph already met and spoke with, but there were also members seated around the room that Triph hadn't seen before. He'd have thought the entire group protested together, or at least in shifts, for the shouting meetings at the docks. It seemed there were more waiting in the wings.

The people were all mumbling, little conversations that quietly filled a room, making it feel more crowded than it was. Everyone went silent as the Sheriff entered. The only eyes that did not look at the man were those that looked away, towards their feet, or at some specific detail on a wall or the ceiling.

The Sheriff seemed to inhale the ambience of the place. Triph heard him sniff in a deep breath. He was silent, dark eyes scanned the room, looking at nothing in particular as they did. He took it in. Took them in. The silent crowd waited. The only scent on the air, the scent that Triph was certain the Sheriff smelled now, was anticipation.

"Close the door," he said. He stepped into the room and filled the space as if he had grown taller. A man in the posse closed the door. The sliding stone scraped against the frame, but not a glance in the room wavered to look toward the sound. The eyes had made their choice. They could look at the Sheriff or they could look away. There was no other object to acknowledge. "There are steps that will be followed for the acquisition of my man."

Triph looked around the room at the religious and the ruffians watching their new leader speak.

"My men here will show you an outfit to arm yourselves. We have the tools of our trade to share with yours on this mission."

"We shall carry no weapons," came the voice of a brave priest in the room.

"You carry stones. These are no different. They are simply a precaution."

"We shall—" began the priest, but the eyes of the Sheriff met his and the man stopped.

"You shall not protest these next days. We need my man to return to port. Wait. Be patient for our gods. The man will return, then we shall as well. Leaving the places of hiding which my men will show you within this city. You will aid the enforcement of the law. I will enact that law. I will remove the heretic from your city."

The Sheriff didn't look around after he stopped speaking. He let the words hang in the air as if they belonged there, ringing in the open space of the room. He found a stool to the side, closer to Triph, but still within the circle of people in the room, and he sat down.

"Why should we break oaths and arm ourselves? To what end do we choose to serve you?" the brave voice spoke again. The priest was not much taller than Triph. He was old and wore the robes of his order. He spoke like an orator. His audience wasn't the Sheriff.

"This Posse Comitatus does not serve me. It serves the law. You serve the law, as I do."

"We serve the gods above. We serve Osnir and his Tower."

The Sheriff took stock of the room. Triph followed his gaze. The priest was gaining traction. Some eyes had focused on him, rather than the choicelessness presented by the Boss's entrance.

"The justice of Osnir is slow. Donar and Irnam judge not of men, and I shall speak no more names. The judgement of gods will come, but my judgement is swift. What is the purpose of man but to quicken the will of the gods?" The priest opened his mouth to retort but the Sheriff wouldn't allow it. "This man is a thief and a killer. Lack of action against evil is an action against justice."

The priest looked away. It was only a second, but it was enough. He had lost.

"What will happen when you have your man?" said another voice. There was no protest in the zealot's speech. This was a follower.

"I will judge him for his crimes with the law of my town, laws of our land and our gods. I shall not find him lacking guilt. He will die."

There were smiles about the room.

The Sheriff stood and looked at Wendel. "Get it done," he said. He left.

Triph sat through the following discussions as long as he could. He could not sit still, though. Never could all his life. Now something worse weighed on him. He thought of Owyn and the giant he had seen. The pair frequented pubs on the docks when they were in town. Owyn had likely already left Kudra, the protestors keeping him away. But the giant? He wondered how Owyn had befriended one of them, anyway. But that didn't matter.

Wendel was speaking when Triph snuck out. He was sure that no one would stop him. He knew the logistics. He was there when the Sheriff told them to the posse.

The streets outside were darker now. Some lamps had been put out or had run out of oil on their own. Even the stars above seemed to shy away behind a thin cloud cover.

He will die.

The three words echoed through Triph's mind. He worked his way towards the docks and their pubs. They weren't a far walk from the shadnel. Owyn had always remarked on that fact: every small town and village they visited, alcohol was close to their temple.

Owyn will die.

Inside the first pub, he found nothing. There were people and drinks and noise, but it was not what Triph was looking for. He wouldn't waste time carousing with bartenders for information.

There was no time to waste. Triph consciously unclenched his jaw; his teeth hurt in the back. Unclenching didn't seem to fix the ache.

The reality of the Sheriff, of what Triph had been aiding in, of what he still felt towards his friend,—all were crashing into Triph as he ran to the next pub, and the next. The same results each time, but with a growing resignation. It wouldn't be so bad to stop and have a drink. What could Triph do? Nothing. He couldn't do anything about the situation, about Owyn. The Sheriff would always win. Next pub. Yes, at the next pub he'd get a drink, calm down some. He unclenched his jaw again.

The giant was walking up the street as he left the third pub. There wouldn't be any drinks. Surely it couldn't be another giant; how many could be in the dockside pubs? The giant seemed to be hurrying down the street, but Triph decided it may not be hurrying. Its stride was simply massive. Triph inhaled and ran after it.

CHAPTER 14

C louds covered the morning, yet work continued. Owyn awoke to questions from the men. Ost had had an idea. He came up with it along with a crewmate named Harol. They didn't share it with the other men, but Ost had smiled at Owyn when he thought of it. "You'll like it," he said. Owyn heard the words "if it works" follow, but he chose to let them remain unthought as unspoken.

"Should we clear the spot?" asked Ost. He'd been silent for a good while after telling Owyn his idea. They stood in the base of the lighthouse, stone scaffolding for the stairways all about them. Above, the sunlight still fought through the clouds to shine down through the small hole to the sky that yet remained open in the spire without its roof.

"Sure," said Owyn. Both men sipped on tea that Owyn had made that morning as they stood. Without the sun, the sea breeze brought cold into the structure. The warm drinks helped, but both men seemed to tense as they walked out into the open space around the lighthouse. The chill wind came more often in the mornings as of late. "But I think I would still like the bucket."

"Sir?"

"Always have a backup plan in case."

"Ah. The Captain would like that."

Owyn smiled. He'd never think himself anything like Doman Sutherland. So garish and loud. A natural-born leader, it seemed. After all, it wasn't as if the sailors beyond Ost wanted to help build this tower. They worked as their Captain directed. Owyn thought of hiding in his lighthouse. Of building something on his own island. Of his want to be alone. He looked out at the tents about the island and the people working around him. Maybe he was more like Doman Sutherland than he thought. Maybe the Captain fell into it all, too. He turned back to Ost. "Any other questions?"

"No. Thank you." Ost approached the construction site and began shouting orders and questions. Owyn ignored the specifics. He took another sip of his tea. It had cooled already in the wind. Something more to deal with.

He looked up at the tower that had been constructed on his island. Owyn didn't feel like he could say that he had built it anymore. So much of the work had been done by others. He took another sip of the lukewarm tea. It looked good, the tower. It was more than he had imagined, somehow both matching the plans he had drawn on the vellum and exceeding them. The stones sat so well atop each other stone. "Bad stone." Owyn shook his head. Tulbër had been right, the stone was good enough for his purpose. It was good enough for his tower. It only took more work to place. Owyn smirked. The structure looked solid from the outside. Sailors worked piling scaffolding now. Towards the top on the outside they went. The stone piles wrapping almost the entire backside of the tower. At the base lay tiles of clay baking slowly in the overcast light. The tiles would be for the roof. Purchased from a merchant vessel before being exported from Kudra to the wider world, he said he gave Owyn a discount. He didn't know enough about clay to confirm. Some of Doman's sailors had begun paint the drier of tiles. They were bright red—bright to the point of being absurd. A bold crimson with flecks of pink and magenta. The color of a jester. Doman had suggested it.

With the shell so close to completion, the inside of the lighthouse needed work now. The oil basin, placing the mirror, Ost's bilge pump idea—that's what the men now worked to complete. The pump made sense in theory, but Owyn would have never thought of it. The bucket was more his speed, and would be a backup now. Owyn finished his cold tea.

Turning away from the lighthouse, out towards the sea, Owyn saw rain. It was far out on the water, like a dark curtain draped down from the clouds above. The rain was far to the south, but the sailors had spoken of the winter rainy season. With clouds above, it could not be far off. Owyn went to his tent to brew another pot of tea. He would share it with the sailors at work, those who wanted some. Most of the men stayed warm with the effort of their work. The foreman would likely join him. He kept his eye in the bay. Even through the rain he thought he saw the Captain's boat. Several calls from the sailors confirmed the sighting. While they worked, Doman sailed in a small boat, one plain mast and a hull without color. Ost had told him it was part of Doman's work with the King. Owyn never would have guessed at seeing the little vessel dart around the bay on sunny days. Doman wasn't alone aboard it—Owyn saw another figure manning the sail some days—but with all the crew working on the island or in the city, Owyn had no idea whom the Captain sailed with.

Owyn walked towards his tent and the stove, but turned back to get a final look at Doman's sailboat on the water. Instead, he saw a rowboat coming back to his island from Kudra. That'd be the men with the loadboat. He'd brew some tea for them, too. That was something he could do, at least. The boat rocked with the chop of the bay, but something felt off to Owyn at a glance. He dismissed the thought and returned his attention to the stove and the tea.

"Ho!" sang a voice, shouting from the boat as it approached and Owyn sat watching while the tea steeped in its pot. He couldn't help but smile. The singing voice cut through the clouds in his thoughts and the sky above. He was happy to see Tulbër. The boat sat lower in the water, looking unfit for the giant's body, but it came towards the island all the same.

"Welcome!" he shouted back as the boat hit the shore and the men got out to pull it onto the rocks. Tulbër didn't wait, splashing through the water as he leapt out of the boat and came ashore.

"Little one, this is marvelous!" he said, giving Owyn a hug. "You can see the light home from the city now, but it does nothing to prepare the eyes for it up close."

"It makes you look small now," joked Owyn.

"It gives you a smile, little one; that is better than shrinking a giant." Both friends shared a comfortable smile.

Ost came over and began speaking to the pair of sailors that had brought Tulbër. He would direct the placement of the goods that they had brought over, but Owyn didn't want work to begin right away.

"I've made tea. Come warm yourselves," he said. He didn't expect the grave look in the giant's lavender eyes. "What happened?"

"The protestors are gone," said a sailor beside Ost.

Owyn grinned. "Really? That's great!" The sailor's face didn't change, though.

"We must talk, little one," said Tulbër.

No one else spoke. Tulbër grabbed the full pot of tea and carried it as he and Owyn walked towards the tents.

"You are in danger, little one."

"Before we even have a sip?" Owyn's smile faded as he saw Tulbër's face. The giant was not joking. "What happened? That man said the protestors were no longer there."

"They aren't. They have left the docks, and this has been good. The last days of loading the boats have gone easy, but there is a darkness hiding. A friend of yours came to me."

"Friend?"

"Another little man. He said his name was Triph."

"Triph is in Kudra?"

"And he is not alone. There are men, he says, who wish to arrest you. They wish to take you back to their town and kill you for your crimes."

Owyn's heart sunk into his stomach as he looked at Tulbër's gemstone-colored eyes. Those eyes pierced into his soul.

"You are my friend, and I trust you, but I must know, little one."

Owyn started to speak, but the giant had not finished.

"Do you intend to commit any crimes, small or large, planned or unplanned?"

"Never again," said Owyn, and he felt the honesty in the statement. The truth. Never again.

"Good little one, good." Tulbër hugged Owyn. "Now that is over, we may drink tea and talk what may come next."

CHAPTER 15

Owyn hadn't come. The Sheriff had held the protestors back. Owyn's men traveled unmolested, yet he still didn't come. There was a knot in his throat. He felt like he needed to swallow, but when he did, nothing changed. The discomfort remained. Owyn hadn't come.

The Sheriff did not have sway in the city of Kudra. He was nothing here—not a man of the city's law, not a man of power. He was simply a man.

Triph watched as that man walked past the line of people waiting their measly chance to enter the palace of the Emperor of Breiar. The Sheriff had no regard for those people. He was not a man who waited unrewarded. His reward had not arrived, and he was done waiting.

The guards raised their arms to stop the man, but with a shout from the angry bald head, they stopped their halt and instead flanked the Sheriff walking with him. He was a force of nature. Pure anger and charisma. A storm of righteousness that would not be stopped by weapons or weak men. The guards could not stop him if they tried. They knew that. They opened the doors for him and accompanied him, if only to limit the damage.

The doors of the great hall opened in front of the posse and they walked in.

"You harbor a fugitive," said the Sheriff to the King.

Triph should not be here. They would not have—should not have—allowed him into the palace of the King. He should never have entered those doors. No one should have allowed him through those doors. Yet here he stood...next to the Sheriff...in front of the King.

"Who are y—" began the King.

"I am the Sheriff and you harbor a fugitive from the law." The room fell silent. Any whispers between the men at the foot of the King stopped. Anyone who had not been paying their full attention to the conversation was now. "The man Owyn. The man whom you not only give freedom in your city, but whose land and work you sanction. That man is a thief and a murderer."

The King was silent. He looked like he had been struck. Surprise at the audacity of the Sheriff lay unhidden on his face. Triph thought the King looked like nothing had struck him before.

The King had never met the Sheriff before.

"I have organized a Posse Comitatus, a militia of free, unpaid men, per the law of your land. We now seek the fugitive and will bring him to justice for the crimes he has committed."

The King looked to his right. There was an empty chair there. It looked cushioned and new. Triph thought it didn't quite match the décor of the room, but the King looked lost without whomever was supposed to have sat there. He turned back towards the Sheriff.

"I have a letter of warrant, notarized by the presiding mayor and judge for whom I am elected to serve." The Sheriff produced a white sheet from his pocket. "This will corroborate my claim."

An advisor approached after the King had gestured him forward and took the sheet, reading it as he brought it to the throne. He whispered something unheard as he handed the letter over. The King read it and frowned.

"These statements are genuine?" he asked. His advisor nodded, but the King looked only at the Sheriff.

"As true as they are horrible," said the Sheriff. "I travel with a witness to the atrocities committed. Interrogation of the man only revealed a further history of crime by the fugitive you have on that island." The Sheriff gestured towards Triph, who soon found that the attention of the entire room was on him. He nodded. He didn't know what else to do. He wanted to crumple under the pressure of all the eyes watching him. The nod seemed satisfactory.

"Very well," said the King before turning to his advisors. He handed one of them the letter of warrant, and the man returned it to the Sheriff, who quickly pocketed it. The other advisors unfroze, some leaving the room, others conferring amongst themselves. "You have leave to utilize my city guard in order to apprehend the criminal. Construction will cease on his project, and those he has helping him will be relinquished of their duties until this man is found. That land returns to the purview of the crown."

The Sheriff did not bow, nor even nod before he turned and left the throne room of the King's palace. Triph offered a quick bow, but had to turn and follow the Sheriff before he lost the man and would have been left alone. He hoped the King wouldn't remember his face.

The city outside felt different now. It looked different. Had there not been clouds covering the sky, the brightness of the sun might have hurt Triph's eyes. The Sheriff did not stop to look around. Triph followed as the man led them towards the docks once more. They had spent the last few days there. The Sheriff had not been there the whole time, but his men, and Triph, had. They had been waiting for Owyn. He had not come.

Two runners passed them on the way to the docks. They came from the direction of the palace and were wearing the clothing of the King's guards.

"The King works fast," said the Sheriff. Triph didn't respond. He heard the man's smile, and he didn't want to see it. The posse around the Sheriff started to break up, each moving into different parts of the city to retrieve the weapons they'd kept there.

As they walked towards the docks, Triph saw the people who had been there the whole time. They had been there before Triph arrived. He wondered what they would do after he left, with the posse, with Owyn captured. With Owyn dead. The protestors tried to hide themselves amongst the people of the docks, but they stood out like a flower in a desert. He could almost smell the stagnant faith wafting off of them, the pious arrogance. Triph had never liked the religious. He had no opinions on religion itself, just those who followed one.

The men and women who had been protesting before the arrival of the Sheriff watched the man with hopeful eyes. Triph saw what hid behind their hope: hunger. They needed something. Their faith did not fulfill them. It could sustain them, maybe, but it did not complete these zealots. They saw more, and they wanted more. Triph thought of the sepht these people must donate at their meetings. What small riches could he rob? That would make him feel better. He hadn't felt better in a long time.

He and the Sheriff reached the docks to see the runners already gone. They were in a boat on the water, the slight chop of the waves in the bay rocking them as they made their way towards a ship anchored in the distance. Triph shook his head. At least the ship they headed towards looked as crazy as he thought the people to be who volunteer for work on the sea. It was covered in garish colors, paints covering the natural beauty of the wood that was used to make the vessel. What a waste. Wood was so rare. Triph had only held the stuff once, and that was for a short time in a rich town. He gathered saliva in his mouth to spit toward the ship before he remembered where he stood, whom he stood next to. The Sheriff would never let that gesture go unpunished. Restraining himself, Triph swallowed and looked out beyond the King's men rowing towards the gaudy ship. He saw the tower. Owyn's tower. It would almost look natural if one didn't know that Owyn had built the thing. It was so far away from the docks, yet still, Triph could see the tower that the man had built reaching towards the sky. The thing was awesome. Triph looked at the spire in the distance and wondered how his friend had done such a thing. They had known each other for so long and the man had never spoken of a dream like this. Not once. They'd lived lives across the continent together. They were thieves, yes, but Triph and Owyn were also friends. Or so he thought. Owyn may have abandoned that idea, but Triph realized he hadn't.

Triph looked at the tower and saw the boat with the message from the King travel out across the bay towards the ship in the distance. It was all out of his hands now. There was another knot in Triph's throat.

"Today is a good day," said the Sheriff.

Triph reentered reality. He looked at the boss. They were alone on the dock. The zealots kept their distance from the Sheriff; most had moved back into the city now that the he had arrived, likely ready to emerge at his signal, but avoiding him all the same.

The Sheriff looked out at the same ocean that Triph did. Both men looked beyond the ships, to the point where the blue sea and the grey clouds combined into a singular, muddled line.

"Rainy season is coming," said Triph. The words came out without thought.

"It'll be good to get home before winter sets in," said the Sheriff.

The pair stood in silence after that. Triph couldn't have guessed how long. They stood until the posse arrived on the dock, carrying clubs in their hands and daggers at their sides.

"Is he coming?" said Wendel. The sound of the words assaulted Triph's ears. Not the words themselves, but the voice that said it.

"The word has gone out. We wait now, as we have," said the Sheriff. His eyes didn't leave the sea. Triph saw he looked towards the spire across the bay. They would wait for hours or even days if they would wait at all. The Sheriff made the time seem as though it weren't an issue. He was close to his quarry. He was close to the job being done. Triph could feel it. The Sheriff was close and they would wait.

There were boats leaving the tower. Triph couldn't discern the people so far out, but they were coming closer. The few he saw were those that had left the island hours before.

There was nothing the men on the docks could do. But this watch felt different. It was more active. It was a job. Triph wondered if that was because of the posse, or because of the Sheriff. He had been here before, but they hadn't. Had they changed the situation, or had they changed the man?

Once on their travels, Triph heard a man of the posse ask, "Why's the Sheriff our boss?" No one had answered. "What town elected him?" said the man. He was rightly beaten. Put in his place. That man stood on the docks now. He was still a part of the posse but no longer asking such questions. He was under the Sheriff. All men were.

As the boat neared, Triph realized the giant was in it. Tulbër. It had told him its name when he had spoken to it a few nights past. It was a friend of Owyn's. How odd. They had never found giants on their journeys together; the things weren't known for their wealth. Triph hadn't thought Owyn would befriend one.

Triph tensed.

The tension wasn't his, but his body reacted as it should. The Sheriff had tensed. The giant was alone in its boat. And Owyn wasn't with it.

Guards walked down the dock towards the posse. They wore different colors than the King's runners had, but they wore the same demeanor. There was an arrogance to them. Triph knew these men well. He'd met them in every town he had ever been to.

"The giant shall travel unharmed," said a brave guard. The posse had not been subtle as they clenched their weapons at the approach of the giant.

"It is an accessory," said the Sheriff. His voice was quiet.

"The Donar-kinder must travel within our city unharmed."

"It has aided a criminal."

"Yet committed no crime. The King will not allow the giant to be harmed." The guard and the men behind him drew swords. Next to them, the men with spears flourished them slightly.

The Sheriff turned away from the giant, still rowing towards the dock, and locked eyes with the guard who had spoken. "You discard the law for a giant?" The man spat the words.

"The King's word *is* the law. The giant passes this dock unmolested."

Triph counted. The posse and the guards stood in equal numbers.
That wouldn't matter. There were other guards, and an entire city
to fight through in order to leave. He thought about fleeing over
the bay, by boat or by swimming, but ultimately realized he was less
afraid of the sword.

"We'll search its boat," said the Sheriff.

"Of course."

"And question it."

"If he chooses to answer."

The Sheriff turned away at that. The guard had won. Triph saw
that. The posse would see a victory for their leader, but Triph wasn't
a part of the posse. Not like that.

The giant landed against the dock. It got out of the boat before
the Sheriff spoke. "Where is the man?"

"Owyn is gone," said the giant. It didn't look at the Sheriff. It
didn't look at Triph. "I'm sorry," it said with a bow. With that, the
giant walked past the posse and the guards, down the dock. The
Sheriff looked as if he wanted to say more, but he didn't. Triph had
never known the man to restrain himself. The giant left and the
guards seemed to relax, and the posse did, too. The Sheriff remained
unfazed. Rigid with emotion—with anger—he yet stood looking
out at the tower across the bay.

"A boat," he said.

The posse reacted.

Two men searched the giant's, boat to no avail, as others scram-
bled to find the Sheriff a boat.

A pair of men rowed them across the bay. Triph sat near the
Sheriff. He wasn't sure why the Sheriff had not made him row, or

even why he was here. He was glad neither of the posse men rowing was Wendel, though.

It took hours.

The chop of the bay shook Triph to his stomach. The feeling of something pushing upwards and out had replaced the knot in his throat. He feared to swallow the saliva that filled his mouth. That would only make things worse. He had felt the same many nights drinking, but he did not vomit then and he would not vomit now. He held the spit in his mouth. If he did not relocate it to stomach or sea, he would be fine. Triph looked over the chop of the bay towards the tower and the distance and forced himself to be positive. He would be fine.

The Sheriff did not seem perturbed by the rocking of the small boat they rode in now, even as the surrounding waves fell in on themselves, white peaks crashing down. Triph imagined overturning on a larger version of one of those little waves. He imagined what was below him in the waters of the bay. He swallowed the saliva in his mouth and the pressure within him pushed further up his throat.

He couldn't let out a breath of relief when they finally landed the boat against the shores of the island. Their journey wasn't over yet. The Sheriff, the two men who had rowed, and Triph all stepped onto land. The tower Owyn had been building loomed above the small party. Its grey stone matched the clouds above. It was lighter than the black rock that they walked on. Somehow, it did not look imposing, though it was massive. Triph liked the roof. They had painted it red.

"Find the man," said the Sheriff. The two men who had been rowing fanned out. There were tents on the island, enough for a full construction crew, but there was no one left on the island. Triph didn't go with the other men. He knew his place here with the Sheriff. He was still property.

The Sheriff led him into the tower. An expanse cut open the curved walls of the structure, big enough that the giant could have entered. The inside was brighter than Triph thought it would be. They had built windows through the walls with regularity, letting in the cloudy light from outside. It felt spacious. They walked around the lower room. Stairs, inset into the wall, spiraled up towards whatever sat under that red roof. There also was a rope ladder hanging down the center of the room. A single rope hung down to the side of it. Triph thought of a gallows joke, but knew to keep it to himself. The Sheriff seemed intrigued by a machine by the base of the stairs. Triph approached. There was a lever, it seemed attached to an apparatus that went into the side wall, behind the stairs, as well as a basin behind it. The rope from above terminated in the basin, Triph saw a stone bucket at the end of the rope. It sat in a liquid.

"Oil?" he said. The word echoed slightly in the enclosed space.

The Sheriff didn't speak, but seemed to almost hum a terse response. He pushed on the lever and a sucking sound came from the oil basin, splashing it slightly. "Hmm," the Sheriff hummed again, then he looked up. Triph followed his eyes, but it was what they heard, not what they saw, that had drawn the boss's attention. There was a soft pitter patter against the stone. They left the tower and walked out into the rain.

A second boat had arrived at the island. It carried city guards. One shouted when they saw Triph and the Sheriff. "On behalf of the King, I order you to leave this island."

"Where is my man?" shouted back the Sheriff. He didn't shout as in raising his voice, losing composure as one does; that was beneath him. He merely spoke, but the words were louder.

"All boats, sailors, and men have left this island. You must leave."

"Where is my man? The criminal?"

"He was not aboard the ship. He may have left with the giant."

This is where Triph would have expected a growl, or a yell—something that would have showed the frustration of the Sheriff. There was none of that. The man seemed to cool down. And that made Triph feel so much worse. "Thank you, officers. We will leave now."

"Safe travels in the rain," said the guards. They would wait and ensure that the posse left the island before beginning their journey back to the city.

The Sheriff turned to Triph. There was a cold fury in his eyes. "Without him here, his crimes are yours."

CHAPTER 16

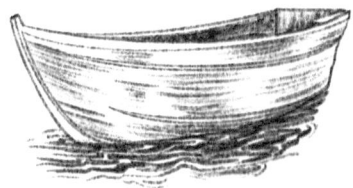

O wyn gasped as he surfaced above the water. Raindrops covered on his face, making him worry for a moment that he was still beneath the waves. That didn't stop him from pulling in a second breath with his lungs. He inhaled life, air—and if a little water came along with it, that was fine. He was alive. Owyn coughed and he breathed, and he knew he was alive.

He crawled up on the rocky shore. He was on land. He was safe. Owyn looked about the wet, rain-slicked landscape and let his face light up in the darkness. He smiled despite everything that had happened. Despite running. Despite losing his dream. He smiled with life. Rain washed over his face, blinking as he looked up at the dim cloudy sky. The rain washed away his smile as he stood and looked out at the bay. Waves chopped across the open water, white-capped curves racing to nowhere. In the distance he saw boats moving across the bay, leaving port and heading to his island.

His island no more.

Owyn stood on the rocky shore of the horn of Turtle Bay. Two towers loomed on either side as he looked out. One of the gods and one of men. In a moment he saw the protestor's fear, their worry. They were so different as he knew them, but at a sight, both unlit, the towers were so similar. Spires to the sky, reaching up and up into the realm of Osnir and Kirad. Yearning for the sky and looking down on the world. He saw their fear in his tower. He saw how one could see blasphemy. Owyn spat at their stupidity. Their shortsightedness had caused his loss. It wasn't his tower anymore. The spit on the dark rock was lost in the rain and washed away into the bay. Anger lost in the miasma of life.

Owyn turned away from the bay and began to walk. The dark rock shore was slick and his feet fought for purchase. He slipped and stood again, before slipping once more. Again and again as he walked. Northbound. Each step a small one away from his dream, his goal, his lighthouse. But each step closer to safety. Closer to a friend.

His footfalls stopped at a strange sound. The waves lapped against the rocks and the rain fell from above, but something in the water sounded different against the shore ahead. He slowly walked forward, peering through the gray light ahead when he saw the source of the strange noise. Water on wood. There was a boat, trapped between two points of rock jutting out of the water. The waves pushed it forwards and backwards from rock to rock, barely moving as the water washed over it.

It looked as if it had been there for months.

Owyn smiled, barely believing his eyes as he walked up and saw his old friend. His hand felt good against the soaked woodgrain of the *Morning Sunshine*. It looked to be exactly the same build as the boat he had replaced it with, like so many other boats he had seen, but Owyn knew. This boat was his.

Rain and seawater filled it, and the wood had worn and splintered against the rocks. The wind must have taken it here after the protestors cut it loose from the docks. He looked about. These rocks somehow felt more familiar as he stood on them. The wind pushed the whitecapped waves directly towards him. He felt the sharp, cool air and the chill of the raindrops and ocean spray hit him. This was where the wind took things. Owyn looked back towards the city in the distance. Lights glowed out from the buildings as people had lit their lamps against the dreary day. He was making his way there, but the city could wait. His journey had a step on it. There would be Sunshine yet today.

The *Morning Sunshine* may have survived the journey across the bay, but the oars were lost. It felt like sin, but Owyn wrenched a wooden thwart out from where it sat crossing the top of the boat. He felt it in his hands. Not too wide, not too thin. It would not be comfortable, but it would work. The boat was damaged, dented, scraped, and splintered, but it yet floated once Owyn cleared it of water. It groaned as he pushed it from the rocks. Wet wood squeaking with pain as it scraped the stoney shore for the last time in this place.

Soaked, breathless, and exhausted, Owyn once again boarded his boat. His boat. The *Morning Sunshine*. If he had nothing, he had this. With the makeshift wooden oar, he followed the shoreline as he did so many weeks ago, lost and unskilled. Was he lost again now? Was he unskilled still? He paddled in the rain, fighting the waves and the wind and his fatigue. He paddled without thinking, without dwelling on the questions circling his mind.

Owyn followed the horn of the bay, paddling as day became evening and the dim cloudy light gave way to darkness. As he reached the point where the horn curved south again, towards the city, towards the docks of Kudra, he stopped. There was no rope to tie the *Morning Sunshine*, but he could not leave it afloat in the bay. He could not bring it in with him either. It would be too much, too obvious who the lone paddler was, even on the northern part of the city, away from the docks and the Sheriff and the protestors.

He pulled his boat ashore, scraping the base against wet stone. The rain-slicked rock made moving the boat easier, but it was still not easy. He found a spot, tucked up and wet only from the rain, not the water of the bay, and flipped over the *Morning Sunshine*. He tucked the makeshift oar underneath it and patted the top of the wooden boat.

"I'll be back for you one day," he said, quietly. His words almost lost in the rain and the wind, but still heard. He heard them. Though he didn't know if they were true.

Owyn turned back to face the city on the edge of the bay.

He dove into the water for a final swim away from his dream.

***

"Little one," said a voice. It was quiet, yet Owyn turned towards it as he came ashore. His eyes hurt. They were red with salt and it felt better to keep them closed. Through tears, he saw Tulbër, waiting for him as they had discussed. "Take my hand, little one. You've made it." The voice sang as it always did, but the song now was different. Owyn could not have guessed what the mixture of pride and sadness sounded like. Tulbër spoke again, his voice that very cocktail of emotion. "Take my hand. We must move."

Owyn did so. Stepping out into the air made him realize how cold his body had gotten. The seawater hadn't felt so bad as he had crossed the bay. Other things were more important in those moments. Now he felt the cold, but other things were still more important. He pushed feelings down. Now needed action.

"Did they follow you?" said Owyn. He was out of breath. The words came out with gasps between each syllable.

"No, but they will. Quickly now."

Tulbër helped Owyn to stand before turning and leading him up towards the city. They were on the north end. There weren't docks here—there wasn't even space to get to the ocean. The shore near the bay here was all rocks and edges. Some alleys ended at the rocks, leading to nowhere. Tulbër and Owyn ran down one of these streets now. No one was about. The wind cut at their backs. The buildings seemed to fall in atop each other, stacked and built at different times. They loomed over the street, as if they would tumble in atop the man and the giant as they ran.

"Where are we going?"

"Quiet, little one."

"No, Tulbër. Wait."

The giant stopped.

"Let me breathe." Owyn's hands were on his knees as he stood still, face towards the cobblestones at his feet. "I swam, sir." Another deep breath. "I swam across that damn bay and now you take me for a racer?"

"You take me for a sir?"

Owyn laughed through the wheezes, then Tulbër broke and laughed at himself. A man and a giant stood alone in the alley, laughing at nothing. Tears fell down Owyn's face. "Tulbër, where are we going?"

"I'm taking you home. They seemed afraid of me. They won't search there."

"Afraid of you?"

"That, and they do not know where I live."

"Oh good. That helps, too."

"You have enough air?"

Owyn didn't. But he nodded anyway, and the two continued down the streets. They were rounding through the city, in parts that Owyn had not been before, and were heading further north, deeper into the city, yet closer to its edge. Owyn didn't look up much. It hurt. He focused on the giant leading him and keeping his lungs full of air. When he did finally look up, he saw the city walls beginning to loom above them. They were really north now. He had spent little time near the walls, only choosing to walk through the city gates the first time before coming straight to the docks. The district near the gates had seemed so clean that it had sparkled. It had shown a traveler all that Kudra could offer. The streets near the walls in this part of town had the opposite effect. They didn't lie about what Kudra could offer, instead showing what the city truly held for some. There was worse than nothing here. There was refuse and darkness; there was an unpleasant feeling in the air. Owyn knew places of crime. He had been a criminal. This place felt right for his old job. It felt too easy.

"We're here," said Tulbër.

The apartment looked like a hovel with more hovels stacked atop it. Tulbër led Owyn past a stone door and into a dark room. The only light that came in was from the doorway, and the cloudy sky and tall walls around the alleyway didn't let much in anyway.

"Take a seat," said Tulbër, pointing to a massive chair at a table near the center of the room. Owyn couldn't see much more than the table, the chairs, and the outlines of things atop the table. He crawled up into a chair that was plainly not built for him as Tulbër closed the door, leaving them in almost total darkness. Then with a spark, an oil lamp on a corner table was lit and Owyn could see the place.

It was cozy despite the size. The room was massive, built for a giant, but Tulbër's things and the relatively small space made it feel almost cramped, full beyond what Owyn would ever put in a space, but with Tulbër, well, it was him. The space was full, but comfortably so. Tulbër lit another lamp, and the room grew brighter still. Owyn watched as the giant moved around, looking uncomfortable with the state of affairs in his home now that there was a guest inside.

"A fire," mumbled the giant. Owyn watched in horror as Tulbër pulled what looked like a piece of a tree and placed it into a well cut into the wall. There were already sticks and small pieces of wood in the well. Then, using the sparker that he'd used for the lamps, the giant set the wood ablaze.

"What are you doing?" said Owyn. He couldn't hide the shock in his voice. He'd almost shouted the question.

"A wood fire for a guest is proper," said Tulbër.

Owyn could only muster a shocked sound. The giant looked at him, and the man closed his mouth. If a wood fire was proper, there was nothing he could say. "Smell it, little one, breath in the air."

Owyn did, and it amazed him. He could smell the fire, but it reminded him nothing of coal or oil. He was used to the acrid, painful dregs of air that came off the flames in the stove he carried, and in all the fires he'd ever smelled. This was different. This smelled good. More than good. The wood fire smelled amazing—earthy, yet with a sharp, crisp bite to the scent. It smelled like some of the herbs in expensive alcohols that Owyn had drunk. It smelled like life.

"Tulbër..."

The giant looked at him. "A wood fire is proper," he said. The fire crackled and popped. The sounds coming off it startled Owyn. "This is the magic of life. It's important that we remember it. That we experience it when we can."

Owyn couldn't look away. "This is magic."

"Some men and Donar-kinder can burn this life within them, in a holy fire. I've heard stories of them. Sorcerers."

Owyn had a hard time seeing the fire. His eyes stung slightly, and he fought against the urge to wipe them. It felt like hiding. He didn't want to hide. "Tulbër, what am I going to do?"

The giant looked at the man, tears beginning to stream down his cheeks. He didn't speak at first. He moved a second chair next to where the man sat and sat by his friend. He looked at the fire, not ignoring the man, but not looking at him. "Tonight, we will watch the wood fire and enjoy each other's company."

"They took everything."

The fire crackled and sang between them.

"They did not."

Owyn and Tulbër were silent then, watching the fire in front of them. Reveling in it. After a while, Tulbër stood, but Owyn did not move. The giant returned with two mugs full of ale. Owyn took his, but did not drink. Tulbër held out his mug towards the flame. "The mountains weep," he said.

Owyn looked down at his mug, the first time his eyes left the flames within the fireplace. He held it up towards the fire. "And so we remember."

"We remember life," said Tulbër. Owyn looked at him, at the added words that had come from him. They tapped their mugs together and they drank, watching the flames as they continued to flicker through the night.

***

"What do you wish to do now?" said the giant.

"Nothing," said Owyn. Tulbër didn't respond. Owyn held his drink. He wanted to take a sip, but not if his friend did not speak. "There's nothing I can do. I have to hide here. It's not like the posse will leave."

"Hmm," said Tulbër. "Maybe." He took a drink. Owyn followed suit. "Maybe."

"What would you have me do?"

"I do not know," said Tulbër, taking another pull from the mug. Owyn followed again. He was beginning to feel the inebriation in his head. It was good, but the worry was still there, pressing against the calm that the alcohol was pushing harder for.

The warm glow of the fire in the room bathed the man and the giant as they sat. There was a tension in the air, but both took a drink and sat in the silent light.

"Come work the quarry with me."

Owyn was about to take a sip, but stopped the mug at his lips. "I can't."

"Why not?"

"Is it even safe?"

"We can make it so. The travel is the danger. The work will be safe, though, little one."

"How can you be sure?"

"The men of the quarry have not assaulted a Donar-kinder. The men barely even notice me. They think not of warrants or criminals. They think of work done. And you can work."

"Why the quarry?"

Tulbër drank again. He let the fire work. Both of them sat deep in their chairs. Owyn was slow in following, but he followed and took another drink. The giant was feeling drunk.

"They need the work as the rainy season begins. The water aids the stonecutting. I began my work there in a rainy season like this. They rush now with all hands working before the quarry floods in the full rain of winter."

"You already left your work there." Owyn felt worse now at the thought of making his friend go back to the place he had left, of making his friend stay in Kudra despite the call of his pilgrimage.

"It is nothing to go back. The journey is fluid on a pilgrimage. And stone is good and solid. My kind come from it, you know? Well, you little ones don't know the true stories, it seems."

"Donar?"

"Our father, yes. The work is good to return to. You will see."

"I'll see," said Owyn. Tulbër realized how drunk the man was. He had slurred the two words into one. He let the conversation stop. Owyn seemed to agree with that. All that was left to do was to watch the fire as it burned in the small hearth. When the flames began to get low, Tulbër stumbled up and placed another log on the fire. It was slow to catch, but as the flame built itself atop the new fuel, the room grew brighter, warmer. The scent of the burning wood had filled the room. There was something magical about that scent.

Tulbër took a lap around the room, putting out the oil lamps that he had lit in the corners. There was soot staining the walls around the lamps, blackening a line towards the ceiling. Completing the circuit of the room, Tulbër refilled his mug. Owyn's hadn't been empty when he had gotten up. The man was probably done with the drink, but Tulbër didn't mention a thing. He sat back in his chair, enjoying the quiet fire in his home with his friend. That was all that needed doing right now.

CHAPTER 17

"Wake up, little one," sang a booming voice. Owyn opened his eyes to strange surroundings. "It's time for work."

Owyn saw the giant but felt that he was in an odd place. Memory came to him slower than senses did. He felt the comfort of the bed he lay in, the sheets he was under, the warmth of the place, the strange cozy feeling of it all. It would have felt wrong, out of the ordinary, but that feeling had lost the battle with the feeling of comfort. That feeling almost overwhelmed him.

"A little bit longer?"

"I've let you sleep long enough, little one. Now get out of my bed. We've got to go to work."

"Your bed?" said Owyn, jumping up as memory and surroundings came together in his mind. "Tulbër, am I in your home?"

"I did not think that you drank that much last night."

"I didn't, uh, well, I was tired, too, and I, uh—"

"It's ok, little one."

"I took your bed."

The giant's eyes said that it was ok once more. "I gave it to you," he said after Owyn did not speak in response. "Now you must get up. We have work to do."

"Work?"

"You agreed to come." Tulbër left the bedside and talked as he walked to another room, preparing for the morning. "I have a rain cloak for you. Don't worry about your clothes."

"That's good," said Owyn, not thinking too hard on the implication of Tulbër's words, but the giant was already out of earshot. Owyn was alone in the bed. The urge to pull up the covers and fall asleep was powerful. It would have won if the pressure to get up and join his friend hadn't pushed harder.

Tulbër had draped most of Owyn's clothes from the day prior over the end of the bed. Owyn got up and grabbed them. They were dry, which was good, but the salt of the bay was still in the fabric. The cloth felt crusty in his hands as he put them on, scratching his skin and waking him up.

The hovel was still dark. There were no windows, and the fire in the hearth had burned down, letting itself go out and leaving only ash behind. Owyn could not believe that Tulbër had truly burned wood last night. It felt opulent, and had it come from anyone other than the giant, Owyn would have thought them boastful, but Tulbër was different. The giant wouldn't brag. It was simply tradition. Owyn saw he was moving around the hovel, placing two bowls on the table set off-center within the room. He went to move the chair that had been facing the hearth over towards the table. Owyn quickly moved to grab the second chair and put it in place.

"Breakfast isn't much," sang Tulbër.

"Anything is enough. Thank you."

They sat and ate a small bowl of mash before they left Tulbër's home. Well, it had been a small bowl for Tulbër. Somehow Tulbër could make even gruel taste good. Mashed oats and nuts, earthy and smooth, topped with the last of the autumn berries fresh from the market. The giant had finished what Owyn couldn't. Before they exited through the stone doorway, Tulbër handed Owyn a cloak. He thought it was for hiding. He hadn't even heard the rain.

They walked the streets of Kudra with the other workers. There was no travel or leisure. It was not a storm, but there was enough rain from the clouds above to put the day to a halt for all who did not have to earn their keep. It quieted the city. Rainwater flowed through the edges of the cobblestone streets, pulling with it refuse and dirt.

They stopped at a crossroads. Owyn almost spoke to ask why until he looked around. They could see down to the palace here. They were at a crossroads with the main street. The street was almost vacant save for the water running towards the palace. Tulbër looked down to the palace, and to the Tower that rose behind where the king of men lived. The Gods' Tower. The rain fell softly against the stones of the city.

Owyn recognized their turn at the intersection. Beyond this, they would be on the road to the quarry, at the edge of the city, towards the work areas that were held within the walls. He looked back at the palace. This was the last place one could see the city for what it was. For what it stood for.

Tulbër continued down the road as he turned away from the palace and the Tower. Owyn followed.

The giant had been right. The foreman didn't notice the extra man appear, and with the rain, everyone's cloaks made him blend in even further.

It was a dark day. The sun fought its battle with the clouds, and some light fell through, but the rain aided the darkness.

"Careful on the way down, little one," said Tulbër. He led Owyn down from the edge of the quarry into the pit itself. The path they walked down was gravel on stone and the water was turning the small stones into a slurry. There was no rail on the edge that overlooked the pit.

At the bottom, they rounded the back of the quarry. There was an alcove carved into the stone ramp they had taken down. Huddled in the alcove was a small group of men, warming over an oilstove. A pot hung on a hook above the flames and some men had metal cups in their hands.

"New man?" inquired one man by the flame, looking at Tulbër and Owyn.

"A green little one," said Tulbër, ducking into the alcove. The giant had to hunch his shoulders to fit. Owyn followed. Out of the rain, with the flame heating the alcove, it was almost comfortable here.

"Good, we'll take him for cutting," said the man. He walked around the stove closer to Owyn and held out a hand. "I'm Berenger. You'll be with me today."

"Owyn," said Owyn, shaking the man's hand.

"Drink some cocoa and get yourself warm; work starts at the next lull."

Owyn looked out at the rain coming down and wondered how one could tell when a lull started. He took a mug from one of the other men and drank. The drink was warm and bitter and rich. Just what he needed. The men talked about the work to come, but also let some silence pass. Owyn didn't speak. He let the world of the workers in the alcove wash over him as he drank the cocoa.

"Lull's here," said one man.

"With me," said Berenger, looking at Owyn. The men all set their mugs down in the dirt by the stove. Some were already out of the alcove, into the rain. Owyn didn't see the lull, but thought maybe it sounded different.

"We will meet here again," said Tulbër.

"Thank you," said Owyn. The giant left the alcove. Owyn followed Berenger out into the rain.

It felt lighter now. The drops were thinner, though just as plentiful as before. His cloak may still wet through, but it would take longer at this rate. It looked a little lighter out, too.

Owyn and Berenger walked across the base of the pit. Men were at work on all sides as they walked. Some were cutting, some were moving stone on hefty platforms with cylinders at the base, many were simply standing in the rain, watching others work and shouting at them occasionally.

"Here," said Berenger, rounding behind a large corner in the wall of stone. "Take the far handle."

Owyn followed him and saw what the man was speaking about. Wedged into the stone wall that they had come around was a long, thin saw. There was a handle at each end.

"You saw through stone?"

"Rain makes cuts easy."

Owyn had no response. He walked to the handle and grabbed it. Berenger raised a hand then grabbed his handle and gave a nod. Owyn pulled while Berenger pushed. Together, they sliced through the stone. It was hard work, but the man had been right. There was something about the water running through the crack, being pushed and pulled with their saw, that made the cutting feel easier than he had expected.

Time passed without Owyn marking its journey. He could not say whether they had cut for minutes or hours. When they reached the bottom of the line, Berenger raised his hand. The man was smiling. He turned and shouted out into the pit. The rain was still falling and Owyn wondered who could have heard the shout. He certainly did not. But after a moment, four men came running up. In their hands was a thick fold of leather and a heavy rope. Two of the men rounded the stone towards Owyn, leather in hand, and unfolded it around the block, dropping some of the sheet into the line they had just cut. Owyn started to help them.

"No," said Berenger, shouting over the sound of the rain. Owyn left the four men to their work and approached Berenger. "You rest now. We're going to be cutting again soon." The man tilted his head upwards and caught rain in his mouth. He swallowed and looked at Owyn with a cheeky grin. "Enjoy the break while you can."

The four men moved the stone block away from the wall, not far, but enough that it was out of the way. They then moved on, leaving Owyn and Berenger alone with their saw and the wall. The older man led Owyn to the wall and placed their saw. They got back to work.

That became Owyn's day. He cut. Berenger called. They rested. Repeat the cycle, completing two more blocks, leaving their saw in the crack of a third block started. Then they were done. After, they met in the alcove. Tulbër was there already, enjoying a mug with the men who had finished their work earlier. The giant said nothing to Owyn as he entered. He merely nodded in welcome. Owyn and Berenger each took a mug of cocoa in hand and stood by the fire. The lull in the rain had lasted the whole day, but they were still both soaked through their cloaks, cold in their bones. The fire made things good. The cocoa made them better.

As they left the pit, a man up top handed each worker a coin for their day's work. Tulbër and Owyn walked home, quiet and tired from the day, but when the giant lit the oil lamps of his hovel, they smiled.

"This was a good day?" said Tulbër.

"Thank you, Tulbër. It was a good day." Owyn was sad as he said it. He'd had good days before, but he hadn't counted them. He'd lived them but didn't take the time to enjoy the work being completed as he did it. He'd sulked during his time working with the sailors and would give anything to return to those days now.

Time continued to pass in this new rhythm. On rainy days, the cutting was good. On days of sunshine, Owyn worked with the men to move the stone that had been cut before. The work was racing now as the rain was coming more often. The quarry would flood soon and the work would stop. Owyn wasn't sure what he'd do then.

Tulbër and he did not have another wood fire, but their nights were comfortable. Beer and conversation in the hovel were always welcome after the day's work. Still, Owyn looked out at the bay each night as they returned from the quarry. Wanting.

It was a sunny day when Owyn saw Doman Sutherland standing at the top of the quarry.

CHAPTER 18

O wyn had never wanted to be on a ship. He'd had a fascination with the sea, sure. It had drawn his mind since he was a boy and heard stories about the lake that never ended, the body of water that went around the entire world. But he'd never wanted to be on it. Near it? Yes. But a ship was a different matter. Still, he could not say no when Doman had asked him to join them aboard *The Small Journey*.

Now, standing on the dinghy at the base of *The Small Journey*, looking at the rope ladder to get aboard the ship and the water between the two boats, he wondered if he should have said yes.

Owyn shook the thoughts out of his head and grabbed the rope. He'd swam across part of this bay in the rain. He could do this. What was some rope? He began the climb aboard *The Small Journey*.

The deck was busy with work as Owyn crested the top of the rail on the side of the ship. Some men looked at him, some were even those who had worked on the lighthouse. None of them put knuckles to their crown now. They continued their work. Owyn marveled at the movement of it all. There was not a man standing still on the central deck. It almost didn't feel true that he was standing on something so huge made entirely of trees. Surely this ship cost more than the King's palace. How many trees of the woodfarm were felled for this one, great, thing? How much must a merchant move to justify the cost?

"Wonderful, isn't it?" said Doman, as he came up from the ladder behind Owyn.

"Captain on deck!" announced one man. Owyn did not see who. But all the men stopped their work for a moment to acknowledge Sutherland with a salute.

"To work!" shouted the Captain. The men returned to their work. "Would you like to see your accommodations?"

Owyn took a moment to realize that Doman was speaking to him. The Captain's voice became almost courtly as he spoke to his guest. Owyn didn't know what to say.

"Accommodations?"

"Well, we certainly won't have any guest of *The Small Journey* sleep amongst the sailors, though their hammocks indeed look comfortable."

The Captain turned, and Owyn followed.

He had come to the quarry to find Owyn. The Captain who had offered help as he crossed the Turtle Bay the first time offered him a chance he'd never thought to have. The Captain said that he was leaving port, and that Owyn could join if he wished. As always, the man's eyes held a mirth that seemed to hide knowledge that only he had. Tulbër had said nothing until he had realized that Owyn might decline. "Go, little one." Three words. Just three words from a friend and Owyn had agreed.

"A short stint to try it out. My treat," had been how the Captain had described it. There had been nothing else to say.

Doman Sutherland, Captain of *The Small Journey*, led Owyn to a door at the rear of the vessel. He opened it and gestured for Owyn to enter. As he did, the Captain turned towards the deck. "Raise anchor and haul her wind!" Owyn heard the order repeated by other men up and over the decking now above him in the room as the Captain closed the door behind him. They walked through a thin hallway until the room opened up. Large windows at the far end of the room let in light from outside. They were at the back of the ship.

"Here will be the officer's mess. You will join us for two squares a day, breakfast and dinner, as we outset; a third shall be provided," the Captain leaned in with a smile and whispered, "but being our guest, you're entitled a lunch through the duration of the voyage."

"Where are we off to?"

"Your room, of course." The Captain led Owyn past the table to the right. A door straight ahead in the wall beside the windows seemed to lead outside, but the Captain continued the turn, back towards a wall with a door beside the hallway they had entered from. Opening the door, Doman revealed a thin passageway with a room to the left. It, too, was lit from a window to the outside. "Here you shall be."

Owyn looked at his room. It looked small, and the bed ran against the outside wall. A small chest sat under the mattress and there was a table in the corner beside the door with cabinet doors latched shut under it. "This is marvelous," said Owyn. He meant it. He'd slept many a night in rooms of an inn that he had paid for. "Captain, this is truly wonderful."

"Down the hallway is my room. Apologies in advance for the snoring, and we'll share an annoyance for the late-night questions from the crew, I'm afraid. No other way to bother me except walking past and bothering you."

"It won't bother at all."

"It surely will, but I appreciate the kindness."

Even anchored, the ship had been moving under Owyn's feet the entire time he had been aboard. His calves felt it with annoyance. He thought he may stand incorrectly for a voyage, but another question came out of his mouth. "What does haul her wind mean?"

Doman Sutherland's smirk must have broken many hearts in the pubs around merchant ports. "Are you certain that you can find your room again on your own?" Owyn nodded. "Then let's return midship."

The Captain turned and led Owyn back towards the door they had entered. Owyn thought he noticed something in the windows of the officer's mess as they walked through it, but Doman moved too quickly for his mind to register it. He opened the door to the outside. The midship deck sat under the sunshine and, now, under unfurled sails. They were moving. Owyn was on a ship that now was sailing across the ocean.

Owyn looked around, head on a swivel. The sails were full and the water was spraying up against the sides of the ship. It was loud. He hadn't expected that. His cheeks hurt.

"Have we left the bay?"

"Not quite, but we have the wind's favor," said Sutherland. He gestured for Owyn to follow, and the man did. The pair walked up the stairs to the decking above where the officer's mess and their bedrooms were and Owyn saw Kudra behind them.

"You've constructed a marvel," said Sutherland, redirecting Owyn's gaze towards an island on the ship's right side. He saw his lighthouse for the first time in weeks. It was not complete, but it was so close. From the outside, the tower looked ready. Waiting to be lit. For a moment, Owyn felt again the mix of pride and shame he had so many times on the island. He had not built it. He had not done what he set out to do so long ago, not lived his dream. He was not alone. *But it is still mine*, he thought. Whether he had built it or it had been built. Despite any word from a king or sheriff. The lighthouse was still his.

The ship was not big, but standing on the deck now, Owyn walked a third of the height of his tower above the sea's surface. Somehow, that felt wrong. They had built so much, the men of Doman Sutherland. The tower looked as though it touched the sky. Inside, stairs worked their way up to a platform to look out on the sea from, a place for a glowing beacon yet unlit. From the sea, it truly did appear awesome. The awe it struck inside him felt wrong. "I didn't, though."

The Captain looked at Owyn. "Sailor," he said, turning to a small room sitting atop the rear of the deck. Inside, a man stood beside a post that rose from a hole in the deck.

"Sir?" called back the man.

"Leave the helm be. We shall handle steering it for the time being."

"Aye," said the man, knuckling his forehead before walking down the stairs towards midship.

"Owyn, grab the whipstaff please," said Sutherland. Owyn did as he was told, Doman following behind him. "Good, get a feel for it," he said once Owyn had the post in his hand.

"This steers?" asked Owyn. The post moved with a surprising ease. As he moved it, he could feel the ship lilt slightly to the right and the left, following his command.

"You *did* build that tower, Owyn," said Doman. "Look out at the ship in front of you. See the decks, the sails, the men; look at the work they are doing. Truly, are they the ones sailing this ship, no? They work far more laboriously than I. Yet would you say that I am not sailing this ship?" He smiled and Owyn looked to see the man's grin. "You build that tower as I sail this ship. There are those who do the work of the matter, as the sails capture the wind and the rudder in your hand do.

"It is semantics, Owyn. That lighthouse is yours, just as the men who built it can be proud that they built it. Don't take that away from them, but don't take it away from yourself in giving credit to their work, either."

"I've never built anything," said Owyn.

"You were a thief before?"

Owyn's head dropped. He knew that the man would have been told, but he wished he hadn't.

"You're not one now," said Doman. "I want you to tell me about it, without shame."

Owyn looked at him and then out at the ship again. The sky was blue—bluer still against the stark white of the full sails. Men moved around the decks, shouting and working, calling and listening. It was a dance on a stage in front of Owyn's eyes. He saw it all from the till. Leaning slightly against the wooden rod, he watched the ship follow his command. His call. He pulled the till back to center, smiling.

"Come, let's eat. Then you can tell me."

Owyn's smile faded. "Can I stay here for a bit?"

Doman put his hand on Owyn's shoulders. "Yes, you may. Charlie!" he shouted towards another man. "Owyn will steer. Keep us on course." The sailor approached, and Doman turned back to Owyn. He didn't speak, but only patted the man on the shoulder once more and walked down the stairs to midship. He shouted directions here and there at men. Owyn could still hear his voice across the ship, above the crashing sounds of the water against the hull and above the sounds of the working men.

"Pull port a bit," said Charlie, pulling Owyn back to the task at hand.

"Which way is that?" said Owyn.

The sailor put his hand atop Owyn's and pushed the till to the left. "That way's port." Then he pointed to the right of the ship. "Starboard that. Straight ahead is fore, behind is aft. Ever been aboard a vessel?"

"Just a rowboat."

Charlie laughed a hacking, coughing, laugh. "That may be an issue here." He slapped Owyn on the back. "We'll keep you from runnin' her aground, eh?"

"How long have you been sailing?"

"Most of me life. I had my time as a stowaway as a boy. I was born in Daughtn, before crewing a vessel." The man took a step back and flourished out his arms. "You can see how far I've made it through," he said with a smile. Owyn didn't, but he smiled back.

"What's it like?"

"What?"

"Living on the sea, living here."

"It be work, man."

"This is just work to you?"

"It be the only thing I can do. What more can a man do? They've got men on land who have my skills, but Cap'n needs men out here with them. So I'm here."

"Do you like it?"

Charlie reached over and pushed the till slightly further to port. "Aye," he mumbled. "That I do."

Owyn steered the ship for hours as the morning passed by. It moved so fast. They had left the bay behind, rounding the corner with his lighthouse, before heading straight towards the west. It felt as if they were leaving Breiar. The land shrinking towards the horizon behind them. Then Charlie had him pull the boat to starboard; the massive vessel turned north under his command. Owyn felt powerful. It was amazing. So many men—who could have been housed by a series of buildings in Kudra—and with a push of his hand, he turned them all towards the north.

Charlie reacted to an order from Doman, who had revisited the helm room, before exiting and shouting some orders to the men on the sails. Owyn couldn't see it all through the small windows of the room, but he saw enough. It was a grand machine of men, working as the ship turned, following the command he had given it through the whipstaff. Men were shouting, hauling in rope, and moving about the ship as the sails turned. They had been leaning to the starboard side of the ship, ever so slightly. Now they remained full of wind, almost looking stationary as the body of the ship turned beneath them. The timing of it, and the amount of work to hold them steady, astounded Owyn.

"Hold here," said Charlie, and Owyn centered the whip in his hands. It fought a bit, but only in feeling, not with force. Charlie left his side and went to a table by the wall, writing something in a notebook.

It felt good to be in control. Owyn held the whipstaff with a light touch. It moved a little, swaying slightly in his grip. He realized that he was but one part of a larger organism. The ship needed him now, someone to steer ;but it also needed people to control the sails, to clean the decks, and to cook the food. And one to command and organize the operation of the entire system.

Doman entered the room, two men behind him. "Charlie, take some rest. Owyn, you're relieved as well." Charlie nodded and left the room quickly, and one of the men took his place, while the other stood beside Owyn, hand out to take the whip. Owyn hadn't realized how reluctant he would be to give up the position, but he left the men to their work and followed Doman onto the deck.

"You shouldn't be cooped up for so long," said the Captain.

"I was enjoying it."

"More than they might, it seems," said Doman with a small laugh. "But we have shifts for a reason. Come."

Owyn followed. They walked out across the deck, men working around them. As they worked, Doman uttered a command and so they did not stop to salute their captain. Something about that felt right now to Owyn. They were working. No need for decorum. He wished he'd known what to say when they'd been working on the island.

Walking across the deck wasn't easy for Owyn. The waves weren't big, but the ship never ceased rocking beneath his feet. It didn't seem to have a rhyme or reason to the motion, yet Doman and the sailors looked as if they had anticipated every rock of the ship as they walked about. Owyn's calves hurt from standing still at the whip. He tried not to think of the pain, how he'd be sore tomorrow, how this was only the first day of the trip. He followed Doman across the deck, all the way to the foremost part of the ship, where the vessel's deck curved into itself, creating a point. The rail about the edge of the deck ended here, but a large wooden point continued out, pointing forward, pointing towards the open sea.

"Look about you, Owyn," said Doman, gesturing for him to approach the confluence of the two sides of the ship. "What do you see?"

Owyn stepped forward, unsure of what to say. He was silent for a time, watching the water, seeing the seam of the horizon, where the sky met the sea, united, but not unified. He watched the ocean break about the point of the ship, cutting through the deep blue water and creating white foam atop waves strewn to each side. The Breiar coast was now to his right, the land both near and far from them now. It all looked so small. His entire world. To the left, the sea spread out infinitely. "I feel like I'm traveling between everything I've ever known and everything that could ever be." His voice was quiet, almost reverent. Doman nodded as he stood behind him. He, too, had seen this, had felt it.

"Breathe it all in," said Doman.

Owyn did, tasting the salt and the humidity in the air.

"Now," said Doman, clapping his hands. "Are you ready to eat?"

A sailor was waiting at the door to the officer's mess. As he saw Doman and Owyn approaching, Doman nodded, and the man quickly disappeared. The room was vacant, save for the table, two chairs, and the glass windows that looked up what lay behind the ship. Doman sat; Owyn followed. Atop the table was a carafe and two glasses—not mugs, but cups made of actual glass.

"I'm uncertain I've ever drunk from a glass before," reflected Owyn as Doman began pouring wine from the carafe.

"Only the finest for a guest of *The Small Journey*." Doman handed Owyn a full glass and began pouring his own. "Well, third finest. The other two we save for emergencies."

The sailor returned, knocking on the door and entering at Doman's word. He had a platter balanced on one hand and hastened to the table to set it down.

"Roast mutton and—"

"Good, good, thank you, Chin," said Doman.

"Sir," said the man, Chin, setting down the rest of the and turning towards the door.

"I'll share our review with you afterwards."

The cook saw the Captain's smirk before he left the room, though the man cleared his face before he turned back towards Owyn.

"Now will you tell me of what led you here?"

CHAPTER 19

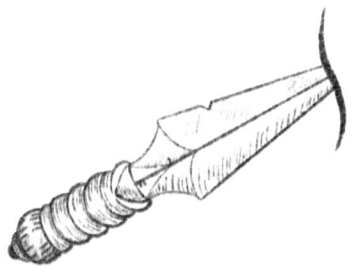

"My oldest friend is a thief," started Owyn. Doman put food from the platter on each of their plates and then took a drink of the wine. "I suppose I'm a thief, too. I'd like to say I was a thief. But—" Owyn paused. Doman hadn't touched the food on his plate. He watched Owyn. He was listening.

"Most of what we did was simple enough. We traveled, we stole, we ate, we drank, we traveled again. Triph used to say, 'There isn't anything to it except for what there is.' And I suppose he was right. It's nonsense, but he was right. Thieving is hard work. Dishonest work, but that doesn't remove the challenge of it. I remember cutting myself on the first window I broke. It was a rich house; glass windows looked into it and I thought to break the glass. My blood was all over the outside of their home. It's a wonder they didn't catch us then."

Doman still had yet to eat. Owyn, too. The Captain simply watched.

"We made our mistake east of Aerdethin. I don't even remember the town's name. It was so small. The Sheriff's niece died."

Doman leaned in closer. Their food was getting cold.

"I always carried a knife," continued Owyn. "Sometimes more than one. You never know the usefulness of one until you need it. Triph thought that the Mayor's manor would be a perfect mark. It would have the wealth of the town, whatever that may be. I didn't like it. I'd been saving up for a dream for a while. The issue wasn't the money; it was the risk I didn't want. But I went along. I always went along." Owyn took a drink. Doman followed suit, eyes never leaving the man across the table.

"He was right in the end. There was an entire wing of the house set aside for business. Mayoral duties, I assume. There was a wing of the manor for this, and this was in a town that hadn't more than a dozen buildings before one had to walk to the farmsteads. Triph was right about the money. I'd been on edge, though. This wasn't our usual burglary. This was big. Triph hadn't spoken to me, but I think he wanted out as much as I did. He'd wanted something.

"I heard a noise before I saw her, the mayor's daughter, and the knife had left my hands before I thought. It was instinct." Owyn took another drink. "I saw her, though. In that last moment while the steel was in my hand. I saw the fear in her eyes. The surprise."

"You killed her?" asked Doman. There was no judgment in his voice, only the question.

"The knife didn't hit. I'd pulled it. I saw her and made certain the blade would not hit. I could not stop the throw at that point, but I could still direct it. It stuck the doorway beside her. But the fear, the shock of it all," Owyn looked down at the table. "She fell. Backwards. Down the stairs behind her. Her neck broke. We had to walk over her body to leave."

There was silence now. Owyn couldn't look up from the food on the table. Doman's eyes could not leave Owyn.

"She was the niece of the Sheriff?" asked Doman.

"She never had long enough to be anything else. We heard as the news of our crime followed us to neighboring towns. The Mayor and the Sheriff are brothers. Both have a penchant for vengeance. For border-town justice."

"This Sheriff followed you."

"As he should have."

Doman reached over the table and pushed Owyn's plate closer to the man. He then grabbed the fork and knife placed by his own plate. "Come now, you've told your tale, now eat."

"She didn't have to die."

"You're correct," said Doman, holding a morsel of food on the edge of his fork, almost touching his mouth. "But judgment is for the next life, and for one's self. Your guilt is your own, and I shan't add to it."

"You would still abide a murderer on your ship?"

"I can't presume you're the first."

"I—" started Owyn.

"Eat, man," said Doman, finishing a bite and skewering another with his fork. "I cannot say if you are good or evil. I don't think men are. But I can say that you've done good around me, with my men. You've built something, and your sins are simply a story to me. If I judged all for their past, I would not have a crew for my ship. Do as your guilt tells you. Be better. But now, your food is growing cold and Chin will absolve you of any sort of guilt with a strike of his own knife if you do not eat it." Doman reached over the table and topped off Owyn's wine.

Owyn took his first bite of the meal in front of him. Doman ate like a starving gentleman. Owyn was slower. He did not feel good, but a part of him felt better. Lighter. He wasn't a good man. Doman may not judge him, but he could do that himself. There was a solace in speaking of the evil though.

They ate in silence for some time.

"Why did you become a thief?" asked Doman, his plate nearly empty. He punctuated the question with a drink from his cup.

Owyn looked up at him without an answer.

"I think it was to help Triph."

Before Doman could reply, there came a knock at the door.

"Come."

A sailor entered. "Cap'n, clouds build to the south."

Doman stood and looked out the glass windows at the rear of the room. Owyn turned and saw that the sky was dark behind them. The Captain thought for only a moment as he looked at the dark sight.

"Adjust course northwest, prepare the storm jib and drogue. Have sails ready to reef in the half hour."

"Aye," said the man with a knuckle to his head before he left the room. The Captain returned to his seat and took a drink of wine.

"I do love a storm. Eat up now' we've got work ahead of us," said Doman, his smile appearing as he set the glass to table. "Finish your drink, too. You asked for judgment? Well, there is nothing closer to the gods' will than a storm."

***

The winds whipped at Owyn's back as he stood atop the deck with Doman. He was told he may operate the pumps to relieve the men as the Captain started those shifts, but for now there was still preparation for the oncoming weather.

Charlie stood in the helm behind them, and Doman yelled orders into the windows. Owyn's eyes were above them, looking to the dozen men atop the sails, rolling up the cloth to reef as Doman had said. They were so high up and the wind was strong down here. In front of the ship, a small crew of men were securing the front sail. It was much smaller than the jib had been. The ship spoke. It groaned as the wind pushed against the timber masts, still pulled by the yet disappearing sails as the men folded them. The ocean was calm beneath them, not still, but calm. The ship was so loud. Wind was louder.

"We'll ride her out as long as we can, get sea room, and heave to if need be," said Doman. He leaned down towards Owyn, trying to speak above the noise of the wind. Owyn knew some of what he said, but most of the terms in the man's orders were foreign. He wasn't even sure what the pumps were that he was meant to run as things got bad.

The storm was on their heels as the ship raced out towards the open water. In front of the ship was a blue day where the sun had won its battle. Behind them was darkness. Between the two, a line in the sky. Owyn thought it looked like something he would have seen represented in a painting or tapestry, but it was real; the storm and darkness were quickly overtaking them. Even with the sole storm jib acting alone, the ship flew across the water. Waves formed at the rear and the vessel rocked and heaved, but always back to front. The motion from side to side was minimal, and Owyn was taken aback by how different the regularity in the waves felt. They were rushing away from the storm on a direct path. Looking to the east, even the land had disappeared. They were at sea now and the line in the sky was not slowing.

There was so much movement, the half hour the Captain predicted seemed to pass in seconds. The storm was upon them.

The men remaining on deck shouted aye's confirming their knots. They were each tied to a portion of the deck. It was a skeleton crew. They still raced forward under the pressure of the wind on the storm jib. Doman headed below deck and Owyn followed. Every sailor was awake. Doman had said this was a lighter storm by his reckoning, but it was the first of the season and the men were nervous.

Below deck was dark. The lamps had been doused to prevent a fire, and the light from the sun was now firmly behind the clouds.

"Ost!" shouted the Captain, and Owyn saw his friend who had led at the lighthouse. The boy with ideas. The leader of a crew. Ost stood at attention. He looked determined now. Owyn had never fought, but he had heard tales of soldiers. This is what he imagined they looked like before a battle.

"Men stand at the pumps and the second watch is ready," said Ost.

"Looks to be third and fourth watches are, too."

Ost nodded.

"Keep strong, count the time well. Second shift to post within half of an hour. I want you ready to swim. But you shan't have to this storm."

"Aye," said Ost, with a knuckle to his head. Doman turned to speak to the others. Aside from Ost, all were something like officers. Owyn did not know all the roles on the ship, but he noted the differing styles of dress. Now was the time for the formality instilled in these men. No one could question an order here.

The ship lurched forward. The sea lifted the stern as if it were the lid of some chest, anchored at the bow, before being slammed down again. Owyn almost fell, but steadied himself against the wall.

Doman finished speaking to his men and turned back towards the door to the top deck. Owyn was in his way. "To the pumps with you," he said.

"I'm with you," said Owyn.

"You wish to ride the storm?"

"I'm with you," said Owyn.

"You asked for judgment. There is nothing closer to the gods' will than a storm," said the Captain as he turned. Owyn followed Doman out through the doors into the tempest above.

Rain was falling without respite, drops the size of coins crashing into the deck as the wind continued to push at the rear of the ship. Another man shut the door behind them. Owyn had made his choice.

Doman looked back only once as he raced across the short span of deck towards the door of the helm. Owyn followed. That the deck was not more slick with the water surprised him. He had expected worse. They reached the door, Doman shouting something into the helm as he entered. Owyn could not hear it as another wave pushed up against the stern of the ship. He saw the door, with Doman standing at the entrance, rise away from him. Fear filled him as a step forward turned into a step up a hill and the helm continued to rise. His foot lost purchase and Owyn realized he was about to fall. He was not tied in as the other men on the deck were. In an instant, his mind cleared. Nothing filled it. Not a thought. He didn't regret his choice to remain with the Captain; he didn't regret any of his life's choices. He didn't think at all. It was only a moment. Owyn fell forward as the water from the wave behind the ship overtopped the wooden structure. His eyes closed instinctively as he braced to hit the deck.

He felt an arm grab him as his knees hit the wooden decking that had been beneath his feet. Instinct over, his eyes opened to see Doman Sutherland pulling at his arm. The Captain had one hand holding the doorframe to the helm and the other outstretched, grabbing Owyn. The ship crashed down as the wave overtopped the rear and water rushed over Owyn and Doman. It pulled at Owyn, trying to take him forward, trying to take him away from the safety of the helm. The Captain held strong. The wave completed its course and, rising to his feet, Owyn stood, pulled into the helm.

Doman closed the door to the room as Owyn scurried in. "Charlie, keep hand to that whip!" shouted the Captain. He needn't have. Charlie stood at the helm, whipstaff in hand and eyes locked forward. His gaze never left the windows of the room as he stared ahead.

Doman dropped a latch on the wooden door, securing it shut before turning towards the same windows that Charlie watched through to steer.

The cacophony around the room made the silence within more palpable. Owyn's eyes went from Charlie to Doman. The helmsman watched the sea, hand fighting the whip as it tried to move with the pressure on the rudder. The Captain watched everything.

"Keep her port," he said. Charlie followed the order, but Owyn saw that the man had been pushing the whip for that turn before the Captain had spoken a word.

There were men out there. Owyn could hardly see them through the rainfall, but as lightning struck, he could see them all. They were so small, tied to the ship that was nothing more than a speck of dust riding on the winds of the sea.

"Level now."

Charlie followed, and another wave took the ship from the rear. A deluge fell over the windows, blinding the helm for a moment, some of the water crashing in. Owyn felt a strange sensation in his lungs as he realized he tasted salt. There was so much water in the air.

Lightning struck with random frequency. It was so close that the thunder immediately followed, shaking the ship and booming through Owyn's chest.

Doman swore.

Owyn was afraid now. The Captain had not uttered an oath or a curse since Owyn had met him. He had said one word, likely to be lost in the storm's noise, but Owyn had heard it.

Another strike of lightning from above. Owyn noticed more men on the deck. They had all tied themselves around the waist with ropes going back into the doors they appeared from. Each was now swapping places with one of the men who had been on deck. It felt like hours had passed, yet it must have been only half of one had if the second shift just now started. Doman unlatched the door to the helm and Ost entered. The rain had soaked the man, but he looked unfazed.

"Owyn to the whip."

Owyn wanted to react, to say something, but there was no time. He relied on instinct now, how men for eternity had survived the wrath of nature and the gods. He took the whipstaff in hand and Charlie stepped back. The man looked exhausted.

"Ost, tighten the luff; the storm jib falters."

The man made no attempt at formality. He turned without pause and headed to the front of the ship. Doman closed the door and latched it again. Charlie had gone to the corner of the helm and sat down, arms limp at his sides.

Owyn understood why. The whip was not light in his hand. It fought him completely. His arms strained to keep it steady in his hands. He was thankful for all the rowing he had done.

"Port, Owyn, gentle now." Owyn followed the orders. He knew he should watch the sea, but he couldn't. His eyes were on the speck moving across the ship's decks. Ost seemed steady despite the water rushing beneath his feet, the rain pelting him from above. He moved without pause to the front of the ship before he reached the man tied to the mast there.

"Steady now, Owyn, starboard for a moment, then true."

Ost and the other man spoke for what seemed like only a second before they moved. The man went out towards one sheet that held the cloth of the jib aloft. He pulled, but Owyn saw that the sail did not tighten. It was loose in the wind and getting worse. Ost had not gone to the sheet with his crewmate. A flash of lighting and Owyn saw he was now scaling the mast.

"Starboard, Owyn."

Ost was now atop the crossbar of the sail. He looked so small, so vulnerable, as he worked up there, but Owyn saw the sail beginning to tighten. The sailor on deck pulled his sheet once more. It was working.

A wave crashed over the deck, as tall as the mast, and hit Ost and his fellow sailor.

"Port, man, port!" said Doman. Water rushed over the windows of the helm. They couldn't see a thing. "Now true, hold her true." Owyn did as he was told. His arms already ached. He could not spare a thought to count the seconds as they slowly ticked away. The water stopped from above and they could see once more.

Ost was still atop the jib.

Owyn felt the relief in the room. The Captain readjusted his shoulders. He stood taller, if that were possible. Owyn imagined the smile on the man's face before he returned his gaze to the sea and his arms to work.

The rain did not cease as Owyn fulfilled the Captain's orders. Wind and wave yet fought to bring them beneath the water, but the ship held. Owyn held. Doman's orders were clear and Owyn followed them without question.

Owyn had not thought of gods or towers until the wind began to slow, and by then he had neither the will nor the energy to think. Were Doman not giving orders, he could not continue. His mind had given out; only his body remained.

As the storm continued to calm around them, the ship rocked amidst the darkness of the clouds above and the sea below. The third shift reached the middle of their time on deck. Owyn had joined Charlie, seated in the helm's corner, when another sailor had entered to take the whip. Another officer had entered to relieve Doman, but the Captain had sent the man back below deck with orders to maintain the men there. The Captain would remain through whatever was to come.

Now lightning only struck well beyond the front of the ship.

Charlie stood and helped Owyn to his feet.

They had made it. Owyn looked through the windows of the helm to see the storm racing away from them.

Doman opened the door to the helm and shouted orders to the men above deck. He then turned to Owyn with the smile of a man half-crazed with joy. "If that were the gods judging your fate, they smiled upon you today."

Chapter 20

Triph stood in the alley behind a pub, hiding from the rain. He liked how the raindrops bounced against the cobblestone road. It looked nice and sounded nice. Why couldn't life be nice?

He wasn't supposed to be here. He had run. Always running. Always. Triph was not supposed to have heard Wendel speaking as he had. The inn's walls were so thin, though—merely a single clay layer. The man had been drunk. Triph had been drunk, too. That's why he ran. The rain and the cobbles were so pretty. They'd sobered him up. Fear had snuck in again. Triph lived his life with a swaggering confidence. As he stared at the rain hitting the ground, head beginning to tinge with pain as the alcohol gave way to the hangover, he realized what a lie that all was.

He got this way more often since Owyn left.

It hadn't started there, though. They had been friends. Owyn had been good for Triph. He always went along with Triph's ideas, even coming up with some of his own. It was great. They'd done so much. Triph had told him to bring the knife. That was one of Triph's ideas. He had so many. They all worked out.

Voices came from the street at the pub's entrance, bouncing around the walls of the alley and disrupting the sound of the rain. Triph pressed himself into the wall, trying to hide in the shadows. The two men who had left the pub walked past the alley without a second thought. Hiding hadn't been necessary. Triph moved on.

He walked without an aim. It was nighttime, and the odds of him running into any of the posse out now during the rain were within a level he'd gamble on. He didn't try to avoid the rain, but he wasn't trying to get soaked, either. He bounced between alcoves and coverings as he walked through the back alleys of Kudra.

Always the back alleys. Never the main roads. One got robbed on the main roads. But the alleys? You could trust folk in the alleys. They all tried to steal from you. They were honest. The people of the main roads tried to steal from you, too, but they did it with a smile and the methods of the rich.

Everyone stole. That was life. You steal all you can until there's nothing left for you to steal or you get too weak to take another breath. Then you die. Everyone died.

But this? This was more than stealing.

Owyn was gone now. He'd gone to work with the giant; one of the men had found that out, and so the group watched him, setting a trap. Then he was gone. But the giant...

Before Triph had run, a fancy man had been spotted at the quarry, a ship captain. Owyn wouldn't have gone on a ship, though. He'd never mentioned a wish for that. Though he'd never mentioned building a tower, either. Had he? Triph was bad at listening when he didn't care about the topic. After the man with the ship left port, Owyn was gone entirely. Search and search. They could not find him. But they could find the giant.

Triph turned a corner and saw a busker asleep in an alcove protected by the rain. The man huddled in layers of ragged cloth. He slept with his instrument held tightly to his chest, partially covered by the cloth, yet decidedly out of the rain. He seemed to care less about the sack containing coins. It lay semi-covered by his body, but Triph would never miss the glint of money. Would the man notice the lighter wallet when he awoke?

His dreams had better be sweet, Triph thought as he walked past the sleeping man. They cost enough. West felt good to Triph. He walked that way. It may have been because the city sloped down in that direction, or that the wind was at his back walking that way. He did not care to think of why; he simply walked. It felt good. The direction. The walking. Triph did what felt good.

He was free, yet there was a weight on him.

He thought of that giant.

He thought of Wendel's words.

He thought of consequences. Of being left behind.

Triph didn't feel good. He didn't feel particularly bad either, but he was not comfortable.

The city began to lower itself, with the rooftops following the grade of the hill on its approach to the bay, and Triph could see the ocean. The sea and sky were dark but still visible, and the light from the open space seemed to illuminate Turtle Bay in a way wholly different from the lanterns in the street lighting the world of alleys and buildings.

"We'll keep the giant till the man returns. Boss's orders."

"He'll come."

Triph would never forget the moan from the giant, held in the second story of the shadnel. He stopped in his tracks. Rain poured over him. It went over his clothes, already soaked, and down into the cobblestone streets. It ran west. Running west was easy. So easy.

A bolt of lightning struck out beyond the bay. Triph saw the waves and the water and the dark miasma in the sky releasing its deluge. Beyond the bay, there may have been a ship. But what he saw was at the edge of the bay: a tower. A tower built by men and a giant. A tower built by a friend.

Owyn may have left him, but Triph was better than that. He may have led the Sheriff here, but that was only to find a friend. A bastard of a friend who abandoned him, but still a friend. Who cared about the consequences or circumstances? He didn't choose to help the Sheriff, but he had. He had wanted to. He had wanted to find his friend. And now Triph wanted to leave, put it all behind him. It had been too easy to sneak away from the posse after they'd nabbed the giant. That thing was a lot to focus on. Triph wanted to leave it all behind—the giant, the Sheriff, Owyn.

"Damn it all!" he cursed.

Triph gazed west, to the sea. It would be easy. He wanted to leave. No, even that wasn't true. He only thought he wanted to. So he turned back to the east and to the city. He did what he wanted to. And he walked back towards the giant. He walked back towards the friend of his old friend. There was nothing else he could do. Determination set on his face as he began to think of a plan. Not actively, but in the recesses of his mind. He was not a planner, but maybe something would come to him. His walk turned into a jog, then, a run, through the rain. His feet clapped against the cobblestones.

He ran towards where the posse was.

To the shadnel.

Triph ran on instinct.

Instinct went out the window when Triph saw a man he never thought he'd see again.

CHAPTER 21

The Small Journey had returned to the Kudran port on the exact day that Doman had stated they would arrive. It had put into Daughtn the same day he stated as well. It was a merchant journey they'd been on. Trade from port town to port town; crates unloaded, and, within a day, refilled and brought back aboard. There was no coin exchanged, but stamps and seals on parchment. "A promise of continued profit runs on trust and on a reliable schedule," said Doman. "Besides, why be late when one can be on time?"

Even with the storm, the man was exact. Owyn hadn't the time to marvel at punctuality. As they approached the port, the Captain told him the score.

"We have the King's orders for this next journey, my friend. The most precious cargo he can dare put aboard a ship, and your friend Ost's least favorite." He smiled at that. "But there will be guards and there will be eyes. I cannot bring you aboard.

"We will take you safely to the north of the city. Watch for our return. This will be a quick journey, a race between storms, so watch for our ship three days from now. I shall send out another boat to the north of the city and we'll take you aboard if you'll have us." The Captain smiled. There was no guile on his face now. He was like a father, proud of his son. Something Owyn never knew, never felt. But here, it felt good.

"I'd like that."

With that, Owyn watched *The Small Journey* leaving the bay. He sat perched on a hillside on the north side of the city, close to the slums that Tulbër lived in. He looked forward to seeing his friend again. But for the moment, he watched the ship, the colors painted on the hull stark against the blue water and the dark grey sky. He could still see the color as the ship rounded the horn with the empty lighthouse. The clouds beyond his island already looked heavy with rain to come.

He stood, unsure if he was feeling joy or sadness. He wanted to smile at the thought of the adventure, the thought of joining the sailors once more, but he still saw the lighthouse in the bay. His lighthouse. Abandoned. Empty. A dream unfulfilled. He regarded the mix of feelings within him but chose to feel none of them. Owyn walked into the city to find his friend and tell him a story. Finally, the smile appeared. It did not matter how small.

Tulbër was not in his hovel.

The cozy home was unlocked. After all, who would steal from a giant? But it was not lived in either. Owyn looked about. Oil in lamps, with evaporation lines set in against them. Food beginning to turn, bought a moment too long ago to eat now. But more than any of the signs, obvious to a thief, there was another feeling. The place felt empty. It felt as though Tulbër were not there. That is what struck Owyn. Not the signs of abandonment, not the dust and the waste, but the emptiness.

His friend wasn't here.

Night was still a few hours away, but this did not look as if just a day had gone by with work. Owyn dashed to the quarry, hoping for any sign of the giant.

"No work here," said the foreman when he arrived. "And I haven't seen Tulbër in a few weeks. Winter's here and brought the flood." Owyn saw that the quarry truly was flooded. Kudra had gained a small lake in the winter. He cared nothing of it, though. Tulbër wasn't here.

Owyn turned back to the hovel, eyes open as night fell. Watching. He was tired, but still his eyes searched. They saw better than others'. They had experience watching.

They saw nothing of a giant in the city as he walked towards Tulbër's home.

Owyn stopped in the darkness. There was a light peeking out from the doorway of the hovel. His heart turned quicker than Owyn ever thought it could, but his mind held his feet at bay. He did not move.

He still had the mind of a criminal.

Trepidation filled Owyn's steps as he slinked forward on the wet cobblestones.

There was no giant in Tulbër's home. Two voices spoke softly within the stone hovel, neither one the singing voice of his friend. Owyn heard the sharp bite of a harsh whisper rising into the tones of normal conversation.

"What'd you get?" said the first voice. It was higher and rang as though the man spoke through his nose.

"Alehouse had a new brew. I picked up enough for the night if you don't drown in it like last." Replied the second. A deep tone resonated as he spoke, but it was hollow compared to how Tulbër's singing voice filled the hovel.

"What else am I supposed to do? It isn't like the little killer is showing up anytime soon."

"Yea but the boss told us to be here."

"And you'd do anything he said?"

"You wouldn't?"

The nasally man was quiet before he told the other man what food he'd brought.

Owyn listened at the doorway as true darkness engulfed the world. No one walked by. No one took notice of the thief missing his friend.

Night dragged on and the pair's conversation slowed. Owyn only risked a single glance within the crack of the doorway. The pair sat in the chair where Tulbër and he had been so recently. How foolish he had been for leaving! He could not risk anything here, though. As one man slept, the second kept watch, alert. Owyn saw the drive in his eyes. It was a look he'd always avoided in a mark.

Owyn snuck away from the hovel as a drizzle began from above.

There were no lamps lit in the roads here. This part of town was rarely lit even in the dry season. Now there was no one to waste the oil for. The streets were empty. Owyn was alone in the largest city in the world. He didn't know where to go. He didn't know what to do. Owyn's tired mind would not think clearly. Images and memories and thoughts flew through it in an unending barrage. Nothing was clear. No, a few things were clear.

His friend was gone.

Thieves or monsters were in his friend's home.

They were waiting for him.

He'd done this to Tulbër.

Owyn noticed his feet were taking him in a direction he wasn't used to. Uphill. He had avoided heading uphill the entire time he was back. The palace was uphill. The God's Tower was uphill. People were uphill. Owyn's feet carried him that direction, anyway.

Alone in the rain, with thoughts he'd rather not have and feelings he wished would just wash away with the water that was falling heavier now, he stopped and turned to stare across the bay. Back to where he felt happiest. Back to where his feelings belonged. Not quite home. He didn't have a home anymore. He didn't have anyone, or anywhere, to go to.

He was alone.

Wasn't this what he had wanted?

No.

Not now.

What had happened to Tulbër?

He wasn't a thief. Not anymore. And he wouldn't abandon another friend.

Owyn didn't look as he moved, but he turned away from the bay. He turned so he walked back up, away from his happiness. His eyes fixed on his feet as they trudged through puddles on the stones as they carried him up. Forward and up. Movement in the city that could not match the movement of his life.

The street crested and dropped back down in elevation. Owyn stopped and looked at where he had ended up. He could see the entire city of Kudra here. In the distance, there were the docks and the bay, the water coming up to the edge of the sandy colored buildings and the darkness of the clouds in the distance, now truly a storm approaching. There were lights in the windows above the ground level and there was the endless sound of water moving through the world of men.

The God's Tower loomed in the center of Kudra. It stood above all the other structures in the city. No matter how great Kudra was, no matter how great the works of men could be, this tower was larger. Wasn't that enough? Couldn't the thing of the gods be content to loom as it did without removing the wonder within the creations of men? Was being made by the gods not enough for the thing that it still had to take from men? Had to take from Owyn?

He stared at the Tower. The scarred structure, damaged centuries before the city was founded and eons before the empire could have even begun, was of another age, and yet it stole from him now. Anger filled him. The gods did nothing for him, yet they took away all he had left. They took away his home. They took away his friend. Owyn sat down, letting the water of the street soak through his pants. He didn't care. He stared out at the Tower, constructed so long ago. It extended upward past the gray clouds of the sky. Rain made the stone of it shine as water raced down the structure.

The anger faded. There was nothing behind it, nothing in Owyn to fuel it. He could not be angry. It was just a Tower. Men had caused his problems, had taken away his dream. One man had taken away his dream.

The Tower wasn't to blame. The Sheriff and the zealots weren't either. He was to blame. Owyn was to blame.

There was a flash of lightning far to the south, still far enough away that the thunder emanating from it would only yell, it wouldn't bombard the city. But the light did. The brightness of nature lit up the sea beyond the city. Owyn saw the horizon past the God's Tower. The wide expanse of the world beyond men and gods filled his vision. His tiny lighthouse, just a speck unnoticed on the expanse. Then the light faded, and the world was darker, dissolved in the distance once more. For a moment, it had been so big. Bigger than the men; bigger than the city; bigger, even, than the gods. Seconds ticked by in his mind, counted without conscious thought. The thunder never arrived, though. The storm was still too far away. But it wouldn't be for long.

There was only one way he could find his friend.

He had to ask for help.

But there was only one group that could aid him. Only one way to find his friend.

He had to ask the monster. The man who tracked him and found him across an empire.

Owyn didn't matter to himself anymore. Tulbër mattered. His friend's safety mattered.

He stood up and looked out across the dark bay. Waiting. Waiting for another bolt of light from the sky. One last look at his lighthouse. Waiting for a final goodbye.

There was no flash.

There was no light.

He said goodbye in the darkness.

It was over.

He didn't know where the Sheriff was. He could search for them or the protestors or the King...or he could light a way for them to come to him.

He looked out at the darkness of the sea where his tower stood.

It was his lighthouse. And it was his way towards the protestors and the posse and Sheriff. Towards his final destiny.

To help find his friend.

He took his first step and looked up. Down the street he saw a face that he never thought he'd see again.

"Owyn?"

CHAPTER 22

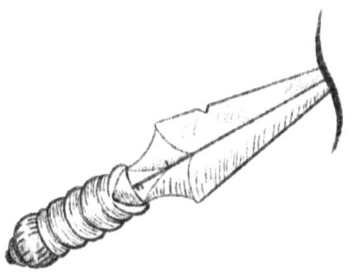

T riph took a step towards Owyn.

Owyn stood still. Triph saw his old friend, his partner. He saw the man who had betrayed him. Rain came down over both of them.

Lightning struck.

It looked as though Owyn saw something behind Triph, but Triph would not let his gaze waver so quickly.

"I'm sorry I abandoned you," said Owyn, eyes returning to Triph.

Triph took a step towards Owyn.

"I'm sorry," he said again.

Triph took another step towards Owyn. The thunder from the lightning strike hit them. Sound washed over them in a shockwave that shook their ribs. The storm was nearly here.

"You're sorry?" said Triph.

"I shouldn't have left you like I did," said Owyn. "You deserved more than that."

Triph was at a loss for words. He thought of the giant's wail as he had run away from the shadnel. He hadn't stopped walking forwards since.

"Do you know where Tulbër is?" asked Owyn, but it was too late. Triph hadn't really heard what Owyn said. He'd taken the rest of the steps forward.

Owyn couldn't believe what his old friend had done.

He didn't need to speak as Triph grabbed him.

The old friends hugged in the rain.

They held each other as the rain washed over them. They held each other as they never had, not once, during their partnership.

Owyn was the first to back away from the embrace.

"Tulbër. My friend. Do you know where he is?" he pleaded as he looked at Triph's face. Owyn looked so tired. Triph had never seen that cast to his friend's face.

"The giant?"

Owyn nodded. "There were men in his home."

"Did they see you?"

"No, but I know they were looking for me. That posse is still in the city. I think they have Tulbër."

Triph swallowed. Owyn spoke before he could open his mouth.

"If you don't know anything, you've got to stay away from me. I'm going to light a beacon that they can't ignore."

"Your tower."

Owyn nodded.

Triph's mind was turning through a mixture of thoughts and memories as he spoke. "What is it? That thing you were building?" Maybe he could yet do something good.

"It's a firetower. Like the woodfarms. It works well enough, I hope."

Triph smiled at the memory, but Owyn continued before he could speak. He shouted above the rain.

"You should get out of here. If you got away from the posse, you've got to stay away from me."

Another flash. The thunder followed almost instantly this time. It shook the rain, seeming to halt the water in the air for a moment before allowing the downpour to continue. It stopped them. In the darkness, Triph saw Owyn for what he was. A man. Just that. Nothing more. He was a friend. He had been a partner. But still, he was just a man.

They'd met when they were boys. Children of a village brothel, they were friends from the start.

"You'd give yourself up to save the giant?" he asked.

"I will. And if I'd known you were in trouble like you were, I'd have done the same for you," said Owyn. "I'm sorry it took me so long to realize."

Triph saw the truth in his eyes.

He knew what he'd do. He needn't bother Owyn with the particulars.

"What's the light for?" he asked as his mind smiled at the good he was committing to do. Owyn didn't even know what a good friend he had abandoned.

"It sits on the horn of the bay. It's impossible to see the rocks below even on a sunny day. Imagine how bad it'd be in a storm like this. The light is a beacon for ships to avoid as they find their way home."

Triph laughed. "Home." He wondered what that felt like. But he was happy for his friend. "You always were too noble to be a thief," he said.

Owyn looked at him. "And you were too much of a scoundrel to be a friend, yet look at the two of us now."

Triph smiled. He would do something good for this man he'd known for so long. Why not be the better man?

He stepped forward and hugged his friend once more. "Wish me luck," he said.

"For what?" said Owyn.

"Never you mind; go light your beacon and give yourself up to save a friend."

Owyn gave a look that Triph had seen a thousand times. Triph wasn't a puzzle. He always understood what he wanted and what was next, even if he didn't know what exactly it'd be or if it'd change tomorrow. Still, his friend never quite understood him. Owyn was too much of a thinker. It was a good thing Triph was a doer. There was good to be done now while Owyn was off thinking about a light and ships and sadness in a storm.

"What will you do?"

"Same thing I always do," said Triph. He leaned back, stretching his spine and popping his shoulders as he extended his arms.

He was going to rescue a giant.

CHAPTER 23

Triph watched Owyn run down the street to the north. His friend didn't have to sacrifice anything. He'd be the noble one now. He arched his back in another stretch. The rain fell onto his face and dripped down his soaked clothes. The water might be an issue, but he smiled anyway. The challenge made it fun.

He twisted. The stretch felt good. Got to be limber. Got to be warm. That was hard in the cold and the rain and the city.

He cracked his neck and closed his smile to the sky.

Time for some thievery.

Triph thought on his vocation as he walked back towards the shadnel. Towards the giant, Tulbër. He hadn't spoken to it—to him. Hadn't learned his name. No, Triph avoided the shame of kidnapping a giant. Avoided the posse entirely and somehow their attention had avoided him, for just long enough to make a run for it.

He saw the building he was looking for. Not the shadnel, but a tan stone building with a pile of refuse next to it just tall enough for the thief to lope up the side of and onto the roof. Within seconds, he was pulling himself quietly up onto the building. Even he couldn't hear his footsteps across the stone roof in the rain. The water may be an issue, but the rain would only help the job.

Thievery.

Triph thought how one could steal a person: steal, kidnap, enslave and worse, yes. Those things happened, but they were not him. He did not abide them. He was a thief. He was not a monster like those who would steal a person from their life, or worse: their life. He merely reminded people how good things were when they had less.

Like it or not, though, he had been a part of the Sheriff's damned Posse Comitatus. He had abided the kidnapping of the giant. Of Tulbër. He allowed the thing and now he would undo the thing. *Damn posse and damn Sheriff!*

Triph thought of the bald man. The dark anger on his face.

He thought of the frustration the man would feel at losing their prisoner.

He thought of Wendel getting yelled at for it, too.

Triph smiled as he bounded from one roof to another. Closer to the shadnel. Closer to the job.

How to rob a temple?

Triph and Owyn had done it before, but that'd been sepht money. *Oh, and the wooden relics that one time*, he recalled. *And was it a temple robbery if you pickpocketed a monk on a pilgrimage?* Triph mused, then shook his head. Always so many thoughts when on a job. Always so much to think about. It was good to have another man around to ground you.

He thought of Owyn and pushed the thought from his mind. That man would do his own crazy things out in the sea at his fire-tower or whatever he wanted to call it. What a fool. Who wouldn't want to keep being a thief? Quitting was for suckers.

Triph hopped onto the shadnel roof.

The building looked no different from its neighbors, save for the cloth sign, one of Irnam, flying above the door—flying hard in the storm's wind, as though trying to break free.

Well, that was it, wasn't it?

Triph smiled. He thought of the best ideas right as he got to the job. Why plan anything out? Planning was for suckers too, it seemed. Owyn liked planning. What a fool. Triph laughed inside. He did that instead of letting the other thoughts of Owyn win out. The worry. The darkness. The shame and the guilt. Nope. He laughed again, even smiling this time, tasting the dirt the rainwater washed down his face as it fell past his open grin.

"Cheap roofs—hate to see what the wind does to it," said Triph to the storm above him as he kicked off the rounded ceramic tiles that covered the seams between the larger flat portions that covered most of the roof. "Real shame when water gets in the little cracks. Good thing it's only a little crack."

Just a lift of a tile here and a tile there and, better than Triph had hoped, a gust shifted the open tiles further apart. "Quite a gap you've got now, kids. Hope that wind isn't too loud."

He couldn't even hear his own voice, but it felt good to say it aloud. It felt good to be doing something. Hunting was for the birds. The Sheriff could keep his day job. Triph loved getting back to his. He kicked off a few more of the tiles and stood at the edge of the shadnel roof. Another gust came and Triph watched as it cut under the open tiles, whistling as it went. Water was pouring into the gaps. He smiled and turned, hopping off the roof down into the alley below.

The shadnel wasn't a big building. A small, two-story affair, re-purposed into its current religious purpose, but built centuries before its current occupants took up residence. Triph hadn't liked his time in there, but it was useful now. The old building was simple, square, open. That wouldn't be easy for the job, but Triph hoped the distraction would do its thing.

He slinked around the corner. The windows were closed, blocked by stone. Triph snuck to the front door. The only door. It wasn't guarded.

There was shouting inside. Triph always thought it was funny the lengths the pious would go to come up with their own swear words instead of using the damn ones everyone else said.

The shouts were a mix of curses and not-quite-swears. He peered in and saw three men running up the stone stairs on the side of the room to the second floor. Water was already running down the steps into the first floor. Even from outside, and over the rain, he could hear how loud it was inside with the wind whistling through his handiwork to the roof.

Triph sauntered into the empty room. He looked about. It was warm. It was bright. It was missing a giant.

Panic struck Triph as he heard the Sheriff's voice among the shouting on the second floor. He hadn't left. He wouldn't leave his prize. Not after Triph had escaped and Owyn had eluded him. That firetower across the bay would get his attention.

"Get that damn thing downstairs and out of my way! You—get those tiles out of the way! Get up there you spineless—"

A gust of wind that Triph could hear from even down here cut off the terrifying man's voice.

So, he was here.

Triph looked about. The room was open. An altar sat in the back with seats set around it. But nothing else. He thought about getting the giant down from the second floor, out and away from that crowd. The distraction was good. He could get up there. He could check it out.

He glanced at the smooth ceiling. Not a gap in sight and not another way up, save for the stairs. Maybe a window outside? No, those would be blocked off just as the ones down here were. Though, maybe not?

Too slow. The hole in the roof wouldn't keep them forever. Triph rolled his neck, stretching, hearing the joints pop. They didn't used to do that so loudly. Oh well. Off the cuff was the best way, anyway. Owyn's plans always took too long. He started towards the stairs and stopped at a noise.

Footfalls on the stone.

Steps in the water rolling down from the second floor.

Big ones.

"C'mon now," said a voice. A voice far too familiar and slimy. Wendel.

New plan.

Triph ducked behind the seat closest to the stairs, just out of sight from the opening above, but close enough to do something. He was near the door. Near enough. He could bolt if he needed to.

Could he?

Triph grimaced. There was no running on this one. He was doing a good thing.

The stone stairs creaked at the steps coming down. Triph hadn't heard stone creak before.

He smiled. Why plan when winging it worked out so well?

Wendel was walking the posse's prisoner down the stairs. Tulbër was wet. His hands were bound. His face was bruised. It looked so wrong without a smile.

"I was only trying to help," said the loud sing-song voice of the creature. They really were marvelous, thought Triph. How could the Sheriff have thought to keep one bound up?

The pair, prisoner and captor, reached the bottom of the stairs.

"Can't have you getting out of those bindings. Boss wouldn't have that."

"I get it. Why use the giant when you have a ladder?" laughed Tulbër. His laugh was louder even than the storm raging on the floor above them and immeasurably sweeter.

The pair walked to the altar. They walked right past Triph. It was good to be small.

Now the roll of the dice. Wendel and the giant reached the altar. One or both would turn, most likely. *Please be the giant.* Wendel turned; Triph was moving before the other man saw him.

The worm of a man's eyes opened wide in shock as Triph ran towards him. Wendel's mouth opened. A shout began. Triph cut it off with his fist.

Gods, that hurt! Why are skulls so damn hard?

Wendel dropped. He let out a little yelp as he did, but Triph hoped the storm cut that noise off from those above. From the Sheriff.

The worm started to shout again.

"Quiet now," said the giant. His voice a low rumble as he stood and loomed over the fallen man. Wendel looked up at them, silent. Fear widened his eyes. He was so small on the ground. Triph couldn't help but smirk. Triph looked over at the giant then back to Wendel.

"Got a blade?" he asked.

Wendel didn't move, but his eyes flinched. Triph leaned down and flipped up the man's shirt, seeing the blade affixed to his belt, right where Wendel hadn't wanted to look. Lawmen slime were so easy. Triph turned to the giant and saw the deep gashes the binding had cut into his grey skin. Guilt loomed above Triph like an unavoidable weight, ready to fall. He was glad he'd limbered up.

He sliced the giant's bindings and felt the guilt on his shoulders crash down on someone else.

Triph was doing something good.

"You," whispered Wendel. Triph turned from the giant to the man, still on the ground. Anger and superiority and frustration all fueled the fire in Wendel's eyes.

Triph just smiled and held up a finger to his lips. "Shh." He turned to the giant. "We've got to run now."

And so they ran, plunging into the rain and darkness of the storm.

CHAPTER 24

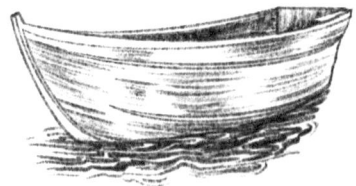

Owyn's steps pounded against the cobblestones. He could not hear them through the thunder and the rain, but he could feel them.

Each step thrummed through the entirety of his body. His back and ribcage vibrated as if Tulbër were speaking. They thrummed with purpose.

He felt so much.

He would light a beacon and give up his dream to save his friend.

The gods may have absolved his sins in the storm aboard *The Small Journey*, but Owyn hadn't absolved himself yet.

The clouds had opened above him; the rain pummeling through to his soul. Wet could not describe his clothes anymore; they were more water than cloth. The lamps of the street were out, doused by the deluge above. Their oil gone. Dead.

Owyn ran based on memory. He had reached roads he knew. There were no people about. The darkness overpowered the signs and the markers.

Kudra was a blur. The city did not matter. What mattered was what was after. The tops of the buildings began to lower themselves below the horizon. It was lighter out past them. Owyn saw the bay. The dark waters fought to be seen. The sky and the storming waves flashed in the lightning, more visible than the buildings that surrounded him. This was truth. This was nature. The walls of society, of men and of giants, meant nothing. This was the battleground of the gods. Owyn turned into an alley and his sight left the ocean and returned to the dark streets he ran through. He raced and raced until he left the city's edge. He ran, not to the docks, but to the north. He ran through the storm towards the *Morning Sunshine*.

The water slapped against the stone shore. The ground was slick as the foam washed over the protuberances that jutted out of the water and pointed out towards the bay. Owyn didn't think. He acted. He flipped the old boat and grabbed the makeshift wooden oar he had ripped from it. It felt good beneath his feet as he sat down. It was his boat. Always had been. He would not steal. Never again. He pushed the *Morning Sunshine* out into the stormy waters.

As he hit the first wave head on, he realized the journey might not be possible.

Water filled the boat, sloshing about Owyn's feet, but there was no time to bucket it out. Another wave hit the rowboat, water breaking against Owyn's back. He rowed, putting all of the strength he'd gained into paddling, each stroke moving him closer to his island. There was no time. He didn't know what was happening to his friend.

He didn't know if his friend was even still alive.

Even during the storm aboard *The Small Journey*, Owyn hadn't truly experienced a lightning strike. He was pushing so hard that other than occasional glances where he opened his eyes to see that the city was still behind him, the man rowed with eyes closed. Saltwater and rain stung them shut, and the strain and focus of rowing fought to keep them shut. Yet even through shut eyes, Owyn saw the bolt of lightning spring from the dark clouds above and cut its way towards the sea. To the end of his days, Owyn would never forget seeing the blood pumping through his eyelids as the light from the bolt burned its way past the thin skin and into his sight. It was so close that the shockwave of the thunder came at the same instant as the lightning strike. The sound only lasted a second before the world was silent around Owyn again, lost in to the vacuum it left behind. And he felt the blast. His lungs hurt as his ribs and spine seemed to vibrate with its intensity. Every one of his instincts screamed to stop. Stay still. Get to safety.

The ocean didn't care about his instinct. Deaf from the thunder, and vision foggy as his eyes fought back blindness, Owyn looked out at the clouds above across the rear of the rowboat. He was deaf, but his ears still told him that this was not correct. Gravity was pulling him backwards, not down. Then the wave crashed over him.

Darkness filled Owyn's lungs as what little sight had returned to his eyes was stripped away. The silence of the world turned into a ringing in his ears. In a moment, it was as if the world had stopped. His body screamed for air, but Owyn did not know which way was up. He floated, still in the water, looking around. There was no way to tell which way was up. His body floated still.

Something in the darkness moved.

Owyn realized that there were shades to the world around him. The sea was dark, but there was something darker in front of him, and it was moving. Fear gripped him and he pushed away from whatever it was, slowly moving in the water. There were two spots, glowing almost. Dim points of light that opened within the shadow in the bay. Eyes. Large eyes—as large as Owyn—golden in the darkness. And they were watching him. They watched him and he watched them. Fear mounting, he pushed again, away from the monster in the deep. His lungs were burning. His back hit something and, for a moment, Owyn's attention was taken from whatever sat in the water before him. When he looked back, the shadow was gone. Whatever monster or spirit hid in the dark waters in front of him had disappeared. It had been massive. Owyn could only recall wisps of the shape that he had seen, only shadows in the darkness.

His body's continued screams grabbed his attention once again and he quickly turned himself to see what he had hit. His boat was floating away in the dark waters. No, not floating. It was sinking.

His boat.

The Morning Sunshine sank deep into Turtle Bay, fading into darkness as it fell deeper into the dark waters.

But Owyn couldn't mourn.

Turning in the opposite direction that the rowboat was slowly traveling, he swam. Instinct led him. It led him to air.

The tempest above had not paused. Waves rolled over Owyn as he gasped, filling his lungs with almost as much water as air. Another wave rocked him as he turned to find himself tumbling between water and sky. There was no line separating the two. There was no way to keep himself entirely afloat. With his body working so hard, there was no more terror to be added. He could not paddle faster. He could not be more afraid. The waves created dark walls that hit him again and again. The rain pelted from above; the sea tossed him from below. His near-deaf ears rang out from the thunder, and his vision had yet to fully recover from the lightning.

Why was he out here?

What was he doing? It was the first thought that had won the fight against instinct. He thought it now as he fought to keep afloat against the chaos. But why was that his only thought? What was he doing?

A wave rolled under him as lightning struck again, this bolt farther in the distance. He didn't register the light or care focus on the majestic crackle of electricity shooting from the sky. He saw the city. Owyn was facing Kudra. He knew what he was doing now.

Owyn turned away from the city and swam.

The storm fought him; the sky and the water both fought him. His lungs screamed and his muscles burned as if they were ready to give out. Owyn fought back, though. "Why" no longer mattered.

He fought.

His hand hit stone.

At the touch of the rock to his fingertips, Owyn's body stopped. He went limp, sinking slightly lower in the water, but most of his body stayed in the air. Looking up, he saw land. He'd made it. Another wave hit him in the back, almost breaking him. He made it, yes, but he had not finished.

With muscles howling, Owyn stood. Dragging himself up, away from the water's edge, onto the horn of the bay. He did not know where on the horn he had struck, but he was here. He turned left, to the south, and walked.

Gods, his body hurt.

His walk turned into a run as lightning struck again. He did not see Kudra. He was not looking that way. He was looking forward. Owyn saw his lighthouse.

Something else flashed as the lighting struck, something behind the horn, beyond the bay. Something he could not see in the dark-

ness: color on the water. It was something that was not supposed to
be here, not for two more days.

Fear filled Owyn.

One more push. Muscles gave way, deferring their fatigue in the
rush. Water crashed against the rock, white spray reflecting the little
light of the stormy world as it struck against the walls of the lighthouse in the distance.

It had been built for this day. He had been built for this day.

Another flash and Owyn's fear surged with confirmation. *The
Small Journey* sailed towards the horn. Doman was not on time. He
was early. The color atop of the black sea was the ship returning to
port.

Why?

No—Owyn didn't have time to wonder why. The beacon now
was not only for Tulbër.

Owyn ran past his fear. He didn't stop as he reached the opening
to the lighthouse. If he stopped, he would die. Momentum was his
keeper now.

It was dark inside the building. The windows cut into the wall
gave nothing. There was no light to steal from the outside. Owyn ran
through the place by memory. Everything was where he had drawn
it. He looked at the oil basin and reached out. *Yes!* There was oil, and
the bucket was in the liquid. He needed nothing more down here.
There was oil. He could do this.

Owyn raced up the stairs that circled his lighthouse. The steps
were slick from the water coming in through the windows. His
feet battled to find purchase on the stone. Owyn slipped, catching
himself against one of the stone steps. His shin was bleeding. Pain.
But pain did not matter now. There was something to be done. He
had battled pain all his life. All do. Why hone skills only to forget
them in battle? Today was his battle.

The top of the lighthouse was open. Rain pressed in on the wings of the wind, cutting under the roof above Owyn's head. He could see again. There was little light in the sky, but Owyn didn't need light to work in *his* lighthouse. In the air once more, he felt the storm. He felt why he was here.

The basin atop the tower had a layer of liquid in it. Owyn reached out and ran his fingers through it. There must have been oil sitting from the construction of the pumps. The fire striker sat ready under the basin. Everything was as he had hoped.

He hit the striker. Sparks flew, fighting to live their brief flash of life as they floated through the tempest of the storm and the wind. None landed on the basin. Owyn struck again. He struck again and again. So few sparks made purchase on the film of liquid in the basin. None lit.

He'd done so much to build a tower holding a flame alight in the sky. He'd done everything right. And now Owyn could not get the flame.

Another throw of sparks hit the liquid and died on its surface.

Nothing.

In frustration, realizing what had happened, Owyn dipped his fingers into the basin and tasted what stuck to them. He did not have to spit it out. Water had filled the oil basin atop the lighthouse.

Owyn wanted to scream. He wanted to yell into the storm. He swallowed his anger.

Rushing to the side of the small platform. Owyn worked the pump that ran to the oil well below. It felt easy, floating in his hands as he worked the bar that operated the pump around and around. Nothing came out. Nothing.

The pump atop the tower had broken, or the sailors had never finished it. There was a pump below, but he doubted he had the energy to go down and carry himself back up the stairs. But that didn't matter. This was why he made the men leave the line with the bucket.

He turned to the rope hanging from above him. It ran down through a hole in the platform. He looked down and saw the line disappear into the dark room below. It was fine. He'd checked it at the bottom. It was there. He grabbed the rope and began pulling it up. Quickly, deliberately, he pulled. It was not quick. His arms screamed with the effort spent. He was so close to being spent. He pulled.

There was a jerk on the line. It was not much. Owyn hardly had felt it, but now the line seemed to come up with more ease. It felt better in his hands, but that only made him feel worse.

The knot had worked itself undone. The line ended and there was nothing more. There was no bucket. There was no oil.

That was it. Owyn let go of the line and fell to his knees. He was done with the fight. He had tried. He had tried so hard, and yet still he failed. Was this the gods' choosing? Was it his? He held his face in his hands. His body was so tired that tears would not come.

Owyn finally gave up.

Through the ringing in his ears, through the wind and the rain, he heard an odd splash. Too close, and too loud to be rain. Then he heard it again. Far too close.

Owyn raised his head out of his palms and saw oil spurt from the pump.

"Need a light?" said a voice behind him.

Owyn turned to see Triph atop the staircase, smirk shining through the darkness.

CHAPTER 25

O rders had never come easy to Triph, but he followed them now. As oil pumped into the bowl, both he and Owyn used strikers to get it lit.

The flame was marvelous. As the shower of sparks touched the surface of the oil, the flame seemed to spring out of nothing. Light fought against the darkness; warmth fought against the biting wind. Raindrops hit the flames and disappeared into nothingness.

"Stop pumping," said Owyn.

"Stop pumping!" repeated Triph, shouting down the stairwell as if it were an order.

Triph looked back at Owyn. The man looked so lost. He was haggard, too, but Triph looked past that and saw the worry on his face. There was a question in his heart.

"What next, little one?" sang a voice from below. Triph wasn't sure he'd ever get used to the feeling of the giant's voice reverberating through his ribcage as he spoke in his sing-song voice. Owyn must have felt it, too. The smile on his face cut through any loss or weakness that had been there the moment before.

Triph was assaulted with a hug from Owyn. He hadn't expected that. Wasn't one enough for a lifetime? It was a day full of surprises. It felt like the hug to end all hugs. What had Owyn been doing to get so strong?

"The giant's right—what's next, boss?" said Triph, squirming in the embrace. Owyn let him go and looked around. Triph couldn't help but smile. Owyn looked ten years younger than he had when Triph first ascended the stairs. That man had been broken. This Owyn had been rebuilt. The fire beside him was growing quickly, the bright orange glow bouncing about the room and onto Owyn. The man may be tired and soaked, bruised and battered, but he was where he belonged. Triph could see that. In the growing glow of the flames on the oil basin, he knew his friend was where he ought to be.

"The mirror!" said Owyn. Triph looked where his eyes fell and saw an enormous sheet of metal. "And Tulbër!" he shouted down the stairs.

"Yes?"

"The pump up here never connected down below. We'll need that."

"It will be done, little one!"

"Now the mirror," he said, turning to Triph.

"You always did make me do the hard work."

Owyn rushed around to the far side of the large piece of metal and glass. It looked heavy. Triph didn't like heavy.

"I don't know if the men completed the base, but we'll have to make it work." Owyn grabbed his end of the mirror. "Ready?"

"If I have to be," said Triph as he grabbed his end and they lifted. He was right; this was heavy. "Why couldn't the giant do this?"

"Because you're the one who came up the stairs. Quit complaining."

"He said not a kind word as we crossed the bay either!" shouted Tulbër from below. Triph looked at Owyn, speaking without words.

"Big ears," Owyn said with a smile in response.

They took the mirror across the small platform towards the now lit basin. The flames had not struggled atop the oil, but were roaring in the center of the tower. It was hot up here with all that fire, even with the storm. Owyn paused; he stood frozen for a second, his mind working on a solution.

"What now?" said Triph, pulling his friend back to the day's problems.

"There's a track around the flame. It should look like a ring."

"Got it."

"Good, place the base in there."

They lowered it. Gods above, it was hot this close to the flame. Triph felt the hair on the back of his hands singeing away into nothingness. There was a thunk and a click as both men forced their ends of the mirror onto the track.

"Okay," said Owyn. He gingerly let go of the mirror, watching it to make sure it stood without fail. Triph had already let go.

"And now?" said Triph.

"Now," said Owyn, sliding the mirror back and forth slightly on the track. "We light up the sea."

Triph stepped back and watched Owyn grasp a handle on the back of the mirror. The ring followed the entire circumference of the basin of flame, allowing Owyn to push the mirror about the basin. It didn't slide gracefully, catching here and there on the metal ring, but it slid well enough. Triph watched Owyn, saw his expression turn from focus to something more, something content. It was a face he had not seen on his friend since they were boys. Had they grown so old? So different?

Owyn wasn't looking at Triph, or at the mirror. He was looking out. Triph followed Owyn's eyes and saw what was affixing the smile on his old friend's face. He left the basin of fire and walked out to the very edge of the platform. There was a stone ring, creating a railing of sorts. Triph let his hands rest on the wet stone. He felt the wind and the rain from the storm hit him as he listened to thunder in the distance.

The light from the mirror was not a focused beam, but it had direction. And with the source at Triph's back, he felt the force of it. It was not day, but it was as close as man and giant could ever hope to gift to the world. The light from the flame danced about the bay, following the direction that Owyn pointed it in. It was like nothing that Triph could have imagined. His friend built this? Owyn, the thief, built this?

"More oil, Tulbër!" shouted Owyn.

"Aye."

The flame grew brighter as oil from below spurted from the pump. The sailors may not have finished the pump atop the tower, but the one below certainly worked.

"A ship, Triph. We're looking for a ship on the west side of the horn. They were too close before. Where are they now?"

"West?"

"That way."

Triph moved himself to where Owyn was pointing. Owyn was still sweeping the light back and forth in an arc. Then he saw it.

"Ship in the distance!"

"How close to the horn?"

"Horn?"

"The rocks, the shore. How close are they?"

"They're close, but they are turning."

"The wind?"

"Pushing them to our left, but they're using it. They're turning with it. They're getting away from the rocks! Gods, those colors make them easy to see!"

Triph felt the sigh of relief that came from Owyn. He kept moving the mirror, though. The man did not stop his work. Owyn said something under his breath with almost a smile: "Doman Sutherland caught himself in another storm." Then louder, he directed Triph, "Watch that ship. Tell me if their course changes."

"And if there are other ships?"

"Are there others?"

"No. That's why I said 'if.'"

Owyn took a second before speaking again. Triph knew the timing, knew he made his friend shake his head again. It was like old times. Triph felt good. Is this what he missed? What was freedom compared to this?

"If there are others, then they should see the light and avoid the rocks."

"This is brilliant, Owyn" said Triph, his eyes on the sea. Owyn pushed the mirror without response. "Owyn?"

"I'm waiting for the remark, bringing me down after the compliment."

"Why? This is brilliant! I can't believe *you* came up with something this smart."

"There it is."

"We're atop a tower, friend. I can't let your ego get much higher than this."

"Why are you here, Triph? Why did you come to the tower?"

"I couldn't run away after finally finding you again," said Triph.

"He grumbled about how noble the choice was the whole time I paddled us over," said the giant from below. "Little thief, try the pump up there now."

Triph looked to Owyn, who nodded toward a metal bar near the platform wall. Triph went to it and began moving the bar. There was resistance as he tried to push it around its circular path, but it moved. He pushed it and pushed it.

The fire flared. "Woah, slow down!" said Owyn. Triph stopped. "It works, Tulbër! Well done."

"There is a bucket down here. Should I tie this to something?"

Triph saw Owyn smile. That bucket had broken him. He saw the empty rope in his friend's hand. That had been the last failure, the final straw at the end of Owyn's sanity. Now he smiled about it. Now it was nothing.

"Fix it on the rope by the oil. We may need it if the pumps fail again."

"Aye, little one," said Tulbër.

Lightning struck outside. It was close, and the thunder followed with a quick crash. It shook the walls of the tower. Looking out now, Triph realized just how high in the air they were. If this thing came tumbling down...He shook his head and tried not to think of it. His eyes hit the sea again. The storm had not slowed. The surrounding tempest still raged. Rain and wind pushed against his body as he stood at the edge of the platform, looking out at the world below.

For a moment, and nothing more, he thought that the zealots may have been right in their worry. There was something about looking down so far that made a man feel like a god. They'd been wrong, though. The gods could never deal with getting hit by a storm up here like this.

Then Triph saw the ship.

"Owyn! Owyn, come here!"

His old friend rushed to his side. They looked out in silence before Owyn spoke, words almost too quiet to hear above the wind. "What happened?"

"I don't know. It was breaking as I looked out."

A mast of *The Small Journey* was towing behind the ship as it moved against the waves. The structure, as tall as the fully grown tree it once was, had completely separated itself from the ship and now floated behind the vessel, still attached to it by a mess of ropes.

"It's pulling them backwards," said Triph. The ship indeed was being dragged closer to the rocks. It sailed with the wind at its back, storm jib full, pushing it away from the shore, but the waves and the mast in the water slowed it too much. It was getting too close.

"They'll cut it. They can still get away."

As Owyn spoke, the ship did just that. It was as if someone kicked a sleeping horse: the ship leapt forward, free of the mast that anchored it and propelled by a wave underneath it. Everything was correct for the ship to fly forward, to leave shore, to get away.

"Osnir above," said Triph under his breath. He was not a religious man. He never spoke the gods' names.

"Is that a man?" Owyn asked, pointing towards a dot flailing in the waves near the broken mast.

"He must have fallen over in the jump when they cut the ropes," said Triph.

Just then, another dot flew from the ship, this one diving into the darkness, charging after the first that fell.

"Another!" screamed Triph.

"A swimmer," said Owyn. He had taken a step back from the edge, turning to go down the stairs, but stopped and turned back towards the sea.

"They won't be able to stop," he said.

"What?"

"The ship, they can't stop. They can't save him."

"The swimmer jumped after the man for nothing?"

"You came here in a boat?"

Triph wasn't following his friend. He couldn't keep up with what was happening. He wasn't a sailor. He had no knowledge of storms and swimming and men overboard. But he nodded at his friend's question.

"Good," said Owyn. He turned and left the platform and rushed down the stairs.

Triph followed, trying not to slip on the wet stone stairs. Owyn had not slowed.

"Little one, what are you doing?" said Tulbër as Owyn reached the bottom.

"The ship cannot save the men overboard, but I might be able to."

"That's insanity. The storm will kill you!" said Triph, reaching the base of the lighthouse.

"They'll die out there. I've got to go."

"No," said Tulbër.

"I've got to go!" insisted Owyn. "You two stay and man the light."

Tulbër shook his head and turned his lavender eyes to Triph. "Little thief, man the light," the giant said as he set his hand on Owyn's shoulder. "You don't go. We go."

CHAPTER 26

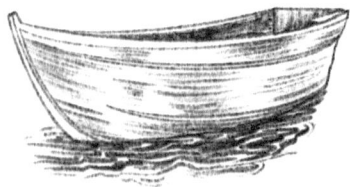

T he rowboat hit a wave head on. Water crashed over the bow, filling the small vessel with water. It wasn't the *Morning Sunshine*, but it would do.

"My feet are wet, little one," said Tulbër. The giant was rowing, facing the rear of the boat.

"Working on it," said Owyn. They had to shout over the crashing of the waves and the howling of the wind. Owyn stood at the prow, as the wave had broken against the narrow point of the vessel, it split to either side of him, keeping him relatively dry. At Tulbër's call, though, he had turned to bail water out of the rowboat with a small bucket that had been in there. He was so tired his muscles couldn't even bear to scream at him anymore. There was nothing left in them but a whimper. They worked because they had to. Because he had to. Owyn was glad that the giant was here to row.

"You work better than your old friend," said the giant.

"He never enjoyed doing anything that took real physical effort."

"He did not avoid fighting to save me."

"He fought?"

They hit another wave. Owyn was leaning down to bail out water as a wave struck him in the back, throwing him face first into the bottom of the boat.

"Are you ok, little one?"

"Doing fine. Keep rowing." Owyn stood and turned to see where they headed. "Starboard, starboard!" he shouted. Tulbër was not a sailor, but he turned the boat just in time to hit head on the oncoming wave that Owyn had seen. Water split in front of them, white foam at the edges of black liquid buffeted the pair in their little boat.

"Water again."

"I know, I know. Keep us straight."

"This can be done."

Owyn continued to bail the liquid, watching their path when he could. The waves and the wind and the rain would not stop. The cold and the rain soothed his aches, or at least hid them. He couldn't think of the tiredness, the weakness. He focused on the water in the boat and the waves ahead of them. Owyn would never have been able to do this on his own. He looked ahead as they sliced through another wave. This one was smaller. The boat handled it gloriously. A light moved about in the sky above them.

His light.

Triph was doing well. Owyn and Tulbër could see the horn of the bay. Other ships would be able to as well. It actually worked. Owyn couldn't feel the tears at the edge of his eyes through the rain.

"Much further?" asked Tulbër.

"I don't know," said Owyn. It was true. Even with the light from Triph, he was unsure how much further to the men who had gone overboard. He looked out beyond the waves and saw *The Small Journey* sailing away from the shore. It would be safe. He'd helped them. Owyn thought of Tulbër and Triph. They'd helped the ship, all three of them. He didn't do that alone.

He couldn't have done it alone.

He didn't have to.

Now they would save the pair who fell overboard.

"Can you make it? How are you doing?"

"Donar built me for this, little one. Don't worry about me. Keep the water off my feet." Owyn heard the smile on the giant's face. They hit another wave, and he continued bailing out the boat. Each lift of the bucket, full of water, hurt. Each lift was slower. Harder.

Owyn heard something on the wind. It wasn't the howling of the air or the crashing of the waves or the pelting of the raindrops.

"Tulbër?"

"She's close!" said the giant.

"She?"

Tulbër straightened his back, sitting up taller than Owyn was standing. "We are coming!" he shouted. His voice shook Owyn. It felt as if thunder had come from their boat. "Call again if you can!"

Owyn heard the scream clearly this time. Two voices, a man and a woman shouted in the darkness. "There!" he said, pointing, but Tulbër was already turning the boat toward the calls.

The light from Triph was no longer moving. It stopped at their boat, dimly lighting the world around Owyn and Tulbër. He saw the pair.

The woman in the water was struggling. Owyn saw her eyes. Those eyes held onto terror as they bounced between him and the boat and the man next to her.

Ost.

Just as Owyn saw his friend, recognized the sailor he had worked with, a wave crashed over the pair and the sea swallowed him.

"Rope Tulbër, rope!"

Tulbër looked at the rope affixed to the yoke he sat on. "Secure."

"Good, grab her!" said Owyn. He had stood, tying the other end around his waist. Tulbër rowed them forward. Closer. Closer, but not there yet. His legs were weak as he stood. His fingers, cold and weak, fumbled with the rope at his waist. Tired beyond tired. The light from the tower shone down on the woman in the water, swimming, but barely just. He counted in his head. Ost wasn't up yet. Seconds felt like hours. Row faster, he thought, but he couldn't say it. He could not put this on Tulbër. He couldn't—

Owyn saw an arm reach up out of the water ahead of them. No head followed. He didn't wait to see more. "You've got her?" he said.

"Aye!" shouted the giant as he leaned to the side, rocking the boat, but not too far. If a wave came now, it would take them all. The giant had the woman in his arm. "Grab a hold of me." Tulbër's voice sang even amidst the storm.

Owyn was too tired to stand. He was too tired to check the rope at his waist. His exhaustion so great he could do nothing but trust that Tulbër had her. Owyn was so tired. He felt dead. He dove into the stormy waters.

Darkness engulfed him as it had before. Fear tried to take him. But not fear for himself.

Owyn powered through the fear, pushing his body through the water. Air didn't matter. The sea didn't matter. This mattered. Without air, without breath or wind or weight, his veins felt something. He was warm in the cold water. His blood still ran, still coursed through his body. He was not dead yet. He would not die this day. Ost would not die either. Owyn's heart pumped harder. Life coursed through his veins. Purpose and reason. He was here, in the water, in the bay by his lighthouse, and, by his choice. He was here to save someone. He could save someone. He could save a life.

The light from his lighthouse didn't seem to spread far into the water below. Owyn's world was varying shades of darkness and his eyes stung from looking through the saltwater. His lungs protested the treatment. Owyn ignored them. He thought of how Ost's lungs would be. Where was he? He saw nothing. He couldn't see anything. Owyn pushed and swam deeper. His lungs yelled again, muscles and joints joining the protest. Ost had said that swimming was a great workout, since it wouldn't hurt the body. Owyn was thankful for that man's teaching now, but he was less thankful for the lie. His body hurt like hell and was letting him know that.

His arm struck something.

Instinct made his hand recoil. Something unknown in the water. He thought of the shadow. Of the great eyes he had seen in the deep of the bay. Everything his brain had been designed to do, to stay safe, said to get away. He reached out beyond that, beyond instinct, grasping for whatever he had touched. It was an arm—at least it felt like an arm. Owyn pulled it closer and through the darkness saw Ost floating, still, beneath the tempest above. He wasn't moving. His eyes were closed.

Owyn kicked and began fighting for the surface. It seemed so easy to find now, not like the struggle when he had tumbled in only hours ago. Before the lighthouse was lit. A lifetime ago. He reached the surface and filled his lungs as the wind and the rain returned.

"Tulbër, he's not breathing!" he shouted to the sky. Immediately, he began getting pulled backwards by the rope around his waist.

He held the sailor tight and kicked in the direction of the rowboat. Tulbër had them both aboard with one sweep of his arm. Owyn set Ost down on the yoke where Tulbër had been sitting. The bottom of the vessel was still filled with water. Raindrops landed on all of them and the wind would not slow about them.

"He's not breathing," said Owyn.

"What do we do?" said Tulbër.

"Something. We've got to do something." Owyn grabbed the man's shoulders and started shaking him. "Wake up!"

"Little one."

"Wake up, please!"

"Little one, what if he's—"

"Wake up!" he pleaded. Owyn knew there were fresh tears on his face mixing with the rain. "Wake up!" He shook him again, but a shove moved him.

"Get out of the way," said a small, strong voice.

The woman who had fallen overboard. Owyn barely had a moment to see her. Recognition at the edge of his memory. Did he know her? His thought faded as she took a deep breath, gulping the storm's air before leaning down and putting her lips to the sailor's.

He thought he could see it, the air move from the woman to the sailor. There was something in the man's shoulders, a movement perhaps. It was not great, but it was something. The women leaned back into the sky, inhaling another breath and passing it once more to the sailor. He shifted now, and she did it again.

"Wake up!" she said, shaking the man and inhaling once more.

He coughed before she could give him the next breath.

"Ost?" said Owyn. His voice was quiet.

He coughed again, water spewing from his mouth.

"You need to sit up," said the woman, helping Ost to do so. "Sit up; breathe; it will be ok." Ost kept coughing until only air passed his lips, the water in his lungs evacuated.

"You did it," said Owyn. Stunned. "You saved him."

"Are you ok?" said the woman. She was holding Ost close. She was shivering as she held him but looked to have no regard for herself. Ost nodded slowly. A mix of awe and gratitude filled his eyes.

Lightning struck in the distance, thunder booming in quickly behind it.

"Tulbër, we've got to get out of this storm," said Owyn.

The giant nodded and helped Owyn move the pair to another yoke. They sat down without a word, holding each other close.

"Rope?" said Tulbër as he sat with oars in hand. Owyn nodded and affixed a length of rope about the pair at their waists.

"We're not losing you again," he said. The woman looked at him and nodded. Did she look familiar? Ost held his eyes on her.

"Thank you," she said before Owyn could answer the thought in his head. Her voice was hoarse.

Owyn nodded. He couldn't respond. He couldn't speak. The tears came again, and he didn't care if they were lost in the rain. They mattered to him. He felt them. He wouldn't lose them in the storm.

Tulbër rowed, and Owyn stood again to do his part. The storm had not let up. Rain and darkness surrounded them on water, whipped into waves by the wind. Owyn called directions and Tulbër brought the boat about as ordered. They hit wave after wave. Owyn pointed them towards the light in the distance. His tower. A beacon now.

"Little one," said Tulbër, his voice loud above the storm.

"Starboard!" shouted Owyn.

Tulbër followed and turned them into the wave. "Little one, the ship returns!"

Owyn turned around and saw *The Small Journey* in the distance. He could almost see the colors painted on the boards in the dim light. It was battling wind and wave and...coming towards the shore?

"What are they doing?" shouted Owyn.

"I don't know. It does not look safe."

The giant was right. The ship was being pulled in so many directions, waves sweeping it along as walls of water hit it broadside and pushed the ship dangerously close to capsizing. The storm jib, billowed out in the wind, pulled it forward, but it looked like there was something else—something hanging from the rear—slowing them.

"What are they doing?" shouted Owyn again. He knew the words were meaningless. No answer would come.

"For me," said the woman at his side. Owyn almost didn't hear her say the words.

"What did you say?" he leaned in close.

"They're looking for me," she said.

Doman wouldn't let someone overboard without a search. Owyn would have smiled if the danger of it all didn't weigh on him. The ship took another wave broadside and the decking dipped towards the water. Doman would risk crew and ship for two people.

"Tulbër, turn us around."

"What?"

"Towards the ship—turn us around. Watch for waves, but we've got to get towards them before they kill themselves."

Tulbër didn't question twice. He stood slightly, surveying the waters about them before hitting a wave head on and turning the boat about in its wake.

"My feet are wet, little one."

"Keep us headed towards that ship and I'll dry them, big guy."

A giant's laughter rang out over the boat. It seemed to sing with the storm around them.

Owyn bailed. Tulbër rowed. The storm raged.

The ship took another hit, but it fought. It stayed the course. Doman would not let that vessel sink; he would fight till his last. But his last may be coming. The wind seemed to shift at Owyn's back. He would have ignored it until he saw the effect it had on the ship in front of them. It was being torn. The sea and the storm had become a monster working to shred the vessel before them. All this to save two overboard sailors. Owyn loved Doman Sutherland, and he resolved to tell the man so the next time he saw him.

Something shimmered. A distraction of the surrounding light. Owyn turned and saw that the light in the tower was shifting back and forth over them. It wouldn't reach great distances, but he could see the almost flicker to it. Owyn's gaze turned back to the ship. They were getting close now. Owyn could see movement, almost that of men, on the rocking top decks. He looked back to the lighthouse, light flickering as it waved over him.

"Triph, you dog," he said, then turned to the woman. "Can you stand?" she nodded. Owyn began waving his arms and shouting. Without question, she joined. Ost remained on the yoke. He had tried to stand with them but the woman gently pressed him back down to lie and rest. "Tulbër?"

"Busy rowing," said the giant, but he joined in the shouting. His voice carried more than the combined efforts of the other two, so Owyn and the woman let their voices fall, but they still waved.

It seemed to last forever, waiting to be seen. Then it changed in an instant. The ship turned sharper than Owyn thought possible. Whatever drogue was at the rear of the vessel had been cut, and the ship turned away from the dangerously close shoreline and pushed out towards the open water. The ship had seen them. Doman had seen them. They'd be safe.

"Tulbër, take us to shore!" shouted Owyn as he kneeled down, getting lower to the boat. The woman sat down once more. Not just a woman. Recognition hit Owyn. He saw the smallest of smiles touch the corner of the girl's mouth as she noticed his realization.

"Are you—" Owyn started.

"Agatha," said the woman. It wasn't a complete answer, but they both knew it sufficed. Owyn opened his mouth to complete the next question. The one he knew the answer to. The one that filled him with joy and with terror. Tulbër's singing cry took him out of his own mind before he could speak.

"Aye there, Captain little one. Please keep my feet dry!"

CHAPTER 27

It would have felt so much better if the sun shined through the next morning, but Owyn welcomed the overcast sky just the same. He sat on the rocky shore of his island, at the base of his lighthouse, looking out at the bay he had crossed last night.

There was a cool breeze, and it made little rippling waves dance across the water of the bay. But there was no rain. Owyn was happy.

He wasn't sure why he awoke so early. His body screamed at him when he had first stood, but looking out on the waters, out towards the city across the bay, he felt good. He'd missed these mornings. Letting out a sigh, he looked at the city. He would have to miss them again.

He wasn't hiding anymore.

Triph had been faster than Owyn. The instant that Tulbër and he had brought Ost and Agatha ashore, he'd raced down from the lighthouse to help them. Through the rain and the water, he'd recognized her. Agatha was not just some passenger aboard *The Small Journey*.

"You're the princess!" he'd exclaimed.

She nodded, her voice still hoarse from the saltwater and yelling.

Owyn saw it. The girl in the chair, the one who had supported him when her father was on the fence. The princess of an empire. "What were you doing on *The Small Journey*?"

"I've been joining their adventures when able to convince my father it will be safe." Her face lit up despite the hoarseness in her voice. "I have been learning to sail." She'd shivered. The rain still fell heavy about them.

"What are you waiting for? Take her to the lighthouse, little thief," said Tulbër. "A princess should not be out in this storm." He smiled at her, and she smiled back at the giant. Then she turned to Owyn. The look in her eyes said so much. Words might not have been able to express the thoughts. She knew. Her thoughts followed his. She'd remembered him even if he had not recognized her face. She knew what would happen and her eyes showed the sorrow mixed with thanks that only a look can give. She turned to Ost. The sailor stood, barely, on his own.

"Are you well?" she asked. The man nodded and she took his arm as they followed Triph up to the lighthouse. Owyn and Tulbër brought the rowboat ashore before heading towards the shelter themselves.

They slept gloriously on the stone floors of the lighthouse, exhaustion taking all of them to the rest that those who have not worked to their breaking point will never know. They faded into the darkness of sleep as the storm continued around them.

Owyn had awoken first. He looked at his friends. Tulbër, the giant, the first person to help him, to offer aid without want on his own end; his best friend. Ost, the quiet sailor that offered to help a man build a lighthouse to avoid shore leave and a woman. Apparently, to avoid a princess, who now slept in his arms on the stone floor. And Triph, his lost friend; old, left behind, but still here; still with him. They all slept now, here, in his lighthouse. His tower. He may not have built it alone, but it was still his. It was theirs.

Owyn was happy. His friends were safe. For now.

His thoughts turned to the future as he looked at the little rippling waves of the gray water.

He was a wanted man. Owyn had to go back to the city. He'd lit the beacon to bring the law here, but he couldn't wait here anymore. He had to bring Agatha home, and there was no quiet way to deliver a princess. Owyn didn't want there to be. She was safe and the people should know; her father should know.

He was tired of hiding, anyway.

The clouds held a tinge of color as the sun rose behind them. It was not the vibrant sunrise in the morning that Owyn had wanted so much to see, but still, it was a good morning. He knew it was his last morning of freedom. He exhaled the chilly morning air, now warmed from his body.

His friends weren't safe with him around. The Sheriff would not stop and the pious in their shadnel wouldn't stop either. They would hunt him. They would tear through his friends to get to him. The Sheriff would not cease without his revenge.

Today was Owyn's last day on his island.

He smiled. He had gotten to light the tower before he gave it up. That was something wasn't it?

And he would give it up.

He built the thing to be alone. But he'd give it up for his friends.

Owyn sat in silence. He smiled and shook his head at the thought of Triph and Tulbër, rowing themselves across the storming bay just to help him. Triph, whom he'd avoided for so long, and Tulbër, who took him in when he shouldn't have. Both were asleep as he sat looking out towards a rising sun on a cloudy day. This felt right.

A sound came from behind him, and Owyn turned to see Princess Agatha walking down the shore towards him.

"Princess?" he said.

"'Good morning' is traditional, I believe," she said. Her voice was still quiet, but it already sounded better than it had in the storm.

"I'm sorry," he said. "Good morning."

"Don't be," she said, sitting down next to him and looking out at the city. "You're just like my father: so jumpy at a joke."

"I don't think I could be compared to the King."

"It would surprise you in how many ways everyone can be."

Owyn turned from her and looked out at the sky she gazed at. The city was across the bay. It provided its own sort of contrast against the white-gray clouds in the sky. The color of the sunrise behind the clouds was fading.

"You can still hide if you like," said Agatha, breaking the silence.

"I'm tired of hiding."

"And you would let that Sheriff take you for whatever he wishes to do in that backwater town?"

"I'd face the consequences of my actions."

A gap in the clouds above Kudra let some of the sunlight through. It made the water of the bay sparkle as the small waves bounced the light around the surface of the bay. It was too late to see the colors of the sunrise, though. The morning had arrived.

"I'll wake the others," said Owyn, standing. "We'll get you home soon, Princess."

"For you, 'Agatha' is formal enough," she said with a smile before turning back to face the water.

"Agatha." Owyn nodded. He turned and walked up towards the lighthouse. Towards his lighthouse.

***

Tulbër, Ost, and Triph woke quickly. The giant had already been awake when Owyn walked into the tower. He had looked at Owyn with a nod, lavender eyes speaking the truth that words could not. He knew what Owyn would do because Tulbër knew Owyn. The man smiled. Triph was still asleep, snoring slightly, but he woke with a touch on the shoulder. Agatha came in and woke Ost. Surprise and joy sparked on his face immediately at the sight of her. She said something quietly to the sailor, but Owyn didn't hear it.

"I'm not going," said Triph, almost before his eyes had even opened.

"Of course not," said Owyn. "We are. All of us. But I'm going in first."

"I won't. They'll take me in. I can't go back to that Sheriff."

"Triph, you can't keep running. We can't keep running like this."

"I can and I will."

"He won't take you if I give myself up," said Owyn and Triph stopped his argument. He saw the look in his old partner's eyes. He knew what Tulbër had already seen. He saw the truth in Owyn's eyes. The decision.

"You can fight or you can walk, little thief, but you're coming," said Tulbër.

"Fine," said Triph. His face was sad, though.

"Good," said Owyn as he slapped Triph on the shoulder. "Now help us with the boat."

Owyn, Triph, Tulbër, Ost, and Agatha loaded the boat and prepared it for the short voyage across the bay.

"You don't have to come," said Owyn. He was looking at Tulbër.
He saw the bruises and wounds from his capture now that sunlight
shined on his friend. "They'll connect you to my crimes and—"

The giant put a hand on his shoulder. "Little one, I'm coming."

"Triph and I will row then. You'll be our guest." Triph looked at
him with a sharp face, but did not protest otherwise. "One more row
across the bay would do me good."

They finished loading into the rowboat. It felt tighter with four
humans and a giant, but it was not overwhelming. Tulbër pushed
them off, and Owyn and Triph began to row together.

The boat was steady and the ride was smooth. Despite the small
ripples and waves that come with the morning, the boat slid across
the water like glass. Triph was not a confident rower, but following
Owyn's lead, he helped keep the boat in line. He and Owyn were
seated looking backwards. Owyn admired his lighthouse.

It had worked.

A part of him still could not believe that his idea had worked. It
saved a ship. It saved a princess! The red roof capped the platform
with the basin and mirror, the stone walls built by so many hands
stretched down to the rock foundation that he had built. It was his.
The lighthouse was more than that, though; it was something to let
go of. It had been his, and that would be enough. Owyn rowed with
a sad smile in his heart.

The rowboat was filled with friends now. That was good. He'd
been wrong about many things in his life. Maybe trying to build the
lighthouse alone was one of them.

"Well, this will be interesting," said Agatha. Owyn's eyes left the
lighthouse behind him and he looked around the bay. *The Small
Journey* had anchored in the bay and must have sent some sailors

ashore. Owyn could see their colors on the docks. He frowned. The posse was already there with the Sheriff at its head.

"How'd he find us so quickly?" said Triph.

"Little thief, we lit up the sky last night," said Tulbër with a laugh.

Owyn remembered the light. His light. The shining beacon he had built in the sky above the bay. They had built it. They had lit the sky aglow during a storm. He smiled.

"And here comes dad."

As if on cue, the King himself could be seen walking down towards the already crowded docks. Guards, and even a few advisors, surrounded him of course, but still, the King was walking.

"You've caused quite the stir, little one."

"We have," said Triph.

"Of course, we cannot forget the little thief."

"What do we do?" said Triph.

"Same thing I said I'd come here to do. I'm done running, Triph."

The man said nothing, but he did continue rowing them towards the awaiting masses.

They heard shouts and jeers as they approached, but nothing directed towards the rowboat. No, the sailors under Sutherland and the men of the posse were slinging insults towards each other. Then they all saw the King, and the shouts ceased.

Owyn and the boat received a silent welcome as the vessel touched the dock. What the reception lacked in volume it made up for in the sheer number of eyes pointed in their direction.

The King broke the silence. "Agatha?"

He ran forward on the docks, the guards closest to him scrambling to keep up. "Agatha!" He reached the boat and helped his daughter out, almost hoisting her up by one arm into a hug. Ost reluctantly let her go, following her towards the King, but stopping and standing near Owyn, Tulbër, and Triph.

The Sheriff took his chance, stepping forward. "Criminals of the realm, you are under arrest." His men were close behind, surrounding Owyn and Triph. "By my order, these men will be tried and hanged," he said as the posse started pulling at Owyn and Triph.

"And by order of the King, you shall unhand them both."

The Sheriff looked at the King. Everyone else's eyes bounced between the two men. The King wasn't a large man. He was imposing by his position and his men. The Sheriff was imposing. The Sheriff said nothing. His men didn't move.

"I said, by order of the King, you shall unhand these men." The King gestured and his guards stepped closer to the posse.

The men of the posse let Owyn and Triph go. They both stepped forward, away from the posse, and closer to Tulbër and the boat. "I grant them both full pardons for their crimes committed within my realm. I forget your town name, but I assure you, it is within my realm. I have heard their crime. A death during a robbery. Horrible. But to risk everything to save another life—" the King looked at Agatha "to save my daughter... I will not have them hanged!" The King smiled with confidence, but it had no effect in calming the air between him and the Sheriff. Tension remained, even in Owyn's spine. A tension that seemed to fill the guards and the posse too.

The Sheriff had yet to speak. He looked ready to burst.

The King had finished, though, and he turned towards a guard. "Raph, please escort the Sheriff and his Posse Comitatus out of the city of Kudra. The rest of you, disperse and return to your lives and work. There is no more violence for you here."

The Sheriff finally burst. "You can't do that! This man killed the daughter of a mayor. This man murdered my niece!" The anger was still there, still with him, the crowd seemed to ignore the King for a moment under the Sheriff's gravitas.

Owyn stepped towards the man. Towards the violent source of law that had chased him across an empire. Chased the thief turned murderer. Chased the accidental killer of his niece.

"I'm sorry," said Owyn. "I am sorry for your loss. For what pain I caused."

The King's men's hands tightened on their weapons as the Sheriff stepped forward. His bald head bright in the sun. The smile that was growing on his face held no light though. The world around the pair tensed, but the Sheriff raised his hands. They were empty. No weapons. Nothing. The Sheriff's face softened. Was there sadness there? He stepped towards Owyn and held out one of the empty hands.

"Thank you," he said. There was a weight to the words. He spoke them quietly, but they still were felt by the crowd, rapt in attention as they watched. The man's whole demeanor had changed in an instant. Down from the fiery anger and into something different. Sadder? Weaker? "For your apology, thank you. I apologize as well. According to this King, I have lost, and I can concede to his word."

The shift in mood scared Owyn. He wanted to hesitate. But he couldn't—not in good faith. This man was offering him a hand, offering him forgiveness. He stepped forward, arm out, reaching for the man's hand, when, without warning, Tulbër jumped between them and decked the bald man. His stone-colored fist sounded like rock as it cracked against the skull of the Sheriff. The lawman dropped to the stone floor of the dock in an instant.

"What was that?" shouted Owyn. He stepped back and looked at his friend. The shock on his face matched that of the crowd.

Tulbër pointed to the soldiers closest to the pair. "Please check his sleeves."

Coming from their surprised stupor, one of the men leaned down to the unconscious Sheriff and pulled back the sleeve of the arm that had been outstretched towards Owyn. In a sheath against the man's wrist was a blade, ready to be used. In that last moment, the Sheriff would have gotten his justice, with or without the King's approval.

Owyn looked at his friend, shocked and happy. He saw Tulbër smile and mouth the words: "Big ears."

There was another cry and the man and the giant looked to see Triph looming over one of the posse, Wendel, holding his face and whining on the ground. Triph smiled at the hurt man, then looked back at his friends and the crowd. He saw the shock on their faces. "He had one, too!"

His Majesty, Rigney the Second, King of Kudra, Emperor of Breiar, turned to his men. "Guards, take this Sheriff to the palace jail to rest off his wounds. Let's see if we can demonstrate how justice is processed in my Empire."

Guards approached the posse, spears in hand but not brandished. There wasn't a sword drawn yet, but Owyn felt the tension of the men: gathered by a Sheriff for a goal, led by charisma now fallen on the ground. It felt as the air had on the sea moments before lightning struck. Everyone felt it. The crowd was ready. Then the first man's head dropped within the mob, and the mob followed. The guards hefted up the passed-out body of the Sheriff and, without purpose anymore, the posse began to fade into the crowd.

Triph jumped for joy, unable to contain his excitement. The crowd that remained let out their held breath. The sailors cheered. Owyn ignored that for the moment, though. He saw Agatha whispering something to her father. The King turned and spoke again. "Your lighthouse is unfinished?" The surrounding crowd silenced and turned at his words.

Owyn nodded. "Yes."

"This despite the beacon we saw last night through the storm?"

"My friends helped me get it working despite its state, sire, but the tower is not yet complete."

"Would you finish it?"

Owyn didn't have to say yes. The King saw his face. "Then you shall receive funding to do so. You've demonstrated the success of your work beyond any reasonable ask. I would have that lighthouse entirely operational as a beacon of safety to our merchants. Cost will not impede you."

"Truly, sire?"

"You shall have that." The King took a step closer to Owyn. Owyn wasn't sure if he should back away. The King kneeled down and took Owyn's hand. "You shall also forever have my greatest thanks." He kissed Owyn's hand. "You saved my daughter, the light of my life. You will forever have the grace of this King."

Rigney the Second stood, no longer simply a king, but a father. A man. Owyn could not speak. He bowed and the King turned to leave. Because of that, he did not notice Agatha quickly approach. He felt the kiss on his cheek, heard the "thanks," and felt happy. Truly happy. But he realized that this wasn't a new feeling. He looked up and as he watched the King's procession leaving the docks, he knew he'd felt this happiness before. It had been with Tulbër and Ost, with Doman, even with Triph. Owyn turned out to look upon the bay. The sun had cut through a break in the clouds and was shining on the water. Owyn would have to cross that bay again today. There was work ahead. He felt good at the prospect.

EPILOGUE

O wyn hung from the side of the lighthouse. He thought the stone walls could do with some color. Tulbër had helped him find the paint. They still visited weekly, but Owyn was happy here. He was content to be working on the lighthouse. It was practically complete, though it'd never truly be done. There was always something that needed work.

The sun shone on Owyn's back as he worked. They'd made it through the rainy season and were back into spring. Trade would increase now, many more ships going to and from Kudra, traveling around the horn. The lighthouse would help on still nights and the stormy.

"Ho!" came a call from behind him.

Owyn turned to see a rowboat approaching, a few men rowing and one, with a rather ostentatious hat, standing at the prow.

Owyn shouted in response, then turned back towards the wall. He could finish painting it later, and here was as good a place to stop as any. He started up the rope that he had tied for himself.

It took him just long enough to get back out of the tower for the boat to arrive and Captain Doman Sutherland, with a few of his men, to be waiting for Owyn's appearance.

Owyn waved as he exited the lighthouse and saw them.

"This is amazing!" said Ost, stepping in front of the Captain towards the lighthouse. He stopped himself though and looked back towards Doman. Owyn followed his gaze.

"I do hate asking to pull you away," started the Captain with a wink. "But Ost here has had it with civilization, whatever that means when one is aboard a ship, and needs a break. He offered to man the lighthouse while you join my crew in his stead."

"You want me to sail with you again?"

"I can think of no other to take the place of a marvelous sailor such as Ost." Doman's smile was genuine and bright. "He taught you to swim, didn't he?"

Owyn thought for a moment. He'd been alone for some time, living and working in the lighthouse. Visits to Tulbër and the city were good, but he had spent time alone in the lighthouse like he had wanted when he designed it. Had he spent enough time alone? He looked down at Doman's smiling face. They needed help.

"Will you visit Tulbër?" he asked Ost.

"With certainty," said Ost. "Bring him back some real stories while you're gone."

"He'd be mad at if I didn't. Keep him satisfied with your tales while I'm away."

Ost smiled and looked up at the lighthouse. "I don't think I've got anything that compares."

Owyn hugged the man. "You know that isn't true." He let his friend go and turned back to Doman. The Captain looked excited, giddy even, like a child in his almost regal jacket.

"Yes," said Owyn. "Of course I'll join you."

He would be happy on a small journey.

The End

THANK YOU

T hank you for reading *A Light Home*. I appreciate each and every reader more than you can imagine.

Please consider rating and reviewing the book on any of your favorite book discussion sites. Publishing is a competitive game, and gaining traction and attention with readers is an immeasurable challenge. If you enjoyed this book—or any book—leaving reviews is one of the best ways you can support authors.

Regardless of whether you choose to leave a review or not, thank you again for taking the time to read *A Light Home*! Owyn, Tulbër, and I appreciate you!

ACKNOWLEDGEMENTS

W hat can I say here that even comes close to my feelings? There are so many people who affected my life to help get this book created and out in the world.

My friends: Andrew, Luke, Cody, Sam, Jake, Derek, Jason, Brad, Jen, Aaron, Alex, Calla, Sarah, Soren, and Sean, who inspired more than a few aspects of my characters. Many of them read advanced copies of this book and their feedback helped immensely.

Carson Lowmiller, the amazing artist who trusted a blind email and a blurb from an unknown artist. He worked with me over *checks notes* eighty-eight emails (!) to get the cover painting just right. I think it's the perfect expression of Owyn and Tulbër and the world they inhabit.

Ryley Wiering, a graphic artist without compare. She took Carson's art and elevated it into a cover better than my wildest dreams.

If this book sells anything, it is entirely to Carson and Ryley's credit. If it doesn't, I'll happily take the blame.

Madi, for the wonderful art beginning each chapter.

My sister, who helped connect me to my proofreader, helped make my author's website, and encouraged me throughout this whole process.

My mother, who let me run wild as a kid and live the adventures I now wish to write.

Woody and Dustin, my editors. I may not have loved every one of your comments, but each and every note and piece of advice made this book better and made me a better writer.

My loving wife, Grace, always supporting me and pushing me. Her support and love is something I wish all of my characters could feel. If everyone felt one-tenth of the love I do, the world would be as wonderful as it is in Tulbër's eyes.

Each of you owns a part of this book. Thank you.

Finally, a last thank you is owed to you, the reader. Without you, this book is merely scribbles on paper. With you, it's a world. It's characters. It's everything I wished it could be. Thank you so much for reading my work.

THE HIDEAWAY

K eep reading for a sneak peek at the next novel set in the world of *A Light Home*!

CHAPTER 1

T he wind blew past Husted and he watched it fill the colorful, dyed sails that flew beneath him. His eyes followed the invisible lines, moving forward, to the sea beyond.

This was freedom.

This was life.

"Land ahead!" he shouted. There was only the thinnest sliver of shore in the distance, but he saw it.

"Ost!" called up a man from below. The ship didn't have officers. It wasn't a military, but there was an informal order to things. "Don't work the watch while you're on break!"

"Sorry, Amel," said Husted back to the man. Amel shook his head but carried on the news to the Captain anyway. There was land ahead.

Ost—Husted to only his mother and himself—looked back out at the sinuous line that separated the sea and the sky on the horizon. It was ground. The ship was a fast one; it was the best ship in the world, thought Ost. It would reach that land soon. The small craft wasn't designed to leave the sight of shore, but that did not stop Captain Doman Sutherland from taking *The Small Journey* away from land and out towards what lay beyond the blue horizon.

He was not Husted here. He was Ost. Half name he chose, half nickname given to him. It was simply him. Husted was his mother's name for him. Not his name here. Not since he left his town and found a home.

He watched the world glide by for a while. He was on break, and the topmast was the best place for that. Alone with the world about him, and the ship beneath his feet, Ost smiled.

The land was growing faster now. It filled the horizon and was getting larger and longer. There would be shore leave at port. Ost would stay here though. There's always work to be done on the ship. Captain Sutherland must allow that. Ost started climbing down, limber body flowing down the ropes with more experience than strength, though muscles beneath his loose shirt told of the strength he'd earned at sea. There was no timekeeping atop the small platform at top mast, but his break must almost be over. Whether it was or not didn't matter if they approached port. All hands would be needed and Ost never missed helping out with the work for the day.

"Don't you think about getting to work, son," said Amel. The stout man was waiting for Ost at the base of the mast. "Your break lasts through port; use it."

Ost looked up at the man. Old, but not much older than the rest on the ship, he was as solid as the timber which built the ship—and as unyielding. "Yes sir," he said.

"If you have an issue, take it up with the captain," Amel smiled. Ost's order to relax had come from Captain Sutherland. Amel slapped the younger man on the shoulder. "Relax, son! Go dice and booze below with Harol. Port will come soon and leave will be good."

Ost nodded. There was no use fighting with Amel. The old man's heart was in the right place. Ost simply nodded and put a knuckle to his forehead.

"Off with you!" said Amel with a smile and Ost left.

He didn't know where to go. There wasn't anything to do that wasn't work. The booze sounded ok, but dicing with Harol had run its course months ago. The man was a good friend and great sailor, but gambling nothing for nothing was less appealing than doing nothing. He looked out at the foredeck and sighed. Beyond the ship was the sea and the sky and the land. The whole world in an image, with his ship at the center.

The Captain was up there, on the foredeck. He was impossible to miss, even on land in a crowd. His ship, *The Small Journey*, was painted in bright, garish colors, and the man had the clothing to match. A long blue coat, the color of flower petals, went down to his calves, revealing dusty red pants, cuffed at the ankles to give his bare feet room to maneuver on the ship. He wore a large, three-cornered hat with a red feather as long as Ost's forearm, flying out backwards from the brim. Ost had no clue what bird the feather had originated from, and he'd seen quite a few strange birds in the ship's travels. Most importantly, the man wore a smile. He was beaming. Doman Sutherland was a man that Ost would do anything for, because the Captain would do anything for his crew.

"Shirking your required break, Ost?" shouted Doman as he turned back to see the young sailor looking at him. Ost simply nodded and walked to the bow. When he passed the Captain, the man put a hand on his shoulder. "You can take shore leave at port, son. You can't work your whole time on my ship."

Ost knew a response, a quick retort came to mind immediately, but he didn't speak it. He knew the Captain was right, even if he didn't like it. "Aye sir," he said, touching the knuckles of his right hand to his forehead. Doman nodded in return and the men walked their separate ways. The Captain shouted at the men working their shift—orders and commands, relayed down the line so that all heard. Ost turned back to the bow, ignoring the orders and the urge to help out.

The ship was flying ahead. The sea was smooth and it broke without resistance against the front of the great wooden structure. None of the spray of the sea reached the deck. It felt wonderful at the front, wind rushing by Ost, and the whole world open before him.

The noise of the Captain and the men calling out to each other as they worked the ship was nothing compared to the sound of port. The shouts of merchants hawking wares, the work being done by the docks and the yells of the workers, and all the sounds of the almost-city beyond.

Daughtn was the largest port on the continent, save of the Empire's capital in Kudra. Colorful flags waved atop many of the buildings, their bright colors, lit at night, a sign to ships of the land approaching. Ost thought them unnecessary, and he was always surprised at how loud a place could be. The shouts and calls of so many people rang out towards the sea, and this wasn't even the loudest of it. The pubs and inns in the town center near a festival day reached a volume he had never heard anywhere else. A city could party.

Down at port though, there was work to be done. Ost ignored any thought of the revels above, in town, and faced on the work at hand. Shore leave be damned.

The Small Journey was not a strictly merchant vessel, but one had to have an income somewhere and trade kept the ship afloat in more ways than one. Income left it able to explore.

"Ost, I do believe that you are a special kind of lazy," said the Captain. Ost hadn't noticed the Captain approach. He had been too focused on the port town ahead. The ship had slowed, its sails being furled and men behind preparing the shore boat and anchor. "You hate work, don't you son?"

"Sir?"

"I think I finally understand. You hate work so much that you'd rather do it and get it out of the way, than let it sit."

"I don't let any of my duties sit, sir."

"See," the captain smiled. His grin was a convincing one; it was impossible to not smile along. "There it is from the siren's mouth itself."

Despite the captain's smile, confusion found Ost's face and started making a home.

"You're lazy, Ost. All sailors are, excepting their Captain of course. You show it differently though. You work so hard because you don't wish to have work over your head. You can't think about what needs to be done while you're in the throes of working something else. Well, I'm ordering you to quit working. Get on that shore boat and take your leave with the other men. Your group is the first to go, and I don't want to find you working when I get to port."

"I don't know what to say sir."

"Don't say anything." The captain smiled again. "Quit being lazy and stop working. Get into town and enjoy some shore leave, son. You've more than earned it."

Ost, conceding, knuckled his forehead and the Captain nodded. The Captain was not going to let the point rest; no one won an argument with the Captain. Ost sometimes wonder if Doman Sutherland held his position simply because one day he had said that he was Captain of a ship, and by his own conviction, the world let it happen. It was better to abide the man rather than bring up the many reasons that shore leave was a waste of time, that Ost was better needed at port. There was work to be done.

He shook his head when he reached the end of the dock, trying to get the argument out of his head. Ost turned back to see Sutherland still standing where he had been. The Captain smiled at Ost and the sailor knew he had been defeated. He turned away from the port and headed into town.

The sound and the rush of the people all about town was worse than Ost had imagined. It was louder and busier than he had remembered. But, that didn't make it bad. In a way, it settled him. The noise was no louder than the shouts of his crewmates, and the crowds of people moving at least had space to get around each other, as compared to the cramped decks. Ost was surprised to find himself smiling as he found some of his crewmen entering one of the inns at the edge of town.

It was a quiet place. The stone walls gave a darker look, one that the coal-filled hearth in the corner fought against, creating a homely feel. It was not full, but folks sat at some of tables, eating their food and drinking their drinks. The noise of the sailors entering brought the attention of the room.

"You staying?" said the stout woman behind the bar. She shouted over the quiet din of the dim room. Ost did not speak, but one of his compatriots did.

"Nay, we're travelling through."

"Then off with ya! Becket's got a brew on down the road. Drink her dry."

"Aye mum," said the sailor, turning on the spot and leading the crew back out into the street.

"What was that?" asked Ost.

"Eh, she don't want folk who aren't paying guests in a bed to drink those who is under the table," laughed the sailor closest to him.

"Harol?" said Ost.

"Aye, Ost, we pair again," laughed the sailor. Harol was as young as Ost, though his skin was fair and his hair already gone. He'd quickly grown the body of a sailor after they'd found him and fed him more than scraps he had been stealing in the night. *The Small Journey* had picked him up as a stowaway as they had sailed round the southern coast, near the Salne port. Ost had never been able to pronounce the town's name correctly, and he didn't want to say it again now.

"You're thinkin' of me home?" said Harol.

"I didn't want to say it"

"You never get it right." They both laughed as they walked now. Harol was a good kid. Lazy, but not in the way that the captain apparently thought Ost was. He was the old-fashioned kind. But he was great fun when they were given—or in Ost's case, assigned—a free moment to spare.

"Here we go!" said one of the voices in front of their little crowd. The first of the men entered the stone building to the right. "Becket?" came a call from within. More of the sailors walked in and Ost and Harol got closer to the opening "Is there a brick?" came another call from within. There was. Ost noticed a red brick, as big as the stones that built the walls of the building, seated by the door.

"Aye!" shouted Harol, noticing the brick slower than Ost, but being quicker to speak.

Cheers erupted from within the building, and Ost and Harol finally reached the open door and saw inside.

Like the inn, no light could enter, save from the small doorway and the few open windows. Unlike the inn, however, this was a home. Lofted on one side was a stone platform with stairs set into the rear wall leading up to it. The main level had been cleared, save for chairs and tables, all stone. These were not extravagant brewers, so the living space must be in the loft.

"How many lads did you bring with you?" shouted a woman standing at the far end of the open floor. She wore a thick wool dress and a thicker woolen apron.

"Enough to drink the red brick dry," said one of the men. All the other sailors laughed and cheered.

The woman smiled. "Well grab a seat. You lot finish the keg and you may get a discount." She disappeared behind the rear wall, down what must be stairs to the cellar.

Harol walked in without pause, and Ost followed. He sat down at a table with two other crewmen. Ost pulled up a stool carved from rock and worn with years of sitting and joined them.

"So the little officer joins us for a drink?" said Terrin. The older sailor sat across from Ost and smiled a mostly toothless smile as he said it.

"He works more than me, but he can have fun," said Harol.

"Not hard to work more than you kid," said Chin, the cook, named for the scar on his face.

"I'm not a kid," said Harol, pouting, his emotions always clear as a smooth sea on his face.

"A stowaway's always a kid until they get their sea legs," said Terrin. "Then you get the chance to graduate to sailor."

"I've had my legs for more than one port."

"Yea, but that doesn't mean we've graduated you."

The table laughed, and their laughs were drowned out by cheers from the rest of the room. The woman had returned, barrel in her arms. Without a word, some of the sailors had jumped up and relieved her of the burden. "Don't just take the barrel, grab the mugs, you mongrels." The men with the barrel did not seem to hear her, but others did. Harol stood and went to the shelf by the stairs where cups and mugs and everything short of a chalice sat in waiting. He grabbed four, as other men grabbed for their tables, and the men with the barrel walked about pouring the ale for all to drink. The hostess disappeared once more down the stairs, shaking her head with a smile in her eyes. Another barrel would be on its way up.

Those with the barrel began to sing as they poured. There was always a song. Ost and his table joined in, and in no time the whole alehouse was singing. They got their drinks and toasted to nothing as Harol sat back down.

Terrin's face revealed the slightest of grimaces beneath a smiling facade as he set his clay mug down on the table. "Ale's ok," he said.

"You've always been picky," said Chip.

"He's always complained," said Harol.

Terrin took another sip. "But I drink like the rest of ya."

Ost took another sip of his drink. He agreed; it was not great ale. It was too malty, without enough bitter to balance it out, and tasted closer to bread gone bad than the magic that happens with a good brew.

The woman—she must be Becket—appeared at the top of the stairs again with another barrel. All the men, Terrin included, took more as the barrel made its way about the room. Tables sung, talked, and joked. Dice and cards came out. Tip, the old carpenter's mate, was doing his balancing act in the corner: tables and chairs seeming to float, only a single point touching his chin or his nose. Feld juggled next to him. In short, it was a party. The men were happy, drunk more on shore leave than the little alcohol within the ale they drank, though they did their best to supplant the lack of burn in the beer with sheer quantity of drinking.

"So this is an alehouse?" Ost asked.

His table had been quiet in the cacophony about them. Not for want of silence, but with enjoyment of all that surrounded them. The trio looked at him.

"Never been to one, Ost?" said Terrin.

"I think not; the taverns and inns feel different."

"It is different," said Harol.

"Worse drink," said Terrin, but quietly so the sound didn't reach Becket's ears. He said it without malice.

"Less options, that's sure. But the party is the same," said Harol.

"Does she brew this all herself?" said Ost, pointing a near empty mug towards Becket, who'd emerged with the third barrel of the day.

"That's an alehouse son," said Terrin. "The money will do her family good. Life's hard on land. She'll brew and sell out, then do it all over again when able. The red brick was the sign a brew's on."

"So there's no consistency?"

"'Tisn't an inn. When the ma'am can brew, she does; when she can't, they'll sell nothing. But I tell you, the family will eat well tonight." He smiled and grabbed the mugs from the table, walking over to the nearest barrel for a refill. Talk of an inn made Ost think of home, his old home, before *The Small Journey*.

"Was this how your home was?" Ost asked Harol.

"Salne had taverns and parties, you remember."

"Some of it."

"Exactly. The wines of Istar are stronger than ales and fruit wines. My people stole that thought and made it better."

"Stronger at least."

Harol nodded with a grin, a memory sitting behind his face. "Don't forget that stuff from the island."

"North of Ali?" said Ost.

"Javat," said Chip.

"That was it!" Harol paused for a sip of ale. "They had some amazing drink. It was like sugar wine, right?"

"It was sweet like rotten fruit," said Ost. "But in a way that tasted good."

"Head didna hurt much the next day either," said Chip.

"I think the Captain still has some stowed," said Terrin. Three pairs of eyes now greedily looked across the table at him. "Barrels marked with a shape like this:" he said, drawing a rough "R" in the air, to the benefit of the illiterate men.

"Think the Cap'n would share?" asked Chip.

"I think it may be for a celebration of sorts."

"That was good stuff," sighed Harol, caught in another memory.

"The fruit juices there, too," said Ost joining him.

"Those you can get anywhere. Salne fruits and Kudran fruits and even inland Aerdethin fruits are all good. But that Javat R. That's the drink to have."

"I wonder if we could swing by that island and get some more?" said Ost.

He didn't speak further. Chip perked up. He was the first to notice the Captain had joined them. Ost turned to see Doman Sutherland standing in the doorway, sunlight beaming behind him, shrouding his face. Even the man's silhouette had color.

"Men, make ready to sail. Mates, gather the crew. We depart before nightfall." Doman did not have to shout. The men heard his voice and began work immediately. Barrels were returned to the wall by the stairs. Becket was paid, tables and chairs straightened. Those who had nothing left within the alehouse exited and began their journey back to the ship. Ost stood and joined this last group, behind Harol, Terrin, and Chip. The men already in the street were shouting, gathering the crew from other alehouses and inns. All had to heed the call or risk being left behind, or worse, face a Captain who had to wait.

"Ost," said Sutherland as the four men walked through the door.

Ost almost jumped. He hadn't expected the Captain to be waiting. "Sir?"

"We sail to Gilles," said Doman. He took off his hat and held it at his side. "This man spoke of you, of your town."

Ost then saw that the Captain was not alone. At his side was a man teetering past middle age with the grace of one who had lived a hard life. It was then that the word struck him. Gilles. The town he left. The town he grew up in. The place he never thought he'd see again.

"Husted?" said the man.

Recognition hit.

"Mister Roe?"

The man smiled. "My, you've grown. Yem can't just sit on you to win an argument now." Roe was caught in his memories, at the edge of laughing at the story playing in his mind.

The Captain placed a hand on the man's shoulder. "Ost, we sail to Gilles for you."

Ost looked at Sutherland, unsure what to say. The Captain nodded to Roe.

"Husted, it's your mama," he said, fighting through to say the words he didn't want to. "She's dying."

ABOUT THE AUTHOR

M. Cosmos Newstrom, Max to his friends, is an author in Colorado, USA. He writes fantasy, sci-fi, horror, and essays. When he's not writing, Max works at the Civil Engineering firm he co-founded, hikes about nature with a camera in hand, or just relaxes with his wife Grace and their two cats, Barbie and Kenny.

Check out Max's writing and newsletter here: